RED OBLIVION

RED
OBLI
VION

LESLIE SHIMOTAKAHARA

DUNDURN
TORONTO

Publisher: Scott Fraser | Acquiring editor: Kathryn Lane | Editor: Jess Shulman
Cover designer: Laura Boyle
Cover images: Hong Kong Street Scene: wikimedia commons/DDMLL; grunge texture: istock.com/lukbar
Printer: Webcom, a division of Marquis Book Printing Inc.Cover images:

Library and Archives Canada Cataloguing in Publication

Title: Red oblivion / Leslie Shimotakahara.
Names: Shimotakahara, Leslie, author.
Identifiers: Canadiana (print) 201900682642 | Canadiana (ebook) 20190068272 | ISBN 9781459745216 (softcover) | ISBN 9781459745223 (PDF) | ISBN 9781459745230 (EPUB)
Classification: LCC PS8637.H525 R44 2019 | DDC C813/.6—dc23

1 2 3 4 5   23 22 21 20 19

We acknowledge the support of the Canada Council for the Arts and the Ontario Arts Council for our publishing program. We also acknowledge the financial support of the Government of Ontario, through the Ontario Book Publishing Tax Credit and Ontario Creates, and the Government of Canada.

VISIT US AT

dundurn.com | @dundurnpress | dundurnpress | dundurnpress

Dundurn
3 Church Street, Suite 500
Toronto, Ontario, Canada
M5E 1M2

To Mr. Wong,
in memory

Alack, 'tis he: why, he was met even now
As mad as the vex'd sea; singing aloud;
Crown'd with rank fumiter and furrow weeds,
With harlocks, hemlock, nettles, cuckoo-flowers,
Darnel, and all the idle weeds that grow
In our sustaining corn. — A century send forth;
Search every acre in the high-grown field,
And bring him to our eye.

      — Cordelia in *King Lear*, Act IV, Scene IV

ONE

The last time I saw my father, he seemed all right — really, he did. He was his old self: a tiny, quail-like man with the gleaming eyes of a guy half his age. We were headed to the bank, the sky white and misty, the tropical air touched by a slight chill that people on this side of the world consider freezing; Ba was walking even faster than usual. The sole of his shoe came loose and slapped against the sidewalk like an old flip-flop, while he just continued on, navigating his way through the crowd of pinstripes.

"Ba, let's get you some new shoes." I tried to pull him into Marks & Spencer, but he shucked off my hand with a fidgety shake of the shoulder.

I followed him beneath the billboards of enigmatically shaped handbags, past the shops on Queen's Road, a sea of diamonds and metallic objects glinting and floating by on the edge of our vision. A watery reflection came into focus and I barely had time to recognize myself before the crowd jostled me forward. The sidewalk seemed to be shuddering, everyone elbowing past, barking into phones. But my wily father had no trouble weaving his way through it all as I struggled to catch up.

After cutting across Grand Millennium Plaza — space opening up enough to breathe, around the ornate fountain — we made our way along Des Voeux into Sheung Wan. Although the neighbourhood had gentrified in patches, it still had the old money exchanges and remittance shops with faded red signs and tarnished gold currency symbols. Dry goods stores here and there, big bins of dehydrated mushrooms, scallops, and shark fins before the open windows.

"Where are you going, Ba?" Grabbing his arm, I gestured at a storefront with rows of bright runners and plastic sandals awash in fluorescent light.

Ignoring me, he kept right on walking. We wended our way into the narrow side streets, past the herbal medicine shops.

Once when I was a kid and had a bad cough that wouldn't go away, even after antibiotics, Ba had taken me to one of these places. We sat at the time-worn redwood counter, the walls decorated with bright paper fans and posters of ox bones and folk legends. After taking my pulse, an old man, who looked like a gravedigger, served me a cup of tea the colour of sewer water and not much better tasting. But my cough had cleared up.

"C'mon, Ba, let's just get you some shoes. I don't have all day here."

His hand slipped into his pocket, fingering the wad of cash always there. Not because he was on the verge of buying anything, not because he was afraid of being pickpocketed. Ba has simply always liked the tactility of money. It's like satin to his fingertips.

We weren't far from his old office, so he ought to have known the area well, yet he seemed puzzled, disoriented.

"It's right around here — *I know it is.*"

Probably, the store was long gone. It was a different, older city he was always seeking, remembering.

Finally, we ended up at Wing On department store, where I encouraged him to try on a pair of black Rockports, but they were too expensive, in his view. He picked up a pair of electric-blue sneakers with three gold stripes along each side, similar to the ones my high school boyfriend used to wear, twenty years back.

They were on sale — hallelujah — this being the real reason they'd caught Ba's eye. And they were comfortable, he claimed. Not that he's ever put much stock in comfort. His own or others'.

I remember thinking that at least in sneakers, he'd be unlikely to slip.

Or maybe it's just easier for me to remember things that way. Me, the sweet, caring daughter, patiently cajoling the old guy, impossible as ever, yet strangely endearing in his stubbornness. Electric-blue sneakers and all.

In reality, on that day, I probably saw him as nothing close to endearing. The self-entitled frugality, the insistence on his way or the highway, the past he's always seeking to resurrect and wear like a badge of honour — all these things would have driven me crazy, his small, inescapable presence casting shadows over my mood.

But in seeing us in a soft, forgiving light, in telling myself these tales that make us seem more like a normal family, I'm doing what my sister's long accused me of doing. I'm like a child seeking enchantment in repeated stories that take on the weight of truth only through an act of imagination.

The tiny cup of green tea on the tray quivers, along with my stomach. It's overwhelmingly strong and bitter, the teabag immersed in barely two sips of hot water. The seatbelt sign chimes on. Mine's already buckled, but I tighten it until it cuts into my hip bones. Not that it'll do much good if we plunge into the ocean.

I glance over at my sister, across the aisle, fast asleep. The man beside her is flipping through *Harvard Business Review*, the reading light casting a warm beam on his mottled complexion. At the beginning of the flight, he was getting chatty — dangerously chatty. I overheard him telling Celeste that he's an economics prof, headed to Hong Kong for a conference. His fingertips gleamed with the grease of chips, shiny as his bald head, as he leaned closer. From a certain angle, my sister's quite pretty. The guy asked her about restaurants and museums; he told her that he's especially interested in having a proper English high tea. Would she recommend the Four Seasons or The Peninsula?

"No idea." Celeste jumped up and rummaged through the overhead bin and slammed it shut. She raked her long hair up into a ponytail, exposing the intricate tattoo of a spider behind her ear. The pretty Celeste vanished in a heartbeat. "You think I'm fresh off the boat?"

The guy got the hint that she wasn't feeling chatty.

Celeste isn't thrilled about going home. It's been quite a few years since she's set foot on home soil. But who's counting, right?

Now I watch my sister begin to wake, a yawn overtaking her face like a tsunami in slow motion. She rubs a knuckle into her eye.

"Ba …? Ba …?" she murmurs.

"What about Ba?"

She's still in the process of awakening, dream world and real world overlapping. "He's … dead, right?" Something contracts in her eyes, leaving behind a glassy film.

"We don't know that yet. We'll have to see how he is when we get there."

"Oh." A confused look. The tear comes to a head and dribbles down her cheek.

"It's okay." Reaching across the aisle, I put a hand on her arm, hot moisture suddenly stinging and bursting in my own eyes. "It's going to be okay. *He's* going to be okay. After all, he's tougher than he looks, right?"

I can't help but see our father as strong as an ox, despite his bad back. Even if he hasn't lifted a finger in decades, he still gives the impression — through sheer force of personality — of someone who could haul a boulder if he had to. Once, years ago, as a teenager, I had the privilege of working for him. My glamorous job was to carry boxes from a warehouse to the trunk of his car. "Bend at the knees when you lift," Ba shouted over his shoulder from the driver's seat, not bothering to get out. "That way you'll save your back. I learned that lesson all too late! Bend at the knees — didn't you hear me? *Save your back!*"

His wretched childhood, his years as a beast of burden. My father's very skilled at using guilt as a tool, a weapon.

"I must've dreamed it. That Ba died," Celeste says.

I forage in my purse for a tissue and blow my nose, then pass one over to her.

"It's not that I'm hoping he's dead, you know," she says a moment later.

"Of course not."

"I really *am* hoping he's going to be okay —"

"*And he will be.*" Now I just want her to stop talking and take another one of those little pink pills that have been keeping her somewhat tranquilized.

The phone call came very early this morning. In the darkness, I stared at the incandescent numbers on my phone; there was something accusatory about their brightness. The caller gave a sputter of gasps and sobs and a garbled explanation in broken English, punctuated with ma'am this, ma'am that. My father is dead, or very nearly dead, Rina was trying to tell me. I rubbed my eyes, but the blurriness wouldn't clear; her words sounded tinny and unreal, like in a dream. And yet I wasn't dreaming, and Rina was saying to me: *He collapsed at the fish market while haggling over a bass.* I sat up in bed, slid on my glasses, and flipped on the light, the sudden clarity of the room — its sharp angles and bone-white sheets — blotting out the last, merciful vestiges of sleep.

Rina could be overreacting. That was the first thing that went through my mind. She's been calling a lot lately over little things: Ba's failing memory, his achy bones, his poor appetite. A letter that seemed to confuse and upset him. I told her not to worry. What can you expect? My father's ninety-four. And the letter was probably just from one of his tenants, complaining about the facilities or giving notice. These things get to him more than they used to. Rina insisted it was more than that and went off on a rambling explanation I couldn't begin to follow.

The plane's engine makes a noise that's vaguely menacing, like the roar of a waterfall or a photocopier that's overheated and about to break down. The sound reminds me of my love for my father: vaguely frightening, formless, persistent, annoying, inescapably *there*. The more I listen, the more I can feel the clouds quivering beneath the soles of my shoeless feet.

I get up to use the washroom, standing in line in the darkness. Every so often, the illusion of night is punctured by a guy in a window seat pulling up his blind, a beam of sun cutting through the cabin like a flashlight across a theatre. For a second, I see a narrow wedge of slumbering faces twitch and cringe and curl deeper into themselves, curl back into the quickly restored shadows.

The skinny woman in line in front of me has her arms crossed tightly, like she's trying to prevent a great many things from escaping her rib cage. Her weight shifts from left foot to right foot and then back again, faster and faster. And then I realize that I've assumed the same posture, the same repetitive, manic jiggle.

My eyes migrate to the emergency exit right beside me, its oversize steel handle beckoning with a strange allure. It's so close. I want to touch it, just to see what it feels like. Just because it's something I'm not supposed to do. But I don't dare, because there's a flight attendant lurking nearby. PUSH DOOR OPEN, SLIDE INFLATES AUTOMATICALLY. In the dim, watery light, that's what the instructions above the big handle are telling me to do. A giant red arrow arcs like a rainbow across the width of the door and points downward. How amazing it would feel to rotate the handle in one continuous motion and push outward and slide down that magically inflating slide into the boundless white-blue ether. Freefall. Skydiving with no parachute. The sheer relief of knowing that after a few harrowing seconds, *this will all be over.*

By the time we land, my body's as sluggish as my brain, everything deprived of circulation. Before the pilot's turned off the seatbelt sign, several folks have jumped up to grab their briefcases and that old feeling of dread and inertia grabs at my insides.

We pass through customs and pick up our suitcases, which are already going around on the conveyor belt, unlike in Toronto, where you're lucky to wait less than twenty minutes. Hong Kong being twelve hours ahead, every cell of my body's behind schedule. My digestive system's in a state of shock. My circadian rhythm's way off, light and colours hitting my retinas all too vividly. As people in boxy suits rush past, eager to get to their meetings and start the day, Celeste and I just look at each other.

It startles me how exhausted she appears. Mauve-grey shadows fall under her large, melancholy eyes, new strands of white weaving up around her temples into her sloppy bun. We're only one year apart — she's thirty-seven and I'm thirty-eight — and when we were kids, people often mistook us for twins. I wonder if

I look just as weary. I wonder what else has been going on in her life lately. She rarely calls me and vice versa. I live and work downtown, while Celeste's out in Markham, and I don't have a car. Sure, sometimes I'll email her ("here's an awesome recipe for lentil soup — perfect for this freezing-ass weather") or she'll text me ("ever try meditation?? bc u cud use it") and we make plans to get together for dim sum, but it always falls apart at the last minute because her cat needs to go to the vet. Or her stomach hurts. Or the tiles in her shower have grown so mouldy they need to be re-grouted immediately, she insists, or else a cloud of germs could envelop her and give her some mysterious illness. Sometimes it feels as though *I'm* the cloud of germs she's so desperately trying to avoid. But at least she never fails to "Like" and write comments with lots of exclamation marks beneath my photos on Facebook. It's easier this way to feel connected without ever having to actually hear about each other's problems, I guess. On this side of the world, our attitude would be shameful, unthinkable, but in Toronto it's somehow okay for everyone to do their own thing.

"So …?" Celeste says, dazed. Buffeted by the crowd, we've begun walking toward the express train, which will take us into Central.

"So …?"

"Do we go to the hospital or the condo first?"

My skin's sticky, covered in a film of its own oils, having been basted in them for the past twenty-four hours. A shower sure would be nice. "When I spoke to Second Aunt yesterday, she implied it's only fifty-fifty that Ba'll make it through surgery."

An unspeakable sentiment hangs in the silence that follows. I recall our conversation on the plane, Celeste's claim that she's *not* hoping he'll die. Of course we're not. And yet — is this too awful to admit? — the prospect of dealing with this man alive is what terrifies us at the moment.

Celeste nods. "Straight to the hospital, then?"

After twenty minutes of sitting side by side, not saying much of anything, we get off the busy train. Glass doors slide open to an underground parking area, where a line of red and white taxis awaits. When I tell the driver the name of the hospital, he asks about the route I'd like to take. It's strange speaking Cantonese all of a sudden; the words and tonalities, with all their complex undulations, feel at once cumbersome and all too familiar on my tongue. Just speaking the language, with its harsh, guttural quality, is making me anxious, turning me into a demanding person.

Glaring sunlight hits my vision as the car takes us up to street level: a dense conglomeration of concrete and blinding, reflective surfaces — banks, hotels, Cartier — interspersed with islands of palm trees and occasional historic buildings, like the old Government House, decked out with neoclassical columns. Pedestrian bridges cut through the air, lifting people across the multi-lane traffic. Soon, we're on the elevated expressway that winds curvaceously toward Causeway Bay, and since rush hour's over, we're getting to our destination with frightening speed. I find myself wishing for a traffic jam.

"The city looks different," Celeste says. "More built up."

Although she's probably right, my eyes detect very little change. Hong Kong's always seemed like this: the new trying to overtake the old, the old never quite disappearing. The luxurious facades of some of these hotels — pink marble and gold curlicue lettering and massive chandeliers right out front — have a blatantly outdated appearance. Memories wash over me. Idealized childhood fantasies of some other bygone era. Scones generously spread with the rose-petal jam our mother adored, her jade droplet earrings skimming the high collar of her dress, the way men used to turn and gaze at her whenever we'd enter the Mandarin Oriental hotel.

Our beautiful mother.

She died suddenly of lung cancer, twelve years back. At least, the whole thing seemed sudden to me, because she didn't tell me that anything was wrong. One evening, on the phone, her voice became weak and incoherent and I demanded to speak to my father — I demanded to know what was wrong. By the time I'd flown over, my mother couldn't speak at all. She placed her cool palms on my cheeks, as I leaned down at her bedside, and she peered in at me as if looking in the mirror, trying to discern her own foggy reflection.

"When were you last here, Celeste?" I ask now.

"Five, six years ago. We stopped for a few days on our way back from our honeymoon. You?"

"I came for Chinese New Year. I always try to come at that time of year." I let that sink in, with all its implications, an ember of resentment glowing in my chest. *Yes, Celeste, I've been coming every year.* Once, when I suggested to her that Ba wouldn't be around forever and maybe, you know, it wouldn't be a bad idea to hop on a plane from time to time, she never replied. All contact between us dropped off for several months.

"You've been a better daughter than me, I guess."

She says this neutrally, not sarcastically. My anger mutes to a soft burning that feels more like guilt.

"Hardly. Coming once a year?" My sense of filial piety — if you can call it that — is half-assed, at best. "And I took a good long break from visiting, for a while."

"That was after Nick came with you, right?"

"Yep." I'm so tired that I'm feeling drunk, and not in a good way. That sensation when the drunkenness just starts to fade, leaving everything tainted by persistent wooziness. But Nick's an old hurt, six years gone, water under the bridge. "He came to ask Ba for my hand in marriage, if you can believe it."

It sounds so silly and old-fashioned it's almost laughable. Celeste does snicker, in fact. "I thought that's what happened."

"As you can imagine, the visit didn't go so well."

First off, Nick Singh was obviously not Chinese. A tall, lanky guy with café-au-lait skin and a craggy nose. Half-Indian, half-Irish, both parents born in Canada. I suspect that my father was put off by Nick's friendly, informal manner, his oversized golf shirt, the softness of his handshake, which Nick wrongly assumed would be the prelude to an embrace. And I know my father was put off, when he interviewed the guy in pidgin English, to discover that Nick was a junior high teacher and yoga instructor.

According to Ba, the decision was mine alone. If I wanted to marry such an unambitious fellow, who was he to stop me? His role, as my father, was simply to offer guidance. Yeah, right. It was pretty clear from the disdainful look on his liver-spotted face that he had every expectation his advice would be taken to heart.

Celeste waits for me to say more, to open up to her, perhaps. About how Nick and I fell apart in the months that followed. About how I didn't visit Ba for three years. When I say nothing, we lapse into silence. By now, we're passing the harbour: a tangle of red and blue cranes and yellow bulldozers, glints of tinfoil water peeking through.

"Jill, don't tell him that I'm not working, okay?" Celeste switches into Cantonese now, throwing in English words here and there, typical of how people in this city talk. Words like *okay* and *anyway* and *cool* and *what the fuck* and *see ya* always get said in English, for some reason.

"*Hiya, hiya* …" Yeah, yeah. I've also slipped into our mother tongue. "But what are you ashamed of? You're going back to school, right?"

"Well. I plan to. I just don't want to get into the whole thing with Ba, okay?"

My sister used to be the cool one, with the OCAD degree and the dirt-cheap loft on Queen Street, back when that stretch by the mental hospital was still edgy and kind of dangerous. She worked as a graphic designer for a marketing firm. With the rise of do-it-yourself software, the company lost a lot of clients. Two years ago, Celeste got laid off. Fortunately, by then, she'd married Eric, a government lawyer, who makes enough to support them. That said, our father also considers Eric not ambitious enough. At least he's Chinese–Canadian, I guess. I have no beef with Eric, though he's always struck me as a strange match for my sister — rather bland, if you want the truth. And it seems wrong that Celeste, of all people, now lives out in the suburbs, while I've taken over her old life downtown.

No one's ambitious enough for our father, when it comes down to it. I fall into that camp, too. I'm an architect, a profession he doesn't at all grasp. In his mind, architects are basically the same as developers. Being a developer's good, because developers build things, developers make money. That much Ba can relate to. What he can't understand is why I've chosen to work for a government agency, the organization responsible for revitalizing Toronto's waterfront. Why am I focusing on aquatic habitats and parks and bike paths, when I could be building skyscrapers and luxury shopping malls and Abu Dhabi?

Celeste turns away from the window, casting me a sheepish look. "So, do we even have any idea what made Ba collapse?"

"He seemed fine when I was here last."

"But I thought you said Rina's been calling a lot?"

"According to her, he's been up at night, pacing around. Complaining about nightmares, complaining about stomach pains, complaining about her cooking. I think she wanted me to come back and deal with him."

"Poor Rina. We're lucky she hasn't quit."

A moment later, my sister adds, "Nightmares, though? I've never heard Ba talk about nightmares before."

She's right. He used to boast about how well he slept, tired out by a hard day's work. "I don't know. Maybe he's gotten more sensitive in old age."

"I very much doubt that."

I shrug, brushing her cynicism aside, pretending that it doesn't bother me. "Psychoanalyzing our father is the last thing on my mind."

TWO

The taxi pulls up in front of the hospital, a thin, tan-coloured tower tucked beside a convent school with a gloomy, mustardy facade. At the end of the street rises a church, designed to look like an ornate Chinese temple, except for the cross at the top.

As I step out of the air-conditioned car, the sauna-like fug hits me all over, followed by a cloud of exhaust from a double-decker bus. I've forgotten just how unbearable July can get.

The ICU, on the third floor, is as cold and brightly lit as the inside of a morgue. My sweat chills to icy dampness. As we enter, a nurse rushes over to hand us baby-blue surgical masks. Shivering, I slip mine on and begin breathing in my own toxins, trapped in the steamy cloud of my polluted breath. A dizzy spell hits me, everything wavering slightly. I count three or four beds, some partitioned by half-drawn curtains. At both ends of the ward are the private rooms for the truly desperate cases. I'm relieved when the nurse guides us to one of the regular beds.

There he is: our father, asleep. So many tubes poke out of his emaciated body that I'm hit — absurdly — with the image of an unborn baby with multiple umbilical cords attached. In the tube that goes straight into his neck, beads of purple blood stagnate. His face appears ashen, more wrinkled than I remember, the sharp edges more pronounced than ever, the gullies under his eyes and cheekbones bathed in shadows. Panic sweeps over me, followed by a shot of outrage. "Can't you … can't you … *do something for him?*"

A rotund nurse steps forward, her white pillbox hat at a crooked angle. "Your grandfather's resting comfortably."

"Not grandfather. *Father. Okay?*"

The nurse looks surprised. She was expecting his daughters to be matronly ladies in their sixties, complete with tightly permed hair, big black purses, and canteens of red date soup in tow. I don't know why I'm so irritated. I should be used to this generational confusion by now — I've only been dealing with it for my entire life.

Our father married very late. The timeline of his life got thrown off by twenty years, due to the Japanese occupation during the Second World War. Ba doesn't like to talk about what happened back then, because he's always been ashamed of how poor his folks were. I've managed to piece things together based on snippets from my aunts. It seems that along with all the atrocities the Japanese army committed during the war — gang rape; torture; the execution of masses of civilians, children included; a meagre ration system that made death by starvation commonplace — they were also in the habit of deporting the unemployed to China. "Repatriation," they called it. Ba's father, who had suffered from poor health since before war broke out, had been out of work for a long time; Ba had been supporting the family since his early teens. Once the Japanese moved in and took over, my grandfather, grandmother, and two aunts — just little girls at the time — found themselves herded onto a crowded boat for China. They sought refuge in the Guangzhou area, where they had family, while my father stayed in Hong Kong and continued to work, sending money over to them each month.

His breakthrough moment came when he realized that the war and all its economic hardships had opened up new opportunities. This part my father's not reluctant to talk about at all. "Restaurants had very few customers, so their tinned goods were sitting around, about to perish. No one had money for a nice meal out!" He began buying up their food at bargain-basement prices, in order to sell it on the black market. Since everything from oil to flour was being rationed, people were famished. "Folks were willing to hock their grandmothers' earrings for a cup of rice."

It was Ba's first venture and he turned a nice profit. An entrepreneur was born.

Toward the end of the war, his parents suddenly died within months of each other. I believe they died of natural causes, but the harshness of wartime life couldn't have helped; Guangzhou, like many other Chinese cities, was occupied by the Japanese. Orphaned, my aunts ended up billeted with relatives. To ensure they were being properly cared for, Ba moved to Guangzhou, where he started a peanut oil business.

The war ended, and Ba dreamed of returning home. But, having sunk all his money into the business, it was best to try to see it through. When his sisters were a bit older, they'd all return home, he must have figured. Hong Kong had been ravaged by the war, so what could be the harm in waiting a few years to let the city recover? Yet without the Japanese enemy to unite them, China's Communists and Nationalists began fighting again; the country's civil war resumed like nothing had happened, throwing Guangzhou into chaos. When the Communists declared victory and "liberated" China, border control tightened up. The moment for absconding had passed. The months turned into years, the years blurred into a decade, then two. This period Ba doesn't like to talk about beyond vague snippets, presumably due to its bleakness. Not until the outbreak of the Cultural Revolution in the mid-1960s did he have an opportunity to escape, under conditions that have always been hazy to me.

Suffice it to say this man couldn't fathom starting a family until he'd managed — by hook or by crook — to find his way back to the good life in Hong Kong.

So Celeste and I are *it*. His belated offspring, born decades too late. We, in our yoga pants and scuffed ballerina flats, are the ones who are supposed to be running the show.

Celeste's off in the corner talking to the doc, a young, stout guy in blue scrubs and white clogs. I go over and start asking questions, but it turns out that this guy — Tony, he introduces himself as — is actually a nurse. He reassures us that our dad is resting comfortably. Tears sting my eyes. Tears of what, I'm not so sure. The operation seems to have gone all right, though it's very early to say, Tony emphasizes, and the doctors should be able to tell us more. When I ask for them to be paged, we're told that they're in surgery. We missed them on their morning rounds. Our best bet is to come back during evening visiting hours.

"What now?" Celeste says.

We look down at Ba's sleeping face. He looks fitful, eyelids twitching.

"We go home, I guess."

Celeste has lost her house key, so I let us in. Swords of sunlight cut across the polished wood floor, from the banks of windows on both sides of the living room. Rina hasn't been slacking, though there's only so much that cleaning can do. The chandeliers my mother chose look more ridiculous than ever, now that Ba's let the place go to seed. A couple of old office chairs, the kind that roll around on wheels, are clustered close to the TV in the corner, where he'd be huddled, under normal circumstances, watching stock prices rise and fall on the business channel. The cushions on the redwood furniture appear faded, yet untouched. The pearl brocade wallpaper is badly peeling at the edges, the ceilings splotched with pale brown stains from a drainage problem on the rooftop terrace.

I follow my poor, shell-shocked sister as she wanders through the condo, yanking open doors. The water damage in her bedroom is worse than anywhere — her old Faye Wong poster looks like it dried after a rainstorm. The smell of soggy woodchips and mildew fills the air.

"I can't believe you let it get this bad, Jill!"

"Hey, visiting more often than you doesn't mean crap. If Ba wants to live this way, who am I to stop him?"

In his bedroom, she lets out a weak chuckle. A broken fridge in the corner has been repurposed as a filing cabinet. It sits beside his rusty-doored safe.

"Now you have a sense of what *I've* been dealing with."

I'm not thrilled about being here, either; far from it. I think of my tiny apartment on College, lovingly furnished with Danish Modern pieces. My framed black-and-white photographs of the old sugar refinery and derelict buildings down by the waterfront. My terrarium with its white sand floor, miniature cacti and crystals here and there. My old-fashioned bathtub with claw feet. My espresso maker. A wave of homesickness hits me in the gut.

But for Ba, real estate's never anything more than an investment. He's living in a penthouse condo on Conduit Road, yet we might as well be in a tenement.

In the living room, I shut the windows and turn on the air conditioner, which is covered in dust. A soft sputtering, no cool air. The noise dies. I flip the switch again. Nada.

"You've got to be fucking kidding," says Celeste.

"You here, ma'ams!" Rina comes out of the kitchen, which adjoins her tiny bedroom. Although dressed in a big turquoise

T-shirt, she appears faded, tired. She's in her late fifties and has aged considerably since I first met her. I'm hoping to catch a maternal glimmer in her smile, but it strikes me as nothing more than a smile of relief. *At last, the negligent daughters are here to take over.*

This is Celeste's first time meeting Rina. Celeste tells her how grateful we are that she was with Ba when he collapsed.

Rina's eyes cloud over. For a second, I think she's going to cry, but she heaves her shoulders, summoning herself. "I so worry, ma'ams, sir gonna die and I get the blame!"

"No, no." I put a hand on her arm. "He's an old man, nearing the end of his life." Is he? My father has amazing reserves — there's no telling what he's capable of. "Whatever happens, happens. You've done an amazing job, Rina."

"Yeah, amazing," Celeste echoes.

And we mean it. In living here for the past three years and putting up with his endless complaining, she's done more than his own daughters ever would. Of all my father's housekeepers, she's lasted the longest. I wonder who's taking care of her own parents, back in the Philippines, or whether they're still alive. I wonder whether she has a husband and kids of her own. Rina claims that she never married, but that doesn't mean anything; these women increase their chances of being hired if they give the impression of being unattached, free of obligations.

As her face clears, she clasps her hands together. "Lunch?"

My stomach is still off from the starchy, gassy meals I had on the plane. Nevertheless, I sit down at the dining room table beside my sister, while Rina brings in steaming bowls of broth and a ceramic dish containing boiled cabbage with ginger slices and tiny, stringy morsels of pork. One of Ba's favourite wartime dishes. Just what you want to be eating in forty-degree weather.

In silence, we eat. Like it used to be when there were four of us at this very table. Celeste scratches the rash that's started to blossom across her neck — not holding back, really digging in, like she did as a kid. She moves on to ravage the skin between her fingers. Just watching her is making me itchy.

"Rina?" she calls over her shoulder.

"Yes?"

"I wonder if you could tell us a bit more about Ba's condition. He hasn't been sleeping well, I hear?"

Rina seems relieved that someone's brought this up. "Oh, your father — he not well!" She taps the side of her head a few times.

"He's been confused?"

"Can't sleep. Bad dream. He talk to self. No one in room. Like talking to ghost."

The back of my neck stiffens, the air heavy and suffocating. "I'm sorry you've had to deal with him like this. He's an old man. Maybe it's dementia."

"It all start with letter. The letter upset sir."

"What letter?"

"I show you after lunch."

Although I nod, I'm not too concerned. The letter's probably just an investment report. Poor profits, that'll get Ba down.

After lunch, we go into my father's study. With all the boxes of old files piled on the floor, we barely have enough room to stand. Now Rina hesitates; perhaps she doesn't want to appear too certain about where things are, like she's been snooping. She gestures timidly at the top drawer of his desk.

Sure enough, there's an envelope addressed to him. Two envelopes, in fact. They don't look like business correspondence. I lift them out of the drawer. There's no return address on either, but the postmarks indicate they were sent from Guangzhou.

A photo slides out of one.

"What is it?" Rina says.

I recognize the place immediately. "Ba's building in Sheung Wan."

The ginseng shop, at street level, has been there for many years. It looks like an old-fashioned apothecary, in the picture. Through the large windows, tall glass jars of massive gnarled roots can be seen on the shelves behind the long counter. I remember, as a child, wanting to go in and poke around, but Ba always said I had no business bothering his tenant. Next door, as the photo shows, is the main entrance, which leads into the lobby, where elevators ascend to the twenty floors of offices above.

Confusion washes over me, leaving a clammy residue. I'm looking at a picture of something so very ordinary, uncannily ordinary. Yet I have no clue what it means.

Ba's office suite used to be on the twelfth floor. I remember occasionally going there with my mom to drop off papers he'd forgotten at home. Mr. Chan, with whom Ba jointly owned the building, had his office one floor below. Ba still talks fondly about how the two of them used to work sixteen-hour days and never complain, because they always knew their investment would be worth it in the end.

Nothing else is in the envelope. "Wasn't there any note?"

Rina shakes her head.

The second envelope also contains a lone photo. It shows a poppy-red armband, emblazoned with a scrawl of yellow writing in Chinese. The face of the person wearing it can't be seen, only a segment of an upper arm clothed in military green.

"What does that say?" Rina asks.

"Red Guard," Celeste whispers.

"Red Guard?" Rina looks at us blankly.

"The Red Guards were a nasty bunch." I'm no history expert, but like any kid who went to school in Hong Kong, I have some idea of who they were. "Mao mobilized them in the early days of the Cultural Revolution."

"Cultural Revolution?"

"It's hard to explain ..."

Nevertheless, I give it a go, while Rina stares at me wide-eyed. The notion of 1960s youth movements typically brings to mind sit-ins and bare-footed hippies strumming their guitars, high on acid, but the Red Guards were another kind of youth organization, one that managed to seize hold of far greater political power. When Mao realized that he was losing his grip over the Party — fraught by schisms over class transformation, still reeling from the disastrous economic policies of the Great Leap Forward — he saw that this network of fanatical high school and university students could be a useful ally.

Rina continues to look confused. I wonder if politics in the Philippines are less stormy.

"Teenagers like to rebel, right?" Celeste chimes in.

"There's more to it than that." But sure, I get what my sister's saying. What teenager doesn't mouth off? The Red Guards were good at making catchy posters that denounced their teachers, profs, and deans for counter-revolutionary tendencies. All Mao had to do was throw his weight behind them. What followed was a period of licence and madness: these kids were free to attack, interrogate, and beat their teachers and elders under suspicion of belonging to the Five Black Categories.

I'm not sure whether anything I've said has made sense. Perhaps it *can't* make sense — it was a crazy time all around. Rina's eyes are like quivering egg yolks, wild locks around her forehead escaping her bun. "Why someone send sir picture like this? *Why?*"

"I don't know. I agree it's weird."

That said, my father's pissed off his share of people over the years. He drives a hard bargain, never takes the short end of the stick. Maybe some retired guy has too much time on his hands?

"Ba never had any connection with the Red Guards back in Guangzhou, did he?" Celeste says.

"You know as much as I do. He's too old to have been involved, isn't he?" He would have been in his forties at the time the Cultural Revolution began.

"I guess so."

"Besides, didn't Ba escape from Guangzhou around then? That's what he always told us."

When my sister doesn't reply, a weightless feeling drifts over my body. The photo slips from my sweaty fingertips and flutters to the ground.

Rina says that she saw Ba looking at the pictures repeatedly. The more he examined them, the more upset he became. That's when he began having sleep problems and his appetite diminished. Pacing and mumbling to himself in Cantonese. "Maybe you ask sir what wrong?"

"It'd only upset him," Celeste says. Yet she's the one who looks upset, deep lines etched between her brows.

"Relax." As usual, I'm trying to play the calm, sensible one.

"I always wondered …"

"What are you talking about?"

She doesn't answer.

A flare of heat in my gut. How it rankles me, my sister's quickness to assume the worst about our father. Even in her silence, I want her to stop — I want to get away from the aura she exudes as she keeps on staring at me, a hint of a knowing, accusatory smile playing at the edges of her lips. But I sense all too vividly what she's feeling, her thoughts seeping into and polluting mine. We both know nothing about Ba's past. About all those years he spent in Guangzhou, before we were born. About how he managed to return to Hong Kong, the city of his youth, the city of his dreams. We learned, early on, that he doesn't like to be questioned. *You have no idea of how I suffered to give you girls this life.*

• • •

A full house this evening. When Celeste and I arrive at the hospital, a little after eight, our father already has an entourage. His two sisters are petite, hunchbacked women in their late seventies, dressed in brightly coloured cardigans. They're crouched at his bedside, fussing and clucking, a couple of our cousins huddled behind. When Celeste and I edge our way to his bedside, our aunts turn to focus on us, with tearful hugs.

Third Aunt's husband bears a steaming thermos of aromatic medicinal soup. Unfortunately, my father can't drink any of it. He can barely breathe, tubes arcing out his nostrils, his voice a light, harsh rasp.

"I'll be back … home … in a few days. Back to … old self."

His sisters smile uncertainly and fuss some more. They're very loyal and attentive.

And yet, it's more than that — it's a debt they're trying to pay, a debt their kids are trying to pay. Everyone knows how much my father's done for my aunts, how he sacrificed his own childhood to work and support the family. Without him, they would have starved to death.

A nurse comes over to do crowd control, ushering people out. The ICU has strict rules about the number of visitors allowed at one time.

Soon, my sister and I find ourselves all alone with our father. There's only one chair and it's full of our aunties' bags, so we crouch down around his bed, our knees killing us. Tears of shame or panic or some other unnameable emotion make everything turn blurry. It's important not to hover above him, as we stroke his withered hands and the top of his bald head, the scalp pinkened in patches, the bones as fragile as eggshells. We must assume a position of deference, his prodigal daughters, here at last.

"You came, Yuk Chu."

Something inside me aches upon hearing him say my Chinese name. "Of course we came. We took the first flight out, Ba."

Celeste adjusts the blankets around his feet. "You gave us quite the scare. How are you feeling?"

"Good that you're both here. You need to take care of business."

And just like that, it starts up: the litany of requests — orders, really. Our father — not a day out of surgery — is itemizing all the things we need to do, from paying bills to collecting rent to evicting a troublesome tenant. It's as though his debilitated state is making him bossier and more controlling than ever. He wants to know how much this hospital stay is costing him. He demands to know why he wasn't taken to the public hospital instead.

"Don't worry about all that, Ba. Just rest."

Celeste shoots me a sharp glance. I know what she's thinking: rest isn't in this guy's vocabulary. Despite the not-so-great look of things, we're thinking that our father is going to recover — of course he will. He's strong as an ox. And then, those damn photographs are on our minds, looming like ghostly projections on the white walls. Who sent them? What do they even mean? It's only a matter of time before we're going to have to show them to Ba.

The surgeon arrives and takes us aside. He speaks to us in English, so Ba can't eavesdrop, I assume. As he talks, onyx and platinum cufflinks glint beneath the sleeves of his lab coat. Doctors at this hospital are far better dressed than the staff at Toronto General, I can't help but notice, and being my father's daughter, I also start worrying about the tab we've racked up. I wonder how much cash is in the safe at home. I'll have to go to the bank tomorrow for a certified cheque. The to-do list gets louder in my head while I'm trying to focus on what the doctor's saying. White blood cell counts. The risk of infection. Our father's been coughing so much that he can barely swallow anything. His choppy vitals can be seen on the monitor, rising and falling in jagged neon lines, like stock markets about to crash.

The doctor pulls a Polaroid from his folder: a close-up of a brown, bloated tube, mangled and bleeding, like a dying worm on the sidewalk after a storm. It ruptured, he explains. The situation turned out to be worse than expected. They had no choice but to amputate the large intestine. It's called a colostomy. For the rest of Ba's life, he'll excrete waste through an opening in his abdomen that connects to a disposable plastic pouch. Keeping the wound clean and free of infection will be of utmost importance.

Celeste puts a limp hand to her stomach, her face the colour of porridge. I, too, feel sick, sick with disbelief. Neither of us has ever thought of our father as frail, wounded. Endangered by his own shit.

"I'm sure it's a great relief to your father that you're both here. Keeping up his spirits will be key."

Keeping up his spirits won't be an issue. That's what I'd quip under normal circumstances, but everything seems to have undergone a landslide in the last couple minutes.

THREE

I stand under the shower for a very long time. The spray doesn't feel nearly cold enough. I wait for it to wake me up and clear my head, water trickling down my torso in soapy rivulets and catching frothily on my limp, neglected pubic hair. Ungroomed, unloved, for years.

As soon as I step out, I'm sticky again, the sweat on my body indistinguishable from the humidity in the air. Although it's just past dawn, it's sweltering already. What's the point of even bathing? Nothing is washed away.

And the abrasive rub of this stiffened, air-dried towel. Every time I come home, the roughness is a shock to my skin. I remember Nick's surprise that we don't have a dryer; wet towels and clothes hang on racks up on the terrace. He thought Hong Kong would be all about cutting-edge technology, but in certain respects, we do things the old-fashioned way. Why have a dryer or dishwasher, when you can have a housekeeper for so very cheap?

Leaving my hair damp and messy, I slip into my lightest linen dress.

Celeste's passed out in her room, snoring up a storm. If only I could be so lucky. I fix myself a mug of instant coffee while staring out the kitchen window at nothing at all.

Morning visiting hours begin soon. But I don't think I can face the ICU again just yet. *My poor father. His bowels blown to bits.* A fiery sensation lights up my sinuses, like I might start crying at any second. His situation still seems so unreal, so cruel.

And then, I remember that I have a legitimate excuse. Didn't my father tell me to go to his building first thing and take care of rent collection? Doing something simple and concrete suddenly appeals to me greatly. Stepping into Ba's study, I attempt to find any kind of rent records amidst the stacks of old notebooks and yellowed newspapers. My resolve slackens after a few minutes of futile searching. Oh, forget it — I'll just talk to the building super and perhaps he can enlighten me. I feel like I need to be enlightened about many things in my life right now.

Conduit Road, the street where I grew up. It winds around the western part of the mountain, and, because the terrain above is too steep to build on, our view of the thick, hardy trees and patches of bald, striated rock never changes. Massive banyan trees arch over the curvaceous street, their gnarled roots clinging to the edges of the stonewall cliffs where condo buildings find their foothold. It's a pleasant enough neighbourhood for walking. My father used to consider it his daily exercise to walk up and down the hundreds of steps, back and forth from work.

And here I am following in his footsteps.

Well, not exactly. Twenty years back, the city built this canopied escalator, which cuts into the side of the mountain and carries you down into Central. Now there are lots of chic stores and restaurants on the mountain streets, unlike when I was a kid and you'd be lucky to find a vinegar shop.

I find myself thinking about the last time my father and I spoke on the phone, a couple weeks ago. He called me, as usual, with a distinct purpose in mind. He isn't like normal dads. There's never any lead-in with "How have you been doing, Jill?" or "What's new in your life?" Right to business, as always. He's been asking about real estate prices in Toronto lately, toying with the idea of picking up an old building, if I can find one at the right price. I'll do up the drawings to convert the place into lofts, oversee construction, and then rent it all out. Maybe we sell some units. He yakked on in his usual way, repeating the things he's been saying to me for years: "You can't make a killing in real estate like you can in currency trading, but over the long run you do okay. And you know how to add value to land — that's what you went to school for, after all!"

So that was Ba's plan. There's a certain percentage yield he's expecting to make and it isn't low. While some daughters bond with their dads over golf and theatre, Ba and I talk rates of return. It's been this way for as long as I can remember.

A strange, shivering sensation passes over me as our conversation replays in my head. Then the photo of his building flashes in my mind. No doubt it was the same calculating business mentality that pushed him to recognize a good opportunity back then.

But what's wrong with wanting to make money? Just because Ba's entrepreneurial to the bone doesn't make him a bad guy.

At the base of the escalator, I head west along Queen's Road, fighting my way through the throngs of office workers. The blinding sheen off facades of flagship stores and corporate towers makes me dizzy, hurting my sleep-deprived eyes. Sweat dribbling down my nose, making my sunglasses slip, I curse myself for not taking a taxi, though at this time of day it'd be impossible to find one. Power-walking farther west, I hit Bonham Strand, where the buildings become older and dingier, festooned with the neon lettering of a different era, the narrowness of the streets casting deep shadows over the gutters. I glimpse the herbal medicine shop where Ba took me when I was a kid, its windows hung with red, black, and ochre posters advertising the old remedies.

At first, when Ba broached the idea of investing in Canadian real estate, I was surprised and kind of flattered, I have to admit. For so long, he's been trying to convince me to move back to Hong Kong. His original expectation was that after university, his daughters would return right away; Canada was never supposed to be anything more than an interlude, a form of insurance. During the lead-up to Hong Kong's return to China in '97, like many people in this city, my parents sought second passports, just in case things took a turn for the worse under Communist rule. They sent me and my sister to board with a Chinese-Canadian family in the suburbs of Toronto during our final years of high school. The shocker for them wasn't really that little changed in Hong Kong after '97, it was that Celeste and I decided to stay in Toronto permanently. We liked the easygoing pace of life, we liked our university friends of Croatian, Egyptian, and Taiwanese backgrounds — everyone unique, hybrid transplants to Canada, even those who'd been there for generations. Canadians are essentially nice, accepting people. Growing up, we'd never known anything like it. And most importantly, I have to say, we liked not having our parents around. It felt like freedom, a fresh start. And so, we stayed and there was nothing they could do to stop us.

As with all things, my father has found the silver lining. The upside of having his offspring in Canada? Real estate's still relatively cheap. Real estate in Hong Kong has skyrocketed to the point that unless you're a mega corporation, it's impossible to acquire anything. Accordingly, I am to quit my job — of course I will, he's always assumed — and start working for him. Maybe we'll team up with investors from this side of the world and I'll start spending a lot more time in Hong Kong. Maybe I'll meet an appropriately ambitious guy and we'll get married and run the family business. That way, my father will get the son he's always wanted. Two birds with one stone.

Just past Cleverly Street, there it is. Ba's building, the same as always.

It's been decades since I've set foot inside. Nevertheless, the lobby feels oddly familiar: the pale tiled floors appear streaked with grime, even though they're freshly mopped; the fluorescent lighting is reminiscent of a laundromat, all the fixtures and furniture so out of date you feel like you've stepped into a scene from a Hitchcock film. It's exactly how I remember it from childhood — nothing's changed, right down to the eerie sensation fluttering up over my scalp. I can't explain why I've always had this instinctive revulsion for this place.

I head toward the far end of the lobby where the super has his alcove, his desk. A thin, bald man with yellowish-grey skin and nicotine-stained teeth. "Ming" reads the name badge sewn to his pale-blue shirt. He looks at me expressionlessly, as though I might be a courier or temp.

"I'm ... Mr. Lau's daughter. My father hasn't been well. I'm here to help out."

"Oh." Ming's face comes to life in a deferential smile. It surprises and disturbs me how easily he accepts my claim — I could be an impostor, I *feel* like an impostor — but perhaps he can see the family resemblance. "I've been phoning Mr. Lau for the past two days, but no one answered. I hope he is okay."

"Look, the truth is my father's in the hospital. My sister and I are going to be taking over his affairs."

"I see." File folders shuffle, pink notes fanning out. "Well, there are a couple things I should tell you about, then."

According to Ming, quite a bit has happened. A water damage problem on the twelfth floor. One of the units has leaky windows —

not good during monsoon season. And another tenant, it seems, has been complaining about the AC not working, threatening to move out.

With everything else on my plate, you've got to be fucking kidding me. I realize, at this moment, how little I know about being a landlord. And how little I wish to know. This was always Ba's territory. I want nothing to do with these grey walls and leaky windows and small-time business owners full of rancorous complaints.

"All right." A sigh escapes my throat, the narrowness of the lobby hemming me in. For a moment, I almost wonder whether Ba planned his collapse so I'd be forced to step up. "Do you want to take me upstairs to show me the problems?"

Ming nods.

As we're waiting for the elevator, I sense my father hovering behind me, like an ethereal phantom, me a little girl again, his hand upon my shoulder. One day, this will all be yours, he whispers, in a cloud of chilly air.

When the elevator doors open, a guy pulls out a trolley and lumbers past. Behind him, a couple of men in suits step out, chatting. The more corpulent one keeps looking at me strangely.

"Jill Lau?"

I smile stiffly. It takes me a moment to realize that yes, there *is* something kind of familiar about this face. Gradually, it comes into focus: not the face of this middle-aged man in fogged-up titanium glasses, but a rounder, more boyish version, cheeks still peppered with acne scars.

Eddy. Mr. Chan's son. Mr. Chan, Ba's old business partner.

"Hey, Eddy."

He shakes my hand, his palm sweaty.

"Jill and I, we go way back," Eddy says to the fellow beside him, a short man in an ill-fitting suit. "Our fathers built this building, back in the day." The note of pride is unmistakable.

A bristling feeling goes up the back of my neck. But that's Eddy Chan for you. The good son, the golden boy. Despite looking more portly and weathered, he's still got the same simpering air he's always had.

One summer back in undergrad, when I returned to Hong Kong for a visit, Ba got it into his head to play matchmaker and I had to endure the most awkward date of my life. After that, I swore off dates set up by my parents forever.

Not that Eddy's a bad guy. We just had zilch in common. Even when we knew each other as kids, he was a quiet, nerdy boy, a few years older than me, and by the time of our date we hadn't seen each other in a decade. When I was eleven, the Chans moved away to Vancouver; a real estate company took over managing their share of the office units. And then, Ba was very upset to learn, some years later, Mr. Chan died in a tragic car accident.

Following in his old man's footsteps, Eddy did an accounting degree, though his real interests lay elsewhere. After graduation, he began working for a development company active on both sides of the Pacific, enabling him to move back to Hong Kong.

I wonder whether he still works for that company or even has a real job anymore. Probably that got tiresome, the hours long. I suspect that like most kids in this city of a certain background, Eddy's gone the route of taking over the family business. The path of least resistance.

"So what are you doing here, Eddy?"

"Rent collection." It turns out that the guy beside him is one of his tenants. "How about you? I'm surprised to see you in Hong Kong."

When I explain about my father's condition, Eddy looks aghast. "That's terrible — is he going to be all right?"

"I hope so. It's too early to say, really." I don't know what else to add, awkwardness gripping my throat. I'm not good at dealing with sympathy.

"Well, if you need any help learning the ropes here, feel free to give me a shout."

"Oh, thanks. But I don't plan to be here long. I have my life to get back to in Toronto."

"Oh? But who'll take care of things here?"

"Um, I haven't given it much thought, really." It's embarrassing to admit this, my thoughts as dishevelled as my uncombed hair. "All this happened only two days ago."

He places a pudgy hand on my arm, as though sensing my fatigue, my desperation, and slips me a business card. "My number. In case you need anything."

"Thanks, Eddy."

But I'm not like you. *I don't belong here.*

On the walk back, I get off the escalator at Prince's Terrace and find Café Lavande. On second thought, I dart down to the 7-Eleven for a pack of smokes before heading to the café.

Sitting at a table on the sidewalk, I sip my iced coffee, with plenty of sugar, and inhale the stream of nicotine deeply.

I brought Nick to this very café once. We were sitting a few tables down, where two teenagers have their heads bent together over frothy glasses. How long ago that warm, overcast afternoon now seems. Nick had sensed, by that point, that my father wasn't so keen on him. He had a befuddled look, like a child awoken from a turbulent dream; the anger, the resentment, hadn't yet set in. I wasn't saying the right things. I wasn't saying much of anything. I just watched the backs of his hands, the big, knobby knuckles, the long, slender fingers that had touched me tenderly. And I thought about how perfectly my face fit into the valley between his neck and right shoulder, how that place made me feel so calm. How he still read philosophy books, just for fun. I wanted to say something nerdy and tragic like, "What would Deleuze say about what we're feeling at this moment?" And then we might have laughed and talked about rhizomes and life under capitalism, in a half-serious, half-playful manner, like a couple of blazer-wearing undergrads.

Instead, we just looked a little past each other's left temple and slurped our cool, foamy drinks in silence. I lit a cigarette and Nick let out a hissing sigh through his nostrils. He might have once been a chain-smoking philosophy major with scruffy hair, but he'd left the worst of it behind years ago. It bothered him that I'd taken up smoking again, pretty much as soon as I'd stepped off the plane.

Later that afternoon, while I'm taking a nap, Celeste bursts into my room, without knocking. Her arms are crossed under her breasts to hold her old yellow bathrobe shut, the belt long vanished. Her hair hangs in clumps, damp from the shower.

"I've been thinking, Jill. We have to speak to Ba."

"About?"

"The photos, of course!"

I sit up on the edge of the bed. "Yeah ... but ... what are we going to say?"

"The million-dollar question." Her arms cross tighter, as if trying to contain some creature running around in her gut.

"You saw him yesterday. He's in no condition."

"Not immediately. But once he's stronger."

"*If* he gets stronger."

"Oh, I'm betting he will. He's *Ba*."

The walls of my stomach contract as I stare back at my sister. Her flared, quivering nostrils and pursed lips make her look like a caricature. So self-righteous, so judgmental. So quick to take for granted that Ba's done something wrong.

"Those pictures obviously upset him," she continues. "They *made* him collapse."

"He collapsed because he's a ninety-four-year-old man."

She doesn't seem to have even heard me. "Maybe it'd help him to talk about things, for once. Get it off his chest."

"Get what off his chest?"

"Someone from the old days has it in for Ba. *Clearly.*"

As Celeste raises her arms, exasperated, her bathrobe swings open and I'm forced to glimpse two acorn-like nipples that perch on breasts a bit plumper and nicer than mine. "Don't you ever wonder how Ba managed to get all *this*?" Clutching her robe closed with one hand, she gestures with the other in increasingly large circles around the room.

I feel the pressure building against my forehead, like in the hours before a monsoon. Why can't she just be grateful that Ba did whatever he had to do in order to give us this life? He endured poverty and privation for most of his life so we wouldn't have to. He poured his sweat and blood into building his business so we could grow up in comfort and do our little degrees in art and architecture and never have to worry about where our next meal would come from. Why can't she cut Ba some slack?

"Hard work," I say. "He worked till he collapsed to give us this life."

Celeste rolls her eyes. For a second, she looks like she almost feels sorry for me.

After she's left, I lie on my bed, staring at the wall. I notice that the fake wood veneer of the closet door has cracked loose and warped over the years.

Although I feel close to drifting off, something keeps pulling me up from the black depths of sleep. A memory. A mirage-like image, soft and dream-like. Yet it isn't a dream, or a mirage. For I know with startling clarity that it happened.

It happened like this.

I'm very young. School's still a novel concept — being surrounded by so many other kids is exhilarating, frightening. Every time I walk into the classroom, the rows of little desks fill my tummy with a hush, my heart thrumming with anticipation.

I write my name on the inside of my exercise book. My Chinese name, Lau Yuk Chu. It's the only name I have, at this point in my life. "Yuk" means jade, the swirly green-blue stone that hangs from my mother's earlobes and encircles her wrists. And "Chu" means pearl, which my mother also wears a lot. Then I'm writing other words in Chinese, following the teacher's instructions, copying in pencil all the intersecting, swaying lines of her black marker on the whiteboard.

It won't be until next year, when I enter grade one, that half my classes will switch into English and a new teacher will assign me the name Jill. Celeste's teacher will call her Mary, but like most kids of our generation, she'll shuck it off, preferring to choose her own. For a while, she'll be Charlotte, then Carlotta. Finally, she'll choose Celeste. Me, I won't be bothered. And besides, I'll kind of like the name my teacher chooses for me, its blank, fresh quality. Nice to take a break from being my mother's little Jade Pearl.

I raise my hand. "I'm done."

"That was fast," the teacher says, standing behind me, looking over my work. Her smile casts warm rays down on my shoulders.

Since I'm the first to finish, I'm allowed to go next door to the playroom, an expansive, cement-floored space with a big sandbox in the centre, a lawn of luscious green AstroTurf off to one side. There's a red tricycle I like. I begin riding around in circles, faster and faster, beneath the skylight, that glorious slip of sky spinning above me. I get off, dizzy, invigorated, and I can see straight up into the blue, blue blueness, no end in sight. Then I'm back on the seat, riding even faster than before, the air like a balm against my cheeks.

As I swerve past the bank of windows, a face catches my eye. A man is looking in, watching me. *My father!* Can it really be him?

Yes, it *is* Ba! He's waving at me, beaming. My heart leaps up through the skylight, somersaulting into the clouds.

Later that week, I see him outside the windows again. It becomes a routine for him to stroll past the kindergarten over lunch hour, once he knows that I'll always be the kid who finishes her work first and gets to ride the red trike.

"Are you out of your mind?" Celeste said to me, when I recounted this story to her.

We were all grown up by then, living in Toronto, in our early twenties. We were at a coffee shop in the middle of a snowstorm, the tile floor streaked with grey slush. Arguing. Arguing about her claim that Ba was never there for us at all. According to her, he never did anything as a father, beyond paying the bills. He ran our family like a business, and that was no way to make kids feel loved. No way at all.

My skin tightened, flushed. Yet I felt sorry for my sister. Because if that's the way she felt, then that's the way she felt. And maybe things were different for her — maybe it was true that Ba had always favoured me. Celeste was never as sharp at school, and she'd always had a bit of a snarky attitude, to be honest. So what could I say? It was a shitty thing to admit, but maybe she'd never gotten as much affection from Ba.

I should've let it go, I should've kept quiet. But I couldn't help it — my instinct to set her straight was just too strong. Thus I made the mistake of sharing my memory of Ba outside the kindergarten window.

"You are so fucking deluded, Jill. I went to that kindergarten too, you know. The playroom didn't even have windows!"

"What are you talking about?"

Celeste smiled grimly, shaking her head. "It had a wall with some stupid mural of meadows and mountains. *No windows.*"

"Whatever." I concentrated very hard on the donut display behind us, the bright, icing-slicked *O*'s. I tried to let the whole thing drop. Let my sister hold on to her delusions.

How satisfied she looked that she'd succeeded in getting to me.

"Besides," I continued, "Ba *told me* about how he used to come to the kindergarten and watch me ride around. I'm not just making this up."

"Oh, right. Like Ba's never told us a lie before. What you remember is nothing more than Ba *telling you* that he came to watch you on that stupid trike. How proud he was of you. And what a great father he was. Wow, he really did a number on you. Do you really think he would've taken the time out of his precious workday?"

A spell of dizziness, uncertainty. My voice like a fragile ribbon. "He might have." For me. He might have.

Back in grad school, I became attached to the films of Tarkovsky. One of my profs mentioned his name during a lecture about exile and "transcendental homelessness" or something arcane like that. So I rented a film and watched it one evening while smoking a joint. It was one of those art-house movies with very little dialogue and long, haunting silences. The sound of raindrops, green bottles rattling in a downpour. If I were to watch it now, I'm sure I'd find it pretentious as hell.

The main character — the rare times that he speaks — has a monotone voice. For much of the film, he's simply wandering the Italian countryside in the company of a madman, slowly walking through abandoned buildings, the rain and mist and smoke from his cigarette giving the scenes a veiled, bleached-out quality.

Occasionally, black-and-white images of another time flash in his mind. A modest house in the country, tamarisk trees in the background. A white horse, a large dog. A peasant woman with two children, a boy and a girl, everyone wearing black shawls over white clothing, as they stand perfectly still on the grass. The boy, the younger child, is blond and innocent looking, but he bears a strangely frozen — unsmiling — expression. Everyone does. In fact, there's something downright eerie about these pastoral images, which represent the main character's memories of his childhood in Russia. His nostalgia, supposedly. *Nostalghia*, after all, is the title of the film.

But if it's nostalgia he's feeling, it's a weird kind of nostalgia, as though the past, or his memory of the past, is largely absent, drained of emotion. All that remains are a few cold images. Where one expects to find yearning, one confronts instead a desire not to look at anything too closely. A desire to turn away.

In the late afternoon, I return to Ba's building to meet with a tradesman I've sourced online. We go up to the unit with the leaky windows and he confirms that it's all beyond repair. I'm looking at dishing out a small fortune for all new windows. Authorizing the work, I hand over the company credit card.

The tenants are none too pleased about how all this is disrupting their workflow. Just as I'm about to leave the unit, the big-haired woman, who acts like she's in charge, grabs me by the elbow. It turns out that the remote control for the AC has gone missing and would I mind replacing it immediately? The thing looks archaic, like a model from the eighties, probably long discontinued. But, being a good landlord, I reply that I'll look into the situation, of course.

I consider checking in with Ming on my way out, then think better of it. If there are more problems, I don't want to know.

Unfortunately, Ming has sharp eyes. Just as I'm trying to slip past unnoticed, he calls out at my back, "Miss! You forgot this."

He hands me a stack of envelopes and a box wrapped in brown paper. I flip through the letters; they're just bills, never-ending bills. I tear the paper off the box. It's a shoebox, though far too light to contain shoes.

The lid pops off — I jump back. The box topples to the floor, its contents scattering everywhere.

A red joss stick.

A piece of yellow paper. The kind burned at funerals.

A square of faded crimson fabric overlaid with patterned stitching, a wisp of cotton batting visible at the neatly cut edges. The corner of a quilt.

A handful of soil, now peppering the ground.

A mouse, stiff and grey, tail and tiny claws outstretched in opposite directions. Frozen by death.

"Holy shit!" Ming's voice sounds distant, as he stands at the periphery of my vision. "You okay, miss?"

I'm nodding or I'm shaking my head — I can't tell which. "Where ... where did this box come from? Did someone drop it off?"

"It arrived by regular mail."

The paper it was wrapped in has fallen to the floor. As I pick it up with trembling hands, I see the Guangzhou postmark and black-pen handwriting. It looks like the same writing as on the envelopes that contained the photos. No return address, once again.

"I'll call the janitor, miss. Get this cleaned up right away."

"Thank you."

He doesn't ask any more questions, for which I'm grateful.

The glare off the polished floor has a mesmerizing quality, as I stand perfectly still, surveying the scene. It's as though I'm merely a shocked onlooker, for a long moment. Although I want nothing more than to hightail it, a little voice in my head tells me to pull out my phone and snap pictures, so I'll have proof this actually happened. As I take several shots, I feel like I'm documenting a crime scene. But it's not a crime scene, it's a funeral scene. The incense stick, the scrap of quilt, the scattered soil, the rough yellow paper burned as an offering to the next world, the small animal corpse. A crude parody of our rituals of burial and mourning.

Then I rush outside into the muggy air and fumble to light a cigarette. As a bus passes by, the ashes blow back and stick to my damp cheeks.

FOUR

I'm tearing up a head of lettuce in a cloud of steam. Rina elbows into me, meat sizzling in the wok in front of her. "Sit down, ma'am. Give me that — I cook it with garlic and ginger."

"No, Rina. I'm making a salad."

Rina's elaborate Chinese soups and stewed casseroles are making my digestive system sluggish. But salad — or anything raw for that matter — is unheard of in the Chinese diet. "I'm no rabbit," my mother used to say. Considering that Ba's been eating like this all his life, I'm not surprised his bowels stopped working and ruptured.

Finally, however, the heat from the stove gets to me and I decide to leave Rina alone to do her thing, sautéing the lettuce. Too many cooks in the kitchen.

My sister's already seated at the dining room table, sipping tea, waiting for Rina to bring everything in. Celeste hasn't even bothered to set the table.

"You okay, Jill? Everything went okay with the window repair guy? You seem tense."

Something about receiving dead rodents in the mail will do that to a person.

I gear myself up to tell Celeste the news, which will send her into a tailspin, no doubt. I can already picture her raking her hands through her hair, her eyebrows jumping up, energized. She'll want to confront Ba. She'll want to call the police. Should we? And say what? Look at the diorama of death we received in the mail? Oh, God. I start coughing up semi-hysterical giggles. Who am I to be judging my sister? I'm as much a wreck as anybody.

"Hey, Celeste? Do you remember Ba ever mentioning any … enemies?"

"Enemies?"

"Yeah."

"Take your pick," she says. "Just look at how many housekeepers he's sacked over the years. What's this all about?"

"A package arrived at Ba's building." As I explain its contents, my sister's petrified expression mirrors what I'm feeling. When I show her the photos on my phone, the fear in her eyes gives over to outrage.

"*Who does this kind of thing?*"

"Someone with too much time on his hands?"

"Ba must've pissed someone off big time!"

"There are plenty of folks who are just plain crazy."

Celeste looks at me like I'm a dim-witted child. "We have to tell Ba."

"You think he'll know who sent it?"

She nods emphatically. "Just like he knows who sent the pictures."

After dinner, we head to the hospital.

At the water dispenser in the corner of the ward, I fill a cup for Ba and add a straw so it'll be easier to drink.

"Too cold." He pushes it away after one sip.

I go back to the dispenser, add a stream of boiling water and stir. "Too hot," he says.

Christ. Clearly, he's feeling more like himself, fussy as ever. I dump out the water and start over. My sister and I exchange tense glances. *We should just ask him.* If he's strong enough to be full of complaints, he's strong enough to answer a few frigging questions.

But every time I get up the nerve, Ba turns feisty about something else. The nurse urges him to eat a bit of congee, which she spoons into his shrivelled lips.

His face contracts in disgust. "Not enough salt."

"You're on a low-sodium diet, sir."

"Well, this is inedible."

"If you don't eat, you'll have to be fed through a tube in your nose."

"So be it."

Another nurse — this one plumper and cheerier — comes over to take Ba's temperature and administer his nighttime meds. If only these ladies would just leave us alone for a few minutes, I could get to what's really important.

There's a shot cup of thick, pink liquid that leaves a chalky taste in Ba's mouth. "*Dreadful.* What're you trying to do to me? Make me choke to death?"

Celeste tries to help Ba brush his teeth. He claims he can still taste the gritty residue and demands to brush all over again. Her lips purse; I can tell she's trying very hard to refrain from saying anything, knowing that if she gets started she won't be able to hold back. I find myself wishing to slow his recovery, longing for some docile old man.

The news on the TV, which hangs from a swivelling arm above the bed, is all about how China's economy is in a state of freefall, despite the government's interventions. Ba is worried, but he's trying to pretend he's not. "It'll spring back. I made a killing in China Life a few years back."

"Rest, save your strength," I tell him.

I flip to another news channel. The president's anticorruption sweep has taken down another "tiger" in the Party, it appears. The photo of the disgraced official, up in the corner of the screen, is from his glory days. The glow of his fleshy face and the sharp angles of his suit, which once made him appear stately, now have been recoded as signs of his duplicity, his guilt.

"The purge continues," Celeste says softly.

Even now, in his weakened state, Ba's eyes light up with fiery enthusiasm, as we hear about how an undercover investigation has exposed this man's habit of taking massive bribes, needed to support his harem of mistresses.

"Good riddance," Ba says.

"You really think this is making things better?" Celeste replies.

Pride suffuses our father's expression, leaving a pinkish glow. "Under the new president, China's on the cusp of becoming the number one economy in the world. What's not to like about that?"

"The economy's not doing so well right now," I say.

"Just a blip. A little hiccup. In six months, by the end of 2015, everything will be just fine. You wait and see. And I'll be checked out of here by the end of the week!"

I wonder if his fortitude's an act. But no, he really does look better since yesterday. The doctors and nurses seem impressed by his progress. So what are we waiting for?

"Ba," I blurt, "we found some interesting mail in your desk."

His eyes veer sideways. A hailstorm of coughing overtakes him, words sticking to the back of his throat.

Then I realize that I'm mistaken. He's not trying to speak at all.

"The two envelopes in your desk, Ba? They contained pictures."

My sister fishes them from her purse and drops them onto the bed in front of him.

He cringes, his eyes dart away. He makes a recoiling motion, like he doesn't want the images anywhere near his skin. "How dare you go through my desk?" Despite his angry words, he appears more defeated than anything.

Celeste withdraws the photos. We all sit in silence for several seconds. In the adjacent tower a ballet class is going on: I can see a dozen young girls in pink tutus running around one of the suites, their arms rising and lowering, like flowers slowly blooming and wilting.

"Don't you have anything to tell us?" Celeste demands. "What's going on here?"

"We're worried about you," I add more gently.

"And also," Celeste says, "a package —"

"Calm down, Ba, just rest," I interrupt, seeing his agitation growing. His face looks very pale and drained. Perhaps we overestimated his strength.

"Time for you both to go home," he says. "I'm tired, okay?"

The curtain around the bed is yanked back by a nurse, her broad, matronly face pinched in disapproval. "What's all this commotion, girls? Your father's right — he needs to rest." She glares at us while we gather up our things, like we must be the worst daughters in the world.

"So that went well," I say during the taxi ride home.

Celeste gnaws at a hangnail while staring out the window. "What did you expect?"

"And we didn't even get to ask about the package."

"Yeah, thanks to you!"

"You saw how upset Ba —"

"*Too bad.*" She crosses her arms in a huff.

"Fine, feel free to take charge, rather than sitting back and leaving all the talking to me. You're in charge from now on."

"Fine. Whatever."

"So …" I say, my irritation fading, "what are we going to do now?"

"Let Ba stew in it. Let him lose a little sleep. You saw his face."

"Yeah, he looked pretty terrified."

Terrified enough to open up to us?

A few minutes later, I receive a text message. I notice my sister watching me with a small, arch smile.

"Terence?" she asks.

I nod. "How did you know?"

"Who else could it be?"

Right. Terence Fok. My one and only friend in Hong Kong. The one guy I've kept in touch with over the years. We've been texting, mostly about Ba's medical situation. Terence has been urging me to make sure I don't get run down, too, his usual antidote being drinks, a night on the town. I've been delaying him, wanting to wait until Ba's out of the woods.

"I don't care if you and Terence have a thing, Jill. You don't have to hide it from me. Whatever he and I once had? Ancient history. We were a couple of horny teenagers."

"Oooh, gross." Definitely an image I can live without. Besides, Terence and I don't have a *thing*. "We're just friends, okay? What's so hard to understand about that?"

"Right. Friends with benefits?"

"Look, the only benefit I get from Terence is that he always orders a good bottle of wine."

In a way, he does feel like an old ex-boyfriend. He knows exactly the kind of French reds I like to drink. Funny to think that my sister's actually his ex. That was a lifetime ago, during undergrad days. Celeste was doing an exchange program in New York, where she met Terence at a party. He was at Columbia taking a finance degree. I came to visit one weekend, but by that point, their relationship was fizzling and he talked more to me than to my sister.

While wandering past wall-size paintings in museums — sun-lit red rectangles and anguished black smears — we chatted about this and that. We were both fond of Roman Polanski and Nina Simone, it turned out. He was reading a book called *The Interpretation of Cultures* for his anthro elective, and had I read it? As we kept talking and strolling — Terence's tall, lean body like a birch tree, rather comforting to stand under — I recall thinking that he didn't seem like a finance major. I even said that aloud. To which he replied that in his family, going to university meant that you had to study business.

At some point, he told me that his father was soon going in for a heart operation, which would involve the valve of a pig. (Although this might seem like a heavy thing to tell someone you've just met, that thought only occurred to me later. He felt like an old friend. From the very beginning, he felt like an old friend.) When I asked whether it was serious, he nodded; his father could die. Yet Terence seemed surprisingly calm about the whole thing. At first, I wondered if he was feigning indifference. But I didn't think so. I sensed that he'd be genuinely relieved by his father's death, as though he felt nothing intrinsic tying himself to the man, their relationship as random as two strangers on a bus. And that made me feel all the more warmly toward Terence, like I could say absolutely anything to him and he'd never judge me a horrible person.

There's a fable Ba used to tell me and Celeste, when we were kids, about how he managed to make it back to Hong Kong after enduring years of drudgery in Guangzhou.

All the odds were against him. His peanut oil shop had long gone out of business. After the Communists' victory, it became difficult for anyone to make a living hustling on what was left of the free market; the government had nationalized all industries. Each individual was assigned to a work unit. Our father, who lacked education, was deemed fit for the job of street cleaner. At least he wasn't being denounced and beaten at community meetings or sent off for re-education to a labour camp, like so many people with a whiff of an elite, capitalist-landlord background. Still, his back ached from all the sweeping and he developed a persistent cough from all the dust and grime. His entrepreneurial spirit languished, beyond occasional dabblings in the black market — helping farmers hawk their excess produce on the sly. But it was small potatoes, quite literally.

Throughout it all, he persisted in working hard, he told us. If he was destined to be a street sweeper, the very best street sweeper he'd be.

Finally, after years of enduring this fate, his diligence caught the eye of a new unit supervisor, who arrived just as the Cultural Revolution was getting underway. "The man came up to me." A dreamy smile, at the memory. "He said, 'I've noticed you working so hard to keep our streets clean, while everyone else here just pretends to work — lazy asses!' We began talking and he asked me where I'm from. I told him I was born in Hong Kong. 'Ah, Hong Kong! The land of opportunity.' The man had friends in Hong Kong, he let me know, under his breath. 'Although I could get in a lot of trouble for doing this, I'm going to cut you a break, you poor bastard.' At the end of the week, he slipped me an envelope that contained a travel permit allowing me to return to Hong Kong, along with one hundred dollars cash. I was so astonished and overjoyed that I broke down in tears."

As with all Ba's tales, there were multiple life lessons to be extracted. "The first lesson is: always work hard, no matter how menial the job is." A bony finger raised in the air. "And never forget the importance of forming relationships. Impressing your superiors is key. You never know when your efforts might pay off. Success in business depends on these things."

It all came down to a few bullet points, à la Dale Carnegie, in the end.

My sister's face would glaze over when he told this story, like she was singing a song in her head to block him out. I, on the other hand, knew it was best to listen and show interest. Once Ba had finished, if I was lucky, I'd receive enough money to buy a candy bar or ice cream cone.

It was a nice story. Though, if I'm honest with myself, I never truly believed it, even back then. Just as I always sensed that Santa Claus didn't exist, Ba's tale had an aura of wishful thinking, subterfuge. But as a child, you're expected to keep up the charade that you believe in the fat, jolly man in a red suit who travels in a sleigh led by flying reindeer. So you don't voice your doubts; you smile, you open your gifts.

For some reason, this attitude of mine continued long after I'd fully realized how far-fetched and utterly implausible his stories were. There hadn't been any generously bestowed travel permit or envelope of cash. Of course there hadn't. These work-unit supervisors were stern people, not likely to put their asses on the line just to be nice.

But on some level, I wanted my father's make-believe to be true, I guess. It was as though his younger self were still alive, if only in my imagination, and I was rooting for that poor wretch to find a way out.

I guess I assumed that in reality Ba was ashamed of the way he'd made his escape. You hear stories of old timers, who, back in the 1960s and '70s, jumped into the dirty waters of Shenzhen Bay under the cover of night and made the long, harrowing swim to Hong Kong. For every person who made it across, scores drowned or were killed by sharks — if they weren't shot dead by the People's Liberation Army first. Their corpses washed up on our shores, flesh scavenged down to the bone by shellfish.

And yet, over the years, enough of them made it across. Enough to satisfy our city's demand for cheap labour in its sweatshops and construction sites.

I awake in the middle of the night, hungry and thirsty, worn out by a strenuous dream. Although I can't remember the whole thing, vestiges hover at the back of my brain: the lid of a shoebox being lifted off, Ba getting all agitated and trembly upon seeing the contents, the dead mouse twitching to life — flying up like a projectile and fastening its tiny, outstretched claws to his nose.... Blinking hard to remind myself I'm awake, I peer into the fridge and find only that limp sautéed lettuce, so I open the cupboard and stare up at rows of tins — beans, pineapple wedges, tuna — and, sure enough, many are past their expiry dates. I don't care. Eating is good. Eating will help appease the gnawing, ulcerous feeling in my gut. I peel open a tin of smoked oysters, add a shot of soy sauce, and scrounge up a pack of crackers, the fishy, salty taste tempered by mealy sawdust. A finger or two of Scotch streams into my glass to wash it down.

Through the living room window, I see that the building next to ours has been covered by a scaffolding of bamboo rods, veiled by diaphanous sheets to keep out the construction dust. They billow in the wind, under the moonlight, as if revealing the high-rise's ghostly, old soul.

Framed photographs look out from our credenza, all old and out of date. My mother selected them.

In one, she's in California at Universal Studios with my father on one of the few vacations they took together. Her hair's in an eighties body perm, her oversized pink shirt as bright as her lip-sticked smile, while my father, shaded by a sun visor, looks subdued.

In another one, she's holding up a certificate for a course she took on elaborate garnishes: white radishes turned into sparrows, carrots transformed into lotus blossoms, a watermelon hollowed out into a lace-edged bowl. I remember thinking the whole thing was pretty silly.

Looking at these ordinary pictures makes me think of another picture. Ba's building. The red armband. The desecrated floor of the lobby — the rodent corpse — flashes in my mind.

I wonder how much my mother knew about Ba's past. If she were alive today, would she be able to say whether he ever had any involvement with the Red Guards? And how did he manage to flee Guangzhou, anyway? A defensive feeling sweeps over me. But I'm not being like my sister — I'm not assuming the worst. My curiosity stems from pride, from love. Doesn't it? I'm proud of Ba.

And yet, the faded luxury of this room — this life — fills me with uncertainty, dread. There are questions I don't dare to ask myself. Insomnia is already wrapping over my scalp like a prickly cap.

If I'd raised any of this with Mom, it's not like I'd have gotten any answers, anyway. She was never one to talk about the past, or anything that made her uncomfortable, for that matter. "I don't have time for all your yapping" was her standard line.

My gaze migrates farther down the credenza to the pictures of her with me and Celeste. We're at the playground, posed on both sides of our mother on the roundabout, as if she's the one who brings us there every day, rather than our nanny.

For as long as I can remember, she prided herself on speaking English with a light British accent and often addressed us in English so we'd have a leg up at school. *Stand up straight, girls. Make sure your teacher likes you. Smile, even if you're feeling glum.* Mom was a high school English teacher, so she knew the drill.

Although she didn't need to work anymore, she kept her job to stave off boredom, I suspect. Then every day after she'd finished teaching, she'd take a taxi into Central and spend the rest of the afternoon trying on clothes at Lane Crawford.

In the photo at the playground, she's still young and attractive, though her skin has begun to darken. She was thirty-one when she got married, old by the standards of the day. Perhaps that's why she appears a tad exhausted in her wedding pictures. Relieved, maybe. Not ecstatic. While my father can be seen making his way around the banquet hall — shaking hands, networking, his face ablaze with his own success — my mother's pale, reserved countenance is harder to read.

Apparently, a colleague at her school had introduced her to my father, and they married just a few months later. I can't imagine it was love at first sight. He was more than twenty years her senior, with terrible table manners that continue to this day.

A woman as pretty as my mother must have had other suitors when she was younger, but perhaps she proved too egotistical for their tastes, impossible to please. Her father being old school, Mom knew that her brothers would inherit everything, so marriage was her only ticket to a comfortable, moneyed life. From that standpoint, Ba wasn't a bad catch. Whatever hardships he'd lived through in Guangzhou, they hadn't affected his entrepreneurial instincts. Since his return to Hong Kong, his acumen and luck had resurged with a vengeance. By the early 1970s, he owned a supermarket business that wholesaled tea and juice to large restaurants, airlines, and hotels. Old British companies like Lipton and Unilever were looking to expand their reach in the Asian marketplace, and Ba found himself well positioned to serve as the go-between.

• • •

I can't say my mother was ever very warm or maternal, though she probably tried her best, considering her own strange upbringing. From a young age, I was aware that she had two sets of siblings, but the elder lot we saw only at funerals, where they were always cool to us. It turned out they were her half-siblings. My grandmother had gotten duped into being something of a concubine. All too late, she'd discovered that her husband already had a wife and kids in China. While my grandfather's behaviour would have been nothing out of the ordinary on that side of the border, this was Hong Kong, under British laws and customs. My grandmother, I would assume, didn't take well to finding out she was, in the eyes of many, the mistress of a scoundrel. By the time I knew her, she was a frail, grey-skinned lady who delighted in nothing so much as the cocktail of medicinal oils she dabbed at her temples constantly, a cloying odour of sandalwood, licorice, and salted fish.

Things got worse when my grandfather decided to move his first wife and family to Hong Kong, in order to protect them from the civil war in China. My mother grew up in a stone mansion at Jardine's Lookout, where one wing was devoted to the first wife's family, the other wing to her own line. That she was the apple of her father's eye turned her into a useful pawn in the ongoing power struggles. Or so I imagine, based on how adept she became at scheming. She never talked about these things; she only ever spoke about her childhood in idyllic terms. How rich they were. How every single one of the children had a separate maid. How her father introduced her to smoking — he said the nicotine would help her to stay up and study. Nice dad.

Fortunately, the hospital has Wi-Fi. The next morning, I bring in my laptop and try to answer a slew of work emails while Ba twitches and snores. Carlos, my HR manager, enquires about how things are going on the home front. The tone of his message is supportive, but what he really wants to know is how much longer I'll be away. Cashing out the rest of my vacation days, I've bought myself a little over a week, much of it gone already. My supervisor has reassigned my work to another project manager, who's letting the consultants walk all over her, I can tell by skimming the emails. Change orders, sloppy drawings. Construction on a large park is about to begin, after a lengthy delay. There's going to be a world of stress for me to deal with when I get back.

Ba no longer seems to be getting better. It's as though the unpleasant talk Celeste and I had with him yesterday has sent him back into decline. He's lethargic, his eyes cracked open in milky slits, his appetite non-existent. At first, I wonder whether he's faking this relapse in an attempt to teach us a lesson. But his weakened state appears real enough. Guilt erupting in my chest, I resolve to wait a bit before asking him about the photos again and bringing up the mini funeral in a shoebox.

I've got more immediate concerns to deal with. It'll be some time before we can leave him on his own. The cardiologist, Dr. Chu, keeps talking about the tough journey ahead, the ever-present risk of infection.

I bite the bullet and ask Carlos for a month-long leave of absence.

At some point, Ba opens his eyes. He stares at the ceiling, unblinking, for a long time. Soon, he'll fall back asleep or turn away, punishing me and my sister.

"How are you feeling?" I ask.

"I've been better."

When he sees that I have no intention of grilling him at the moment, his face relaxes a little. Celeste looks over at us from her chair in the corner and I wonder whether she's planning to launch into the dead mouse, but she settles back and stares down at her phone.

Ba's voice is like a wheeze, an effortful wheeze. "The first time ... I saw her ... I thought she was the most beautiful woman alive ..."

Awkwardness creeps over me. Grossness. Who is my father talking about? Some old flame?

"Rest, Ba."

"I knew that if I could marry her ... I had it ... in me ... to rebuild myself from nothing ..."

"You're talking about *Mom*?"

I wonder if the meds are messing with his hormones. When she was alive, Ba never showed Mom any affection, not in front of us, that's for sure. They never went out on dates. Occasionally, as a kid, I'd hear them talking in hushed tones behind their bedroom door, and I'd strain to catch some note of intimacy, of love. Maybe it was there and I just couldn't detect it. Or maybe Ba was incapable of expressing his love for her until she was gone.

In any case, his timeline's way off. My mother couldn't have given him the strength to rebuild his life, because he was already rich when she married him. But that's not something I can say, of course, so I just stroke his hand and let him continue his odd reminiscence.

"I always thought ... she'd be here beside me ..." His eyes mist up, his chin jutting out, trembling. He feels cheated, sorry for himself. "That's why I worked myself ... to the bone.... The money ... was supposed to be for her ... after I'm gone ..."

A balloon of air escapes my sister's rubbery lips, disdain bristling from her bony shoulders.

"It's okay, Ba. Mom knew she was well taken care of, thanks to you." I stroke his forehead while shooting Celeste a cold glance.

But I understand why she's pissed off. Ba's claim that his workaholic behaviour was solely for his wife doesn't ring true, in her mind. And I can't deny she has a point. The main reason Ba worked so hard is that he likes to work. He loves nothing so much on this earth as making money. He's happiest when he's reviewing his investments and studying the fluctuations of currencies and commodities around the world, contemplating what to sell and what to buy. He follows international politics for this purpose, too. A regime falls, markets crash, and the falcons swoop down to carry away the spoils.

After a bout of coughing, he continues trying to speak: "If your mother were alive ... we could go travelling together.... She always wanted to ... go back to Paris ..."

"Oh, *please*," Celeste says. "You *hated* travelling. All those museums bored you to tears. Whenever Mom wanted to go anywhere, you always said you couldn't afford the time away!"

He flinches. Instinctively, my hands have reached out to my father, my arms shielding him from my sister's harsh words. Up close, I can see the dead flakes of skin clinging to his nose, the grey, discoloured patches on his cheeks, like the outer layer of an old onion. Staring at the ceiling, he makes no attempt to defend himself or tell my sister off. His eyelids drop shut. *This is exactly how he'll look when he's dead.*

"I can't take this anymore — this joke of a family!" Celeste storms out, bumping into a metal cart on her way out.

Several minutes later, Ba opens his eyes and finds me still there, watching over him.

In the days after Mom's death, Celeste and I went through her clothes, separating the things to give to charity from those we wanted to keep. That's when we discovered the cache of photo albums at the back of her closet. I pull them out when I get back to the condo.

Our mother? A girl of thirteen, in her high school uniform. Chin raised, she smiles directly into the camera, with all the confidence of a girl who knows she's pretty. The dark A-line skirt emphasizes the slenderness of her waist. Her white ankle socks and black flats have a girlish look, yet there's something contrived about how she's angled one foot behind the other, toes pointed outward in a balletic pose. She's grown accustomed to being admired and making the most of every opportunity.

She developed more range as she got older. In some photos, she looks shy and a little bewildered, a white scarf wrapped around her hair. In others, she's dreamy looking, contemplative, a tad wild or vivacious, as though she's watched her share of American films. Sometimes she has friends with her, other well-dressed girls from moneyed backgrounds. Sometimes the friends are boys. By twenty, she has the look of an Asian Jackie Kennedy — the tousled bouffant hair, the oversized sunglasses — but instead of tailored suits, she wears short *qipao*s in bold, dramatic prints: magenta swirls against black, white peonies on aubergine.

I wonder about the person taking these pictures, especially during the year she spent in Europe. In those photos, she can be seen smoking and drinking red wine at a sidewalk café in Paris and standing in Piazza San Marco in Venice, in front of the basilica, the sun reflecting off the domes and spires and her bare right shoulder. She's always depicted alone, yet there's a feeling of intimacy in the way she looks at the photographer. The Europe photos appear less posed than the others, as though they capture private moments, sides of my mother she never intended to share with anyone except this photographer — her boyfriend, her lover, perhaps. It's impossible for me to imagine her looking at my father in quite this way. Her smile is relaxed, silly even, as if she and this man have reverted to being little kids together, having just disentangled themselves from a sloppy kiss.

It's this young woman — the party girl, the lover, my mother before she was my mother — who catches hold of my imagination, makes me want to get to know her. By the time she'd become my mom, the light had been extinguished from her eyes, the anticipation vanished from her step. And so it's a phantasm I've conjured in my head, I guess, when I think I recall myself as a young child clasping my beautiful, fun-loving mother's hand as we'd enter the tearoom of the Mandarin Oriental hotel and all heads turn.

FIVE

"So when are we going to talk to Ba about the package?" Celeste asks. She stands in the hallway, still in her pyjamas.

I cross my arms, my wrists aching. My desire to procrastinate has never been stronger. "You really think he's strong enough?" An image of his face, so listless against the pillow, fills me with pity and dread.

She sighs, rubbing her eyes like a sleepy child. "Well, in that case …"

I can already sense in my bones what's coming next.

"I'm sorry, Jill — I just feel like crap today. Mind going to the hospital on your own?"

"What the hell …? Don't you want to talk to Ba about the package?"

"*You* talk to him, when you're ready."

"Why does it always have to be me?"

With a pitiful smile, Celeste clutches a hand to her stomach, as though she's getting the most awful menstrual cramps.

One hall pass turns into another. Over the next few days, she continues to mope around and visits Ba only once, staying for less than an hour. My irritation simmers. Okay, so our father refuses to talk about the past and sees his life through rose-coloured glass. Just because Celeste's pissed off doesn't mean she's off the hook. And Ba doesn't hesitate to let me know that her negligence has been noted.

When I confront her, indignation fires up her expression. "What's the big deal? Ba's always preferred your company, anyway. Seeing me just reminds him of what a screw-up I am!"

I try to let it drop. Now is not the time to pick fights.

In her own way, Celeste helps out. We divide up the to-do list and get into a routine. She can't stand dealing with the banking, bills, rent collection, or building repairs. In general, anything to do with money makes her skin crawl. But she doesn't mind running around to buy the bags of adult diapers the hospital expects us to provide. She's quite fine making the soup Ba wants brought to him every evening, so I let her do her thing with the cauldron of figs, mushrooms, and dried tangerine peel, letting it simmer like a witch's brew for hours.

Meanwhile, I'm at the bank shifting funds around, withdrawing staggering sums to cover the hospital bills. I'm running to the post office to pay off his phone, electricity, and credit card bills — everything late, so late. Ba's become absentminded, more than absentminded. He'd never have let things slide like this in the old days. Then I'm sourcing electricians and plumbers for the repairs that constantly need to be made to his building. And I'm chasing down tenants who seem to have forgotten when their rents are due, based on what I manage to deduce from his inadequate records.

Ba used to have the rent-collection schedule memorized. When I question him about certain outstanding cases, I expect his face to regain its alert glow. Instead, panic appears to wash over him. "Have you … made out proper receipts?"

"Ba, how can I make out receipts if I haven't collected the rent yet?"

"Well ... check my files. Everything should be there. And make sure to write out receipts. And deposit the cheques into the right accounts. And bring me receipts from the bank to prove it!"

"All right already."

A pinprick of fear bounces across his eyes, his voice splintering. "I shouldn't be dealing with numbers and money, in this state. You ... you have to do it."

A shocking admission coming from my father.

Files? What files? Going through all the cabinets in our condo, I find everything a bloody mess. Ba is of that generation that never throws anything out. Papers have been stuffed into drawers in his study until they won't close. The overflow's in boxes on the floor. More overflow is in the old fridge in the corner of his bedroom and stashed in drawers that ought to contain his pyjamas. His accounting consists of ringed notebooks, "1989" and "1992" written in ballpoint pen on the covers, the years in between somehow missing. He's never owned a computer, just his trusty old calculator and abacus in the corner of his desk.

While sorting through it all, I'm on the alert for any clues about Ba's pen pal. If Celeste's right that somebody from the old days has it in for him, it's possible we're talking about a previous tenant. Maybe the guy moved to Guangzhou? It's not uncommon for Hongkongers to retire to that area, where property's far cheaper.

But I find nothing in Ba's records to point in that direction. No forwarding address in Guangzhou, no mention of that city at all. It's hard enough to piece together a list of our *current* tenants.

My sister isn't terribly appreciative of all my efforts. The sight of Ba's files strewn across the dining room table wins me a long, irritated sigh.

"Having fun being his secretary?"

"Someone's got to do it, Celeste."

"Really."

"Otherwise, the money stops flowing." Duh.

"By the way, Eddy Chan called." An unnatural tilt in her tone. "He asked how you're making out. He said you should feel free to call him, if you have any questions about the building."

"That's nice of him, I guess."

"So now you're going to be just like Eddy?"

"*Oh, for fuck's sake, Celeste.*" I gesture at the mass of dogeared folders and papers. "You think I'm enjoying any of this?"

"Why do it, then?"

"What? You want the whole business to collapse?"

In the humidity, the tendrils at her temples are unfurling like strands of seaweed. "Some people might be happy if Ba's business collapsed. If that whole fucking building collapsed. Like whoever sent that package!"

I never wanted to deal with any of this. My sister's full of crap. I have just as much of an aversion to Ba's money as she does. I'm not like Eddy — it's been fifteen years since I've taken a dime from our father. In fact, that's what pushed our relationship onto the rocks in the first place.

I still remember the delirious thrill of defying him, of shocking him speechless. It was the winter after I'd finished undergrad. I was working for one of the larger architecture firms in Toronto, doing some of the usual CAD monkey stuff, but also starting to distinguish myself as one of the kids who could actually design. Going back to school for my master's was on my mind. When I mentioned this to Ba during one of our rare phone conversations — long-distance rates were still high back then, so he didn't like to waste money on idle chitchat — he began throwing his weight around. I knew it was happening before he'd even breathed a word. Something about how the currents of silence seemed to shift, like the quiver in air molecules in that second before a slap across the face.

"Don't you think it's about time you came back to Hong Kong? Time for you to roll up your sleeves and work with me to make some real money."

I remained perfectly quiet. Ba probably took this as a sign of acceptance, assent.

"After you've worked a few years in Hong Kong, if you still want to go back to school, then we'll talk. And I'll probably give you the money. And if you want to study abroad, why not New York or London? That'd be more fun than Toronto and you'd make more useful connections."

As usual, the carrot and stick routine, nothing veiled about it. The threat of being cut off. The reward of grad school somewhere glamorous and exciting.

An eerie calm slipped over me, the walls of my bedroom so white and pure they seemed to be glowing with an almost supernatural quality. After spending my whole life being bossed around by this man, it dawned on me that there was nothing he could do to me. "See, Ba, here's the thing. You mention covering my school bills. But I have no intention of taking money from you. *Ever again.* I wouldn't dream of it."

A wallop of silence, surprise, incomprehension.

"It's time for me to stand on my own, don't you think?"

"But …"

Just like that, the all-powerful threat of disinheritance ceased to be a threat. I'd stolen it away from his clutching, trembling fingertips.

"You have no idea what you're talking about, *you ungrateful fool.* When I was your age, I would've killed for the opportunities I'm offering you. And you just —"

"But I'm *not* you, Ba. I guess that's the problem."

Click.

For nearly two years, we didn't talk at all. Well, that was fine — we saved on the long distance, right? And I got rid of my Jetta and learned to take the subway to work. I moved out of my two-bedroom apartment at Yonge and Bloor into a leaky, tumbledown house at Ossington and Dundas, shared with three friends. I squirrelled away savings, I stopped eating at nice restaurants, I learned how to cook chicken fried rice and pasta puttanesca. It was no hardship, really. We had fun in that house, not that any of us were there very often. By working long hours, I got a promotion and raise, and I even took on extra drafting work for another design studio on the side. It felt good to be doing this on my own, as though with every luxury I renounced and every dollar I saved, I was getting a little further away from my family and being reborn, bit by bit, as a better, more authentic person. The money that sustained me belonged to me alone; it was pure, uncorrupted. I knew its source as intimately as I knew the ever-present ache between my shoulder blades.

It was easy to ignore Ba when my mother was still alive. He wasn't alone. She was there to deal with his crap. After her death, however, I noticed a new neediness creeping over him. Despite the gulf that remained between us, despite the abyss of ill will, he swallowed his pride and began phoning me more often, under the guise of wanting to talk about the stock market. Really, he was just lonely, I guess.

About a year after my mother's funeral, some neighbour tried to set my father up with his sister, who'd also recently been widowed.

"The lunch date was a disaster," Ba announced to me on the phone one evening. "The woman was fat — double my size! I'm not joking. And she had hair on her upper lip."

"But maybe she was nice? It'd be good for you to have a companion. What did you two talk about?"

"Oh, nothing of any importance. And don't you worry. I have no intention of remarrying. You needn't worry about your inheritance being jeopardized."

In truth, I would have been relieved if some kind, hardy widow were willing to take him off my hands.

Over the years, I suppose our quarrel faded, to some extent, anyway, though neither of us really budged an inch. I did as I pleased. I completed my master's, I stayed in Toronto, I worked at various design studios and organizations. From time to time, I taught adjunct courses at U of T. Ba continued to hold the opinion that I was a fool for wasting my life, but he never pressed his point as aggressively as he had the first time. He knew that he couldn't push me around. And that — ironically — made him respect me. A respect that's grown over time, old age mellowing him slightly. These days, he seems to believe more ardently than ever that I'm just the person to take his business into the next phase.

And so, it's as though we've come full circle. Me a little girl again, Ba whispering in my ear that one day his kingdom will pass down to me. Me riding my tricycle so fast that his face becomes nothing more than an immaterial blur at the edge of my vision, easy to ignore most of the time, possibly just a figment of my imagination, anyway.

Gradually, the colour's returning to my father's face. In addition to congee, he's able to eat a soft custard, which boosts his energy level slightly. Although his prognosis remains uncertain, he's allowed to move out of the windowless ICU to a regular ward on the fifteenth floor.

Ba gets the corner bed with a view of the street below. Not that he can see anything, lying flat on his back. The heaps of ant-size people weave around one another and the stagnant traffic. At least it's something to look at while I wait.

Wait for what? I wonder.

There are two other patients in the suite, since Ba refused to splurge on a private room. A preadolescent boy with bad skin peeking out from beneath a red hoodie. Playing away at some game on his iPad, he doesn't appear sick at all. In the bed across from him lies a pale, well-powdered woman, who has the icy polish typical of the businesswomen strutting around Central in their Ferragamos. Her magazine-perfect face looks strange above the hospital gown. She doesn't seem ill either, as she talks loudly into her phone, bossing around her husband or house-keeper, demanding that a certain pair of slippers be packed. I'm trying to signal that she should keep it down, but she keeps right on yakking.

I lean closer to my father's ear. "Remember my old kindergarten?"

"On Robinson Road." The fondness in his voice is unmistakable.

"You used to come visit me over your lunch break, right?"

"That's right."

"And I'd be riding my tricycle."

"You were very fast ... such a quick learner ..." His chuckle turns into a fit of wheezing.

"I took after you, I guess." I extend a tissue below his lips, so he can spit out the phlegm glob.

That damn woman's now on the phone with some fancy res-taurant, rescheduling a dinner engagement. When her voice cre-scendos, I jump up and nearly grab the phone. *"Do you mind?* My father's trying to rest here."

She looks at me like *I'm* the crazy woman.

Back at Ba's bedside, I use a damp cloth to wipe his forehead. "Do you recall what colour my trike was?"

"It was ... blue, wasn't it?"

"Oh, um, I think it was red, maybe." This lapse doesn't mean anything, of course. Ba can't be expected to remember such details.

"I knew, even back then, how clever you were."

His struggle for breath gets worse, as if to remind me that he's a dying old man. It's only a matter of time before everything's going to fall to me. It doesn't matter that I tried to walk away — walking away is impossible.

I pull the curtain closed around his bed and lean down next to his ear. "You know, Ba, you can talk to me. I'm here for you."

After the cough subsides, he nods.

"I'm not a kid anymore," I continue. "You can tell me the truth — I can take it. *I need to know.* You don't have to make up tales about a nice supervisor who gave you a hundred bucks and helped you leave Guangzhou. I mean, seriously, Ba. Who would ever do that? What *really* happened? You swam across the bay at night?"

My father looks at me quizzically. "I'm not that strong of a swimmer ... and more importantly, I'm not an idiot."

"Okay ...?"

"Haven't I taught you anything? If I were going to try to escape — I'm not saying this is what happened, but hypothetically speaking — *I would plan ahead.* I wouldn't just jump into shark-filled waters and hope for the best!"

"And what might this plan entail?"

"Befriending someone with power. The power to grant me a travel permit and a bit of cash to begin my new life in Hong Kong."

In the silence that follows, I stare out the window at the glimmer of harbour peeking through the mirrored high-rises. It's as though he really does believe this is the truth. And maybe, at some level, it *is* true. The closest he can come to telling me the truth.

I don't even know what I'm hoping he'll tell me. That the money I'm about to inherit is clean, pristine, earned by nothing more than the sweat of his brow? Or that it's irredeemably tainted by … what? What's the point of obsessing about all this, anyway? Money's just money. Yet its history — more than its value — seems to be what matters most to me, in my gut.

"It couldn't have been easy for you to get back on your feet in Hong Kong, Ba. You were struggling to get by, right?"

He nods ruefully.

"In times of desperation, sometimes it's necessary to play dirty. I get that."

My father remains silent, impervious.

"Those photos we talked about," I press. "Someone from the old days sent them to you, isn't that right? Someone you knew in Guangzhou?"

Looking away, he doesn't deny it.

I'm on the verge of telling him about the mouse corpse, but his croup resumes and I can't help but hear something pleading in his every gasp for breath.

And then, I notice that Ba has turned his head toward me, his eyes like dull coins. He's trying to say something, with great effort. Leaning down, I edge my ear closer.

"Has there been …?"

"Has there been what, Ba?"

He cringes as though speaking hurts his throat. "Mail … any more mail?"

Relief hits me, even as I feel myself cringing, too. "To tell you the truth, that's what I've been wanting to talk to you about."

"*Oh*. More … more pictures?"

"A package, this time." I explain the contents, carefully watching him.

"It was … like a … gravesite?"

He seems to take the news stoically. Then, in a blink, everything changes, something frantic pouring over his gaze.

"*Why?* Why would someone do that, Ba? Do you have any idea who sent it?"

Shaking his head, he closes his eyes.

"I don't know what to do, Ba." I need him to tell me what to do. "Should we go to the police?"

At first, I think he's just crossing his arms, but then I realize it's more like he's clutching his chest. His cheeks have become flushed, dewy with sweat, and his eyes are glazed as though he's been thrown into cold water and left to tread for far too long. While they're looking right at me, it's like they're not really seeing me.

"What's happening, Ba? *Are you all right?*"

He just gasps for air, shaking.

"Nurse! My father!" I yank the curtain back.

SIX

"**O**h my God — what happened?" Celeste is rushing down the hall toward me.

I'm slouched in a chair outside Ba's room. "It wasn't a heart attack, according to the doc."

"Then what *was* it?" My sister pulls her cardigan around her body, looking like she's just rolled out of bed.

"A panic attack, maybe."

"A panic attack? That's it?"

"I know. I can't believe it either."

But as my words sink in, her face changes until she looks like she could be on the verge of a panic attack, too. "You confronted Ba about the package, didn't you?"

"He wouldn't tell me a thing. He just freaked out — clutching his chest." I find myself getting all choked up. It's not a good feeling to know that you pushed your father into such a state.

"Where is he? Can we see him?"

"They've taken him off for some tests. That cough of his isn't getting any better." I insisted, in no uncertain terms, that Ba be thoroughly checked out. Hospitals are crawling with pneumonia and other vicious germs.

An hour or two later, the respirologist comes to talk to us, but I'm unable to focus on what he's saying, his words skating over the surface of my tired mind. The gist seems to be that they're waiting for test results. I sense that the doctors are only trying to placate me, going through the motions. They're convinced it was just a panic attack, nothing to get too worried about.

For the remainder of the day, while Celeste and I sit at Ba's bedside, we're on our best behaviour. We don't ask him anything; we barely even speak. We sit in silence, watching his sleeping, quivering face, occasionally adjusting the blankets around his feet.

The next morning, I'm back at my father's bedside. He doesn't appear any better.

I'm leaning down to give him a sip of water, and he grabs my wrist with unexpected force — liquid sloshes all over the blankets.

"Any more mail?" he whispers.

I shake my head.

An hour later, he asks me again, like a man possessed. And a half-hour after that, the same desperate question. How I wish I hadn't told him anything. My repeated reports that there hasn't been any more mail don't calm him at all. Some shadowy figure has gotten lodged in his consciousness, tormenting him with trains of thought I can't begin to follow.

"If gold and jade are in the coffin ... the mouse'll have ... a rich afterlife ...?"

"What are you talking about, Ba?" I hesitate, unsure how far I can press him. "The package, Ba? Do you know who sent it?"

For a moment, it seems like he's almost laughing. A strange, weak bleating. Then his eyes fall shut.

He remains drugged up, his temperature slightly up one day, down the next, then up again. When I mention to the head nurse that my father doesn't seem entirely lucid, she tells me it's not uncommon for the elderly to suffer delirium after being bedridden so long.

Even if he manages to recover to some degree, I wonder how likely it is he'll ever walk again. Being confined to a wheelchair would depress the hell out of him.

When Celeste and I try to help with Ba's rehabilitation, we don't get a lot of co-operation. We urge him to sit up and blow through this toy-like contraption with little coloured balls inside, left by the hospital's occupational therapist.

"My back hurts."

By now, I've developed a grudging respect for the occupational therapist, and I try to imitate her camp-counsellor vigour. "C'mon, Ba. Just one breath. I know you can do it!"

As the air flows into the tube in a half-hearted wheeze, the blue ball floats upward by an inch, hovering like an old balloon, before plummeting. My poor father's drained by the effort.

Maybe it's time for him to go. Maybe death would actually be a blessing.

The instant the thought crosses my mind, I'm slammed with a wallop of guilt, an all-too-familiar haggard face in the mirror. Is Ba's relapse what I've been wishing for all along? Is that why I insisted on telling him about that damn package?

At last, Ba has been tucked into bed. He has his cup of water, at just the right temperature, and the TV is softly on. His eyelids look heavy. Celeste and I are about to leave.

The curtain around the bed is suddenly drawn back, a face peeking in. It's Third Aunt, her gunmetal-grey hair freshly permed. A younger guy, who looks vaguely familiar, stands beside her.

"Hope we're not interrupting anything?" she says.

"Not at all." I jump up to offer my seat.

She shakes her head and rests her ample tush against the window ledge, her gaze focused on the man I suddenly realize must be her son.

I haven't seen the guy in decades. In my last hazy memory of First Cousin, he's a teenager leaning down to ruffle my hair, a metallic, mangy smell about him. But I must have seen him since then. He was always nice to me and Celeste when we were kids, despite some weird tension between Ba and him, which probably existed because First Cousin never made much of himself, in Ba's view. The guy's dressed in his work clothes: old jeans, construction boots, navy-blue T-shirt with the logo of the company where he's been an electrician for most of his life. He hasn't lost the air of a surly teenager, standing before us as if awaiting judgment even though he's got to be close to fifty. Poor guy, forced to pay his respects, dragged along by his mother.

"So?" Third Aunt prods, still staring at him. "My son has something to say. He's come to make amends."

When First Cousin opens his mouth, nothing comes out.

My father keeps silent, unreadable.

What on earth does First Cousin have to apologize for? Not living up to Ba's expectations? Like any of us can do that. But when I glance over at my sister, she doesn't look terribly surprised. She appears sad, frustrated. I can't tell, however, whether these emotions are directed at First Cousin or Ba.

"I'm sorry I stopped coming over for Chinese New Year, all those years ago," First Cousin manages to say at last.

It never struck me as all that strange that he'd stopped coming over, because — let's face it — my father's not the most pleasant guy to be around. Lots of relatives have stopped coming over the years. Ba likes to play the patriarch at these occasions, doling out all kinds of advice no one's asked for — telling folks that they've messed up their lives by studying the wrong things at school, ordering them to go back in this or that program, expressing surprise that his niece can afford a lavish vacation when she still has a mortgage to pay off, does she not? Not a year goes by when Ba doesn't snap at some little kid for bad behaviour, then reprimand the parents. First Cousin's certainly not the only one to skip out on these cheery occasions. These days, we're lucky if half a dozen relatives show up.

But Third Aunt's eyes continue to bore into her son.

Now First Cousin starts crying — really crying, knots of emotion distorting every inch of his ruddy skin. "I'm sorry," he manages to say, wiping away mucousy tears. "After all you did to help me …"

I'm embarrassed for the guy. More than anything, though, I'm confused.

Sure, my father helped First Cousin out, along with that whole wing of the family. When Celeste and I were little, they still lived in Guangzhou. I must have been five or six when I met them for the first time. First Cousin came over on his own and Ba gave him a place to live and helped him get a job as an electrician's apprentice. Then Third Aunt, Second Aunt, their husbands, and other kids followed. It was the early '80s; the Cultural Revolution was over by then and the Party was back-pedalling and condemning the whole thing like it'd all been a big mistake, a social experiment gone awry. The peasants, it turned out, weren't going to rise up and remake society as a beautiful utopian vision. Life over there was tough. Not surprisingly, plenty of people wanted to move to Hong Kong.

"I should have done more to help you out over the years, Uncle," First Cousin continues, trying to get hold of himself. He crouches down at my father's bedside, so that he's positioned below Ba.

After a long moment, my father nods. It's not clear whether he has accepted this strange apology or he's simply agreeing that yes, First Cousin should have done more over the years. Or maybe he just wants everyone to leave. Ba looks away, as if to signal that the visit is over.

"Would you like to go across the street for some lunch?" My words sound surreal and absurd after everything that's just happened.

"Not today, thank you," my aunt says. "My son needs to get back to work."

"What the fuck was that all about?" I whisper, as we're waiting for the elevator.

Celeste laughs bitterly. "Ba finally got what he's wanted all these years."

"What does First Cousin have to apologize for?"

But the elevator arrives and we find ourselves crammed on opposite sides of a woman carrying a massive potted fern.

Across the street at Fairwood, we stand in line to order our rice and pork bowl sets. It's too noisy to talk, so I wait until we're carrying our steaming trays into the bright-orange interior.

"What does First Cousin have to be sorry about?"

Celeste sits down and looks at me incredulously. "You really don't know anything about this?"

"About ...?"

"Why do you think he stopped coming over for Chinese New Year? Why do you think all contact with him suddenly dropped off?"

"I assumed the guy was busy. He had his own life."

"Yeah. And that was the problem, from Ba's perspective."

Celeste has always been much closer to that side of the family. First Cousin's younger sister is the same age as her and they used to be almost like sisters, which made me jealous at the time.

"Do you remember when Ba brought that side of the family over?" she continues. "We were just little."

"Yeah. First Cousin came on his own, at first."

"That's right. Ba paid smugglers to bring the kid over, when he was only fifteen."

"What? *Ba paid smugglers?*"

Celeste seems amused by my shocked reaction. "Well, what did you think? How did you think he made it over here?"

"How should I know?" As a child, I didn't give any thought to how our cousin managed to immigrate.

"This is China we're talking about. It's not like anyone could just say, 'Oh, I think I'll up and leave now' — particularly back then. So smugglers were the easiest route. After First Cousin had gotten on his feet in Hong Kong, the money he earned as an electrician went toward paying the smugglers to bring the rest of the family over. And Ba contributed the lion's share, I'm sure, because the whole thing couldn't have been cheap."

The light seems to have changed tone, ever so slightly, bathing the skin of all the strangers around me in a harsh, waxy veneer. My shock fades somewhat, though; stories of circuitous migrations are not at all uncommon in this city, so why should my own family be any different?

I hear myself say, sounding remarkably composed, "I still don't understand why Ba and First Cousin had a falling out."

"In Ba's eyes, the kid was indebted to him for the rest of his life. So whenever there'd be electrical problems at his building, he'd call First Cousin up out of the blue and expect him to drop everything and come over. He'd call late at night, on Sundays — it didn't matter, when Ba wants it done, he wants it done *now*. You know how demanding he is. After running around like that for ten years, First Cousin had had enough. He was married by then, with a baby on the way. One day, he just stopped answering Ba's calls."

"And Ba, being Ba, was furious."

"As far as I know, their visit today is the first time they've seen each other in over twenty years."

My brain's gone woozy, overloaded by all this unwanted information. Celeste keeps looking at me like I'm even more out of it than she thought. Blinded by my hero worship of Ba.

Yeah, okay, maybe I've been a bit slow on the uptake. But so what? "Ba did do a lot for that side of the family. If it weren't for him, they'd all be —"

"Oh, spare me. You sound so much like him it makes me sick!"

"What are you talking about? I never —"

"If Ba really wanted to help that side of the family, why didn't he ask First Cousin to come live with us? A fifteen-year-old boy, all alone in a rooming house. *Nice.*"

"Well, when Ba was fifteen he was already out working, supporting his entire family. That's probably what he thought. And like you would've given up your bedroom for our cousin!"

"I might have. Think about how Ba treated that kid — *his own nephew.* It's no wonder someone's sending dead mice in the mail."

I stare at my sister, her words settling heavily. She knows what I'm thinking, but she starts shaking her head. "No, First Cousin wouldn't have sent the package. He's a sweet, mild guy. Not vengeful."

"Not vengeful, because maybe deep down he's grateful for all Ba did."

"*All Ba did?*" The scorn in my sister's voice makes me back away from the table, from our cold meals. "He could've done a lot more, if he'd wanted to, but instead he preferred to let them all live in the middle of buttfuck nowhere, in a tiny apartment that didn't even have a toilet!"

At least, here, I understand what Celeste's referring to. We visited Second and Third Aunts and their families shortly after they'd all moved to Hong Kong. Their apartment was far away in the outskirts of Kowloon. The main thing I remember, like Celeste, is that their unit had no toilet. Mom had to take the two of us to a communal washroom shared by the entire floor. I wonder now why Ba didn't do more to help them find better accommodations. Probably because my mother never liked that side of the family and Ba's capital was tied up in his own ventures. And he'd just spent a shitload of money paying off the smugglers.

"You just don't get it," Celeste continues, "because you've always been Ba's favourite."

"That is so not true."

"Ba's always seen *you* as his heir apparent — he always put *you* in charge of the tea deliveries, Jill."

"Oh, right — the joy of lifting boxes!"

When we were kids, she never wanted anything to do with Ba's business. And for Christ's sake, I didn't want to do it, either. From time to time, when some restaurant or café would place a last-minute order for tea or juice, it was too minuscule to merit delivery by truck (or Ba was too cheap to pay for it). Instead, on Sunday afternoons, he'd expect me to drop everything and help out. He would drive us to the destination, jabbering on in his usual manner about currency fluctuations and new avenues for turning a profit, and when we'd get there, he'd bark at me to lift by bending at the knees to save my back from a lifetime of agony. If only we'd had a brother, then he'd have gotten stuck with this grunt work, but Ba had only me and Celeste, and *she* certainly wasn't going to break a sweat for him, now was she?

SEVEN

Until now, I've been putting off seeing friends. Or to be more precise, my one friend. But after this latest screaming match with my sister, I'm ready for a stiff drink.

I meet Terence at nine at The Upper House, in Admiralty. In this crowded city, it's best to find secluded hotel bars, which hover, aerie-like, on the top floors of skyscrapers affording stunning views across the harbour. While in the elevator, my ears lightly popping, the sea of yellow umbrellas that went up outside on the pavement last year during Occupy flit into my mind and I feel uncomfortable — guilty, almost — about how much we're about to blow on a few cocktails. But this place wasn't my choice; Terence decides these things. And he let me know, on the one occasion we discussed Occupy, that he was right out there under those umbrellas, being part of history in the making. If it had gone on a lot longer, he'd have been as happy as anybody. The dip in the stock market worked to his advantage, allowing him to pick up stuff on the cheap. That's democracy for you, Hong Kong–style. Terence talks jokingly, but it's hard to tell if he means it. Conversations about politics tend to blur very quickly into chatter about the economy; people in this city are much more comfortable talking about money.

The hostess leads me into the dimly lit interior, toward the continuous bank of greyish-blue upholstered benches winding like a snake across the length of the venue, Kowloon's skyline sparkling on the other side of the harbour. Terence is nestled against a pillow, holding the house specialty, an Earl Grey martini.

The guy looks the way he always does. A tad glum, gaunt through the face, dressed all in black, his jeans not quite as fitted as they used to be, now that he's relaxing into the ease of middle age. His hair is shorter and more geometric than when I last saw him in February. His expression is blank, lost in thought, though it flickers to life when he catches sight of me.

We embrace and he towers a head above, stooping slightly. I sit down and order a vodka martini, craving familiarity more than novelty.

When he asks about my father, I decide to give the short, sanitized version for now: Ba's recovering as well as can be expected. Terence doesn't press, sensing that I'm more in the mood to escape from my problems than rehash them at the moment. Enough alcohol may reverse this, however.

"So how's business?" I ask.

Terence owns a yakitori bar. It's good, very authentic — a noisy, crowded joint like the kind they have in Tokyo. Walls covered in tatami. The grill behind the bar fuelled by coal, not gas. The sauces are homemade and you come out with your clothes smelling like you've spent the night in front of a bonfire.

"Business is *okay*." He says this like it could mean any number of things, none of which is okay exactly, cryptic as always.

I wonder if he's bored. Terence is a smart guy. When he first moved back to Hong Kong after his degree at Columbia, he worked for a few years as a fund manager, but he burned out or lost interest or something. He went on a long backpacking trip in Nepal and, at the end of it all, decided to fall back on the family business. His folks own quite a few restaurants and bars across the city. Terence helps manage them, while taking care of the family's investment portfolio.

They've got hostess bars and gambling dens, too, I've heard through the grapevine. Terence never talks about that end of the business, which his older brother handles. Celeste once told me that the Fok family has gangster ties. Or *had* gangster ties, back in the father's day. Terence — in his well-tailored jackets, with his penchant for watching Gordon Ramsay cooking classes on YouTube for hours — strikes me as a far cry from any gangster.

"I'm thinking of opening a sake bar in the space above my restaurant. A late-night venue. Intimate and cozy, jazz music. The kind of place you'd take a girl on a cool first date."

"Well, if you're looking for an architect …?"

"I thought you loved your job in Toronto."

"Oh, sure." I hesitate, surprised by the excitement stirring inside me. "But I'm never too busy to do an interesting project on the side."

"So you *are* thinking of setting up your own practice. It's in your blood, after all."

I make a face. "One project, Terence. A small project. I can handle that without uprooting my entire life."

"Looks like it's been uprooted already. Did they give you a leave of absence?"

"They weren't thrilled about it, naturally."

We order more drinks. The alcohol works its way into my bloodstream, soothing me into pleasant numbness.

"Are things any easier this time around?" Terence says, referring to the last time I was here for an extended period, when my mother was dying.

"Oh, it's just different. Mom was practically dead by the time I got here. She wasn't a fighter, she didn't fight to hang on. The complete opposite of my dad."

"You're not going to be able to go home anytime soon, then?"

Is that a hint of hopefulness I detect? "Probably not."

Home. Wherever that is.

I ask Terence about how things are going with his girlfriend, Julianne. An air of remoteness drifts over him. The same air that always takes over whenever he talks about women, even when things are supposedly going well, which isn't the case right now. He and Julianne haven't seen each other in almost a month; she's been travelling a lot on business. Or maybe just pretending to travel, in order to dodge his calls. "I've been ready to end this thing for ages, but I can't if I can't get hold of her."

"Guess that's why she's been avoiding you."

"I wouldn't dump her. I'd let *her* dump me. That's the gentlemanly thing to do. Less guilt, less blowback."

I snicker.

"Well, wouldn't *you* rather do the dumping?" he says.

"I'd rather the guy grew some balls and told me what's on his mind."

But that was Nick's approach. In the end, he was the one who pulled the plug. And that was a shitty feeling, too.

"Women in this city are too high maintenance," Terence continues. "I'm not up to dating anymore."

"You should know that from dating Celeste!"

He looks uncomfortable, and I regret having brought it up.

"The only problem with staying single is that I'll get stuck living with Mom forever. And as I said, Hong Kong women are high maintenance. Mothers being the highest maintenance of all."

"Fathers can be high maintenance, too."

"Yeah, but let's face it, yours is old. He's not going to linger on for decades."

"Let's hope so, for everyone's sake."

I'm tipsy now, more than tipsy. Kowloon's skyline looks like a forest of Christmas trees, lit up with a neon brightness that appears to be trying too hard, and it suddenly makes me sad.

"The hardest thing is I have no idea what my father wants from me right now."

"You're here. That's enough."

"I wish. He wants more, he's always wanted *more*. The way he looks at me, while lying in that hospital bed, it's a desperate, pleading look. Like he wants confirmation that he's been a good father. Like he wants to be cleared for every nasty thing he's ever done."

"Fathers," Terence says, like that one word says it all.

"Mine appears to have made some enemies over the years."

I'm approaching the right level of drunkenness to tell him about the dead mouse and photos. In fact, I'm just drunk enough that as I launch into the story, the whole thing strikes me as kind of funny, in a sick, sad way.

When I get home, I'm not feeling so well. The giddy sense of escape offered by the alcohol has faded and now I just want to hit the sack. I'm surprised to find my sister still up. She's locked herself inside the bathroom and when I tap on the door, she tells me to go away. A second later, I hear her heaving and puking.

"Celeste, are you okay?" Although I haven't forgotten about our fight, some other impulse is overriding that at the moment. She really sounds terrible. "Did you eat something bad? Are you coming down with a bug?"

"Just leave me alone. I'll be fine."

Okay. Looks like I'm going to bed without brushing my teeth. I pop out my disposable contact lenses and let them fall wherever they fall and shrivel up like slips of dead skin.

I hope my sister's not getting all weird about her weight again, fantasizing pockets of fat where there's only skin and bone, puking herself to wafer thinness.

My head thuds onto the pillow, but my mind's too agitated to drift off. If Celeste's not well tomorrow, it'll be me going to see Ba on my own.

Turning on my side, I try to calm myself by hugging a pillow, the conversation with Terence replaying in my head. At first, it seemed like he was trying to be comforting, trying to reassure me that a dead rodent isn't anything to get too bent out of shape about. When he was a kid, his father received a cake box full of shit in the mail, he said. A month later, a second box of shit arrived. Whether it was animal or human shit they could never figure out.

"There are plenty of weirdos out there, Jill. These people have their stupid fun and that's it."

"Did you ever find out who sent it?"

"Not for certain. I had my suspicions, though." A trace of a bleak smile, drawing me into a sense of intimacy. "A business deal had gone sour. Billiard halls. One of my father's old partners was trying to break off on his own, but his venture failed miserably, due to my father's actions. The guy was pissed. Things got rather ugly for a while."

I didn't know how to respond. This was the first time Terence had ever alluded to his family's unsavoury past. "What happened?"

"Dunno exactly. But the cake boxes stopped arriving. And the guy disappeared."

"What do you mean? The guy left town?"

With a shrug, he downed the rest of his drink. "All I can say is that no one ever heard from him again."

. . .

"I'm not sure how much more we can do for your father, to be honest," Dr. Lam, the respirologist, says. Although late middle-aged, he dresses like a hipster in a black Paul Smith jacket whose fluorescent detailing keeps distracting me. "And wouldn't your father be more comfortable at home in his own bed?"

"Seriously? Isn't it way too soon? Ba's nowhere close to being back to his old self."

"Um, your father's ninety-four. And he's recovered remarkably from the operation."

"What about his recent attack?"

Dr. Lam's eyes soften in a way that doesn't come naturally, a practised look. "All the tests came back fine, Jill. Old people can be emotionally sensitive.... It might've been a nightmare that set him off. The worst of his illness has passed and his condition's stabilized for the time being. You can hire a nurse to take care of him at home."

A man of Ba's age is in a palliative state anyway — that's what the doctors probably think. If spending his remaining days on his own couch means so much to him, who are we to begrudge him these small, parting pleasures?

My father, not surprisingly, is thrilled by the news.

"Don't you think it'd be better to wait, Ba?"

"No, I want my own blankets and pillows.... And I want Rina to make steamed fish ..."

I stare down at my father's bedridden body, frail as an invalid child's. This is nothing like how I imagined he would be upon his return home.

But the news seems to energize him, his face revealing a vestige of its old intensity. "I'm going to live for another four years. The doctor says my liver's in perfect shape, as good as the liver of a young man."

"Oh? Well, that's good, I guess."

Ba doesn't appear too pleased by his self-diagnosis. He treats it more like a duty the world has imposed on him, this duty to keep on living, surviving.

"When I was a boy, my first job paid only five dollars a month." Wide-eyed as an owl, he expects my rapt attention, like I haven't heard this story millions of times before.

"I thought it was ten." During my childhood, Ba always pegged his salary at ten dollars per month, but over the years it's somehow been halved. Who knows, maybe he's adjusting for inflation.

"It was a grocery store," he continues. "Stocking shelves, sweeping floors. Knew I wasn't going to get anywhere with that."

"So you went to that bookkeeping office." I nudge the story along so he won't tire himself out. "You showed the manager your test scores from your last year at school, right?"

"Yup. Then I asked for a job. The man looked at my scores and said" — Ba furrows his forehead, mimicking the guy's astonished expression — "'Young man, with marks like these, why are you not in school?' I shook my head. 'We are very poor, sir. My father cannot afford the school fee. I have to work.' You know what the man said?"

Yes, I know, of course I know. But so as not to spoil his enjoyment, I shrug.

"'What a pity ... what a pity ...'"

The animation seeps from Ba's face, bitterness and fatigue setting in. I don't know why he insists on always returning to this same pathetic story that only makes him feel like crap.

He closes his eyes, drifting off. If he were more energetic, there'd be more he would say, no doubt. He'd tell me about how in addition to working at the grocery store, he cleaned the bookkeeping office at night.

• • •

When my father awakes, he looks troubled. Perhaps he had a bad dream.

"It'll be good to be home. That way, if more mail arrives …"

"There hasn't been any more mail, Ba. Just drop it, okay?"

A tremor passes through the air between us. Soon, I'll be compelled to wheel him down to the lobby many times a day so he can peer into the mailbox himself.

"If you're so concerned, Ba, it'd help if you talked to me."

"It has nothing to do with you."

"Nice try."

The fear in his eyes lingers. "Things weren't supposed to end like this for me. But for you … for you … it's not too late."

"What are you talking about?"

"You're no spring chicken, you know."

"Gee, thanks."

"There's one thing I want you to promise me, in case I die tomorrow."

Oh, God. Here we go again.

"Promise me that you'll stay in Hong Kong … get married … start a family."

"That's three promises, not one."

"Well, I can ask for three, can't I?" As something tickles his throat, he starts hacking up a storm. I wonder if he's faking, in an attempt to win my sympathy. "My work on this planet isn't done yet. I … I haven't accomplished all I wanted to."

"I don't see what that has to do with me getting married and having kids."

"Future generations, a grandson … wouldn't that be nice?"

Not grandchild, but grand*son*. My jaw clenches. That old, familiar tightness in the back of my throat. It gives way to a burst of laughter. The last thing I need is a little clone of Ba following me around from beyond the grave, clutching at my calves.

"Well, Ba, what can I say? I'm single. You might have better luck talking to Celeste. Plus, I can't promise you I'm going to stay in Hong Kong. My whole life's in Canada. You know that."

All his features pinch together in a lumpy knot. "Do you know how much real estate in this city's gone up?" He tells me how much he paid for our condo, over forty years ago, compared to how much it's worth today. "Can Canada say that? And taxes there are sky high."

For a brief second, I consider raising the point that boys with poor, sickly fathers can't go to school and have a decent shot in life unless somebody pays the taxman. But why waste my breath? The only lesson this man has learned from his Dickensian childhood is survival of the fittest.

"Plus," Ba continues, "we never get snow here. Not like in Canada."

"I don't mind the snow, Ba. It's actually kind of pretty."

When I first visited Toronto, over twenty years ago, I remember being struck by how flat and empty and grey everything appeared. That was my first impression. It was hard to believe this was Canada's largest city. Even the high-rises appeared strangely low compared to what I was used to, and they were spaced so far apart that they had the solitary air of lone trees. Nothing like the forests of high-rises in Hong Kong. And where were all the people? According to the taxi driver, Yonge Street was the longest street in the world. But if Yonge was such a big deal, why did it have this eerie, post-apocalyptic calmness to it? Whole blocks went by and I saw only a handful of folks trudging along in their puffy zipped-up coats, past the convenience stores and auto shops and cottage-like houses still bordered in garish Christmas lights.

It was February. The air was frigid like I'd never experienced before. The asphalt had a chalky appearance, but I knew it couldn't be snow, because snow was supposed to be fluffy and fly away, wasn't it? At least that's how it looked in movies.

A hard veneer came over my mother's face in that first taxi ride as she stared out the window and pressed her lips together, magenta lipstick feathering into the fine creases around her mouth, the sunspots on her complexion like faint, indelible stains. At that moment, she probably wished she'd listened to my father, who'd remained in Hong Kong. He didn't think any of this was necessary; he was simply indulging her desire for a Canadian passport. So here we were. Me, my mother, and Celeste, who was already snoozing on my shoulder. After this brief visit to get the ball rolling, the plan was that we'd move to Toronto over the summer. With the help of an immigration consultant, my parents were going to buy a condominium, and my sister and I would begin our final years of high school in this bleached-out, frostbitten wilderness.

As it turned out, Mom had another plan up her sleeve — for herself, in any case. A tour of the Eaton Centre and then a trip up to Holt Renfrew left her very homesick. Consequently, she held off on purchasing that condo and rented a serviced apartment at Yonge and Eglinton instead. The three of us moved in at the beginning of the summer. In August, however, she announced that she'd be returning to Hong Kong the very next week. She'd found a nice Chinese-Canadian family for us to board with, out in Markham.

If Mom felt at all guilty about leaving us behind, she hid it well. I was seventeen, my sister sixteen. When Mom was only fourteen, she and her younger brothers had been sent to live in an apartment all by themselves with only a maid to take care of them (presumably because my grandfather's first wife no longer wanted another woman's kids in her face). "You girls are old enough to take care of yourselves," our mother said, with a brusque energy that made her permed hair flounce outward. Self-reliance and the ability to adapt to quickly changing circumstances were the most important skills in life, according to her. Funny how she proved about as adaptable as a hothouse flower where moving to Canada was concerned.

Whatever bitterness I felt at the time got shoved aside in the flurry of activity to get us settled. Autumn in Canada was actually rather pretty, I discovered, with spacious suburban front yards and tree-lined streets, leaves lit up in fiery blotches. The older couple who owned the house where Celeste and I boarded were pleasant enough folks, but we both kept to ourselves, retreating to our rooms right after dinner.

Every day, we took the bus to Markham District High, a sprawling red-brick building where the halls echoed with slamming lockers and high fives and whoops of glee that never had anything to do with us. That was fine by me; I was content to let the noise of strangers bubble up and flow past. I immersed myself in my studies, I took long walks, I read a lot. Since I had already covered most of the curriculum in the maths and sciences in previous years, I had time to read for pleasure — existentialist authors, in particular. I liked how Camus's characters were cut off from the ordinary world and laws of morality, ensconced in the solitude of their own demented minds.

To my surprise, I didn't miss Hong Kong much, its crowded streets, hung with giant neon signs and billboards of airbrushed complexions, skyscrapers looming like mountaintops, the onslaught of sweaty bodies streaming out of subway stations. That other life was still there; it never really faded from my mind. But I didn't feel any yearning to return to it. At the same time, it wasn't like I had a surge of affection for my new surroundings. If anything, what I felt was calm, cool indifference. I could live anywhere, because I wasn't homesick. I'd never had any true sense of "home." This realization offered a strange, diffuse comfort. Everything around me assumed a bright, immaterial quality, as if composed of nothing more than projections of coloured light: a pale, wintery street, the last bit of sunset glaring off ice patches, an old TV in a dim, musty basement, an alarm clock ticking away on a bedside table, my hand reaching over to pick it up. Even those ticks — those tiny increments of sound — seemed arbitrary, fleeting. I drifted through the days, aware only of the randomness of the world around me, one place interchangeable with the next.

Over time, I managed to make a few friends at school, other exiles from Hong Kong. But I knew these connections wouldn't survive the semester. Having these kids to chat with in Cantonese over lunch hour and to drive me to the movie theatre didn't make me feel any less alone, if you want the truth. And I was quite all right with that, because I'd discovered that I rather liked being alone.

"When am I ...?"

"Relax, Ba. The doctor says you'll be released early next week."

I'm glad that I've got a bit of time, at least, to get the condo in order. I'm stocking up on adult diapers. I'm running around to buy rubber handles to attach to the shower wall, along with a lot of other equipment my father needs. And while I'm in this hamster-on-a-wheel mode, I figure that Rina and I might as well throw out a ton of crap. Boxes of empty bottles and jars stashed under the kitchen counter, saved for God knows what. Threadbare, yellowed undershirts, crammed into a dresser. Yesterday, the internet guy came over, as did the AC repairman, who restored our living room to a bearable temperature. What a joy not to be damp and sticky all the time.

And then there's Ba's building, of course. Checking in with Ming every couple days, I take note of all the things that need to be repaired and the squabbles between our tenants that he seems to think I'd want to get involved in, for some reason. Friction over the mess in a shared washroom. The disgusting smell of burning meat in a hallway, coming from an office microwave every lunch hour. I nod and smile tightly, Ming's long-winded reports registering in only a vague way. But I let him go on, dreading the end of the conversation, when my stomach always gallops in that moment right before he hands me the stack of mail. And yet, there's nothing of any consequence — just bills, flyers. Maybe Terence is right, maybe these things die out on their own.

Occasionally, I glance at Facebook to catch up on the lives of my friends and colleagues in Toronto. They lead such happy, normal, balanced lives. Family picnics on Centre Island. Canoeing at the cottage. My old roommate's gotten married, Vegas style. (I wonder if she's giving the impression they eloped only because she doesn't want her Facebook friends to feel bad about not being invited to the wedding.) A basement has been renovated. Blueberry muffins have been baked. Two babies have been born, a dog has died. Nick and his new girlfriend have moved in together and she has a pixie of a daughter with blond-white hair and an irresistible, shy smile.

That all-too-familiar handwriting, the Guangzhou postmark. A long white envelope, light as if it contains nothing at all.

I'm not at Ba's building, I'm at home. It's late in the day, so the area of the lobby around the mailboxes is full of people returning from work. I rush toward the door to get outside, not wanting to run into any neighbours, incapable of hiding my horror, my strange sense of humiliation. The doorman looks up as I rush past, my heart pattering madly.

A few streets down, I find a parkette with an empty bench. By now the envelope's damp from my sweaty fingers and while I open it, I have to hold the letter delicately at the edges to avoid smearing the ink.

It's in Chinese. It's been so long since I've read anything of any length that for the first several moments the characters appear cryptic, meaningless. An endless tangle of black lines.

Then, all too quickly, the ink becomes decipherable:

Dear Comrade,

You probably thought you'd gotten rid of me, since I haven't been in touch for a while. True, I was getting bored and thinking of moving on to more pressing matters, like tending my garden. However, as you of all people are no doubt aware, the stock market has taken a nasty tumble in recent weeks. While men like you can ride out the storm, for folks like us it ain't so easy.

In view of the long history our families shared, I feel well within my rights to turn to you in our time of need. You were once very skillful at hunting down and capitalizing on our family heirlooms. That's why we no longer have anything to hock and make up for our shortfall.

For most of your life, you probably thought little of your misdeeds. But I'm hoping that now, in the wisdom of old age, you will recognize the error of what you did to us and try to redress the situation.

And so, let me come to the point of this letter, without wasting time on niceties. My son is currently at university in Hong Kong. His name is Ma Kaiming, though most people, I understand, call him "Benjamin" these days. He is a bright, diligent student. Due to the plunge in the stock market, no one in our family is able to help the boy out with his tuition and living expenses.

We trust that you — acting out of the goodness of your heart, no doubt — will step forward and help out. My father always considered you someone who could be depended upon.

A certified cheque for $700,000, made out to Ma Kaiming, is what the situation requires. The cheque should be mailed to:

PO Box 53466
General Post Office
Hong Kong

Since fall tuition is overdue, it would be best if we received the cheque by the end of the week.

Considering that what we are asking for is so little, why not settle the books once and for all?

Respectfully yours,
An Old Friend from Guangzhou

EIGHT

"**N**o, I don't think I'm going overboard, Terence. Blackmail isn't an exaggeration at all!"

Terence pops a dumpling into his mouth, flushing at the hot explosion of juices. It takes him a moment to recover. Or maybe he's biding his time, trying to word his thoughts delicately.

"The thing about blackmail is it usually requires some kind of actual threat."

"The whole letter is dripping with threats!" I pluck it off the table and begin skimming it again, somewhat manically perhaps. Where did all those menacing words disappear to?

"*In view of the long history our families shared, I feel well within my rights to turn to you in our time of need,*" I read. "What's that supposed to mean? What is this long history, exactly?"

"The two families were friends. Friends have history together."

"*We* are friends. My dad and this guy are *not* friends."

I bite into a slice of translucent jellyfish, which slithers over my tongue like something still alive. We're at an old-school Shanghainese restaurant. White tablecloths and grey carpet and fluorescent lighting, like the place hasn't changed at all since the 1950s, when it was a Shanghainese members-only club.

"Let me tell you how a threat is structured. The letter would say: if you don't pay up, someone's going to come and smash your kneecaps. Or turn you over to the police. Or at the very least, expose you to your family. Some nasty consequence would be laid out. This letter does nothing of the sort. It just appeals to your dad's conscience."

"Because Ba supposedly stole a bunch of their heirlooms!"

"The letter doesn't say he stole them. It says he hunted them down."

"Hunted them down and capitalized on them." I keep chewing the jellyfish, which now tastes like soggy plastic.

"Well, do you think there's any truth to it?"

"No, it's absurd." Sure, my father dabbled in the black market, but he's no thief, for Christ's sake.

"Remember, it was a crazy time back then." Terence's voice seems to be floating, unanchored, as though he isn't sure how far he should press his point, how much I can handle. "I'm assuming the letter writer comes from the landlord class. Or *came* from the landlord class, before the Cultural Revolution swept all that away."

"Why do you say that?"

"The reference to family heirlooms."

"Oh … right." It's as though the details of the letter are only now catching hold in my exhausted brain, the shock finally wearing off. "Didn't most heirlooms get destroyed around then? During the … what was it called? Attack the Four Olds campaign?"

I try to remember what the Four Olds were. Old customs, old culture, old ideas … and there's one other old that escapes me now. A bunch of kids in Red Guard armbands ran through the streets, ransacking temples and houses, slashing paintings, burning books, smashing furniture, and anything else they could get their hands on — all to prove their allegiance to Mao and the country's utopian future. Intellectuals and anyone else tarred as bourgeoisie or capitalist roaders were harassed, interrogated, beaten.

"My sister-in-law's father was targeted," Terence says. "He was forced to kneel for hours during struggle sessions while confessing his so-called crimes, wearing some ridiculous hat, in front of the whole community. Can you imagine? Eventually, the guy had had enough and he killed himself."

There are similar stories buried in my family, I tell Terence. Second Aunt's husband came from the landlord class. Although she never talks about what happened back then, she harbours great bitterness. One of her sons died from the flu when he was little, because no doctor could be found to treat him. Doctors shied away from treating anyone of a bad class background.

"I can't believe they wouldn't even help a sick little boy." Terence shakes his head, bewildered. "Lovely country we live in."

Although I'm nodding, my mind's circled back to what we were talking about before getting sidetracked. "If all the old treasures and heirlooms were smashed, why does the letter say my father 'capitalized' on them? What does that even mean?"

"Perhaps not all the stuff actually got destroyed. The Party had a few secret collectors, I'm sure. They probably managed to protect a bit of the loot for themselves. Some of the stuff might have made its way into private collections, through the black market."

"That'd be right up my father's alley."

I think of how proudly he used to recount his enterprising adventures. When it comes right down to it, I don't think he's ever seen much distinction between the black market and the market proper. For him, it's all just the market. And the market has always been his oyster.

Maybe that's how he actually won his freedom — the travel permit and cash to return to Hong Kong. Did he take part in some smuggling scheme? Were those spoils the origin of his fortune, his fresh start?

And now, one of the folks he ripped off wants payback.

A restless sensation grabs hold of me, my skin turning hot and itchy, like I'm drunk, even though I've only had one beer. "So maybe my father did help himself to a few old vases that would've gotten destroyed anyway. I doubt that whatever he took is worth anywhere close to seven hundred K."

"That's Hong Kong dollars, remember." Terence tips his head back, doing some mental calculation.

Dividing the figure by six, I arrive at roughly a hundred and twenty thousand Canadian dollars.

"Sounds about right for what a year of schooling costs here," he says, "tuition fees and apartment included."

"The kid'll be living well. An apartment with a view of the harbour."

"Fine, they're highballing a little. Maybe the money's meant to cover more than one year. And the father has stock-market debts, too."

"It's weird how he hasn't even tried to conceal his son's name. Benjamin Ma. He could've asked for the cheque to go to a corporate account, at least. What if I were to take this letter straight to the police?"

"And say what? You're being blackmailed? As I was saying, it doesn't sound very threatening. It reads like one old man reaching out to another, cashing in on an old favour, settling the books, as the letter says. And these people are simple folks. Corporate bank accounts and anonymous money transfers aren't on their radar."

"Huh."

"You don't sound very convinced."

My hand jostles the teacup, knocking it over, brown water seeping into the tablecloth. I watch the stain expanding and losing colour. I think of Ba's troubled sleep, his terror of slipping away into the abyss. Maybe whoever wrote the letter thinks that Ba will jump at the chance to make up for whatever he did. Cleanse his conscience.

"Why don't you ask your father what to do?" Terence says. "Read him the letter, see what he has to say."

"He's in no state." An image of him clutching his chest and seizing up again fills me with dread.

"Well, I guess you're on your own, then. My advice? Bring your old man home from the hospital and let him die in peace."

Rina's still up when I get home. She's in the kitchen, making herself a cup of tea, and asks whether I'd like one, too.

Shaking my head, I turn away, unable to bear her bright gaze.

She senses something's up. "Ma'am? Are you all right?"

I hesitate. With the language barrier between us, I don't feel capable of explaining the possibility that Ba ripped off a bunch of heirlooms during the chaos back then. Also, part of me thinks that Ba is coming home to rule the roost; he's still Rina's employer. It seems wrong to undermine him by exposing his shady ventures. Or maybe I just don't want to admit that my father is a crook.

It was a mad, confusing time. Ba, being Ba, couldn't help but sniff out enterprising opportunities from the rubble and ruins. He must have thought that all the old treasures were going to be destroyed anyway, so what difference would it make if he salvaged a few and used them for his own ends?

Ba's a survivor, a scavenger. Growing up in poverty wires a person's brain very differently, I believe.

"Nothing's happened, Rina. Nothing for you to concern yourself with."

Her eyes fall downward. "Ma'am, your sister told me about dead mouse."

I brush aside my irritation with Celeste. Well, I suppose Rina would have found out sooner or later. When Ba comes home, he's going to be asking her to check the mailbox multiple times a day.

"You know who sent it, ma'am?"

"I have no idea." I make an effort to keep my voice calm, indicating that I'd like her to do the same.

But the poor woman doesn't seem to notice, her lips pinched like they're trying to hold in an inflating balloon.

Then it occurs to me that maybe she knows something. Maybe she has her own suspicions about who sent the package. After all, before Ba's collapse, she's the one who spent the most time with him. "Did my father ever say anything …?"

She begins shaking her head, pacing back and forth. "Sir never tell me … but … but …"

"But *what*?" Grabbing her by the arm, more roughly than intended, I manage to get her to stop moving. "What is it, Rina?"

"Every week, you know how sir want me to come with him shopping for food so I can carry bags?"

It's ridiculous how controlling my father is. In any other household, the housekeeper would do the shopping on her own, but Ba worries that Rina won't bargain at the market aggressively enough or she'll pocket a bit of change.

"Well," she continues, "a month before sir get sick, I notice someone following us behind. A man."

"Someone was *following Ba*?"

A feeble nod.

"What did this person look like?"

"Maybe I mistake. I don't know. That why I not come to you before now, ma'am."

"It's all right, Rina. Just tell me what you saw."

"Sir and me, we walk along Robinson Road to ParknShop. It start raining, so I turn around to put up umbrella. That's when

I notice man in white T-shirt, baseball cap. In ParknShop, I see him in aisle again. Then at fish market, too. A few weeks later, the same man following again!"

"Are you sure it was the same guy?"

Although Rina shrugs, her eyes remain fearful and quite certain.

"Well, what did he look like?"

"Chinese man."

That hardly narrows things. "How old?"

"Not too young. Not old, either."

"Around my age?"

"Maybe. No, younger. A bit."

"Short? Tall?"

"Your height, ma'am, maybe."

About five and a half feet.

"Fatter, though. Not *fat*. Hard." She grasps her upper arm.

"Muscular, like he works out?"

A hesitant nod.

"Did he ever try to approach Ba?"

"No, just watching us. Sunglasses on. But inside supermarket, he take glasses off for a second. And then, I notice …" Rina points to the edge of her eye.

"There was something weird about his left eye?"

She draws the shape of a large teardrop. "Brown spot."

"He had a birthmark?"

"A birthmark?"

"Yes, a birthmark. That's what it's called."

We continue staring at each other, though there doesn't seem to be anything else to say.

"Thanks for bringing this to my attention, Rina."

As she turns to go, I reach out and grab her wrist. A thought darts through my brain, quick as a lizard. "I'm just wondering — this guy you saw? Do you think he could be a university student?"

"I don't know …?"

"But he's around that age, right? Younger than me, you said."

She nods.

After she's left, I wander into the living room and perch on the edge of the sofa, my brain in overdrive. It makes sense that the kid — Benjamin Ma — would want to track down my father and see where he lives. Follow him around to get a sense of his daily routines. Get a feel for how much money our family could be fleeced for. Fury, mixed with a confused sense of injustice, surges over me. Even if Ba did seize his start-up capital through underhanded means, that doesn't mean that all our money's tainted. Ba still had to work hard, using his brains and instincts. I wonder if Benjamin even goes to university or if that's just a cover story, a scam — no different from Ba's tale about how he escaped from Guangzhou. These people have the nerve to accuse my father of being a crook, but how do I know that they're not the real crooks? It takes one to know one, after all.

"At least now we know what we're dealing with," Celeste says, clutching the letter. While sipping her first coffee of the day, she rereads it, with all the concentration of a lawyer assessing a damning piece of evidence.

It startles me to see how calm my sister appears. More than mere calmness: her face emits a flushed glow of superiority.

"Whatever the case," she continues, "we know that Ba's guilty of something. Sounds like he ripped off these people's heirlooms. And probably a lot worse."

"We don't know that." But a nauseous feeling assails my gut, as last night's conversation with Terence echoes in my head.

"So what now?" Celeste uses her pyjama sleeve to clean smudges off her glasses. "I say we pay up. There's more than enough blood money to go around."

"You must be joking."

My sister returns my gaze, perfectly straight-faced.

"We have no idea whether there's any truth to this," I say. "To these … these allegations!"

"Oh, please. Just think about it for a second, okay?" Her eyes glint with sudden anger, frustration. "I've had suspicions since we were kids. Haven't you? If you're honest with yourself?"

When I remain silent, my sister looks at me with disgust. Like I'm either a perfect coward or too stupid for words.

"No one makes that much money so fast," she says. "Think about it, Jill. Ba returned to Hong Kong in '68, destitute, jobless. By '72, he owned a supermarket, this condo, and half an office tower. Where did all that money come from?"

I'm beginning to recognize a different side of my sister now: a steely, practical, ruthlessly logical side. How I yearn for the whimsical, scatterbrained Celeste.

A glum, lethargic look passes over her face as we sink into silence. "You know, I really don't want any of it," she says at last.

"What are you talking about?"

"Ba's money. *The blood money.*"

I sigh. Why does my sister always have to be so melodramatic? "Look, it doesn't matter which one of us manages it. I'll take care of the money for both of us. That goes without saying."

"That's not what I mean. I really don't want it!" Her shoulders tremble as though she's trying to shake off a ghostly chill or a terrible premonition. "You take it. You'll do with it whatever Ba wants you to do and continue the cycle of profit-making carnage."

Again, I sigh, weariness hitting me.

"You know," she goes on, "all I ever wanted when we were kids was for Ba to stop counting his money and talk to me, *see me.* 'Hey, Celeste, I see you've taken up the flute. What made you choose that instrument? And is everything going all right at school? Do you like your new teachers?' But do you remember what he'd be doing Sunday afternoons?"

Of course I remember. Sunday was the one day of the week Ba took off. Yet he'd still be working as he puttered around the condo in his old clothes, calculator tucked into his cardigan pocket, never far from his fingertips. He was calculating interest rates, he was double-checking the math on his investment gains and losses, he was reviewing the housekeeper's shopping receipts against the amounts she'd entered in the ledger book. And many other things, I'm sure. Everything in life was a calculation, in our father's eyes.

"You know how much I came to hate that calculator?" Celeste says, throwing up her hands. "It was me — *I* was the one behind the defective batteries he kept getting stuck with. Remember how pissed off he'd get?"

I remember all too well. Every few Sundays, Ba's calculator would die and he'd be forced to walk all the way to Central to buy new batteries. It baffled him how he kept getting cursed with lemons. How livid he'd become, demanding that store owners give him his money back.

"That was you? You kept fucking up his batteries?"

"I'd wait until Ba was in the shower. And then I'd open his calculator and remove the batteries. I'd cut ever so tiny pieces of clear tape and place them over the ends, before putting the batteries back inside."

A giggle wells up, quickly swallowed — disloyalty leaving an unpleasant taste in my mouth. "Wow. Nicely done. You definitely succeeded in ruining Ba's day. Many days."

The sarcasm in my voice makes her aura of satisfaction fade. A sunny glare takes over. "Oh, don't look at me like that, Jill. Ba deserved it every bit. You know he did."

• • •

From Queen's Road, I wander into Landmark, past Louis Vuitton and up a couple escalators that lead to Manolo Blahnik. From there, I make my way into the core of Landmark — which is really just a fancy, monumental name for a luxury shopping mall — and edge my way around the perimeter of a giant, light-filled atrium, populated by Marc Jacobs, Alexander McQueen, and Dior.

I'm not in the mood to shop, or even window-shop. Right now, I just want to walk alone for hours, until my feet turn numb. And this retail labyrinth stretches for miles — beyond the atrium, a glass bridge leads across multiple lanes of traffic toward a silver-clad building marked ARMANI. Why would I dare to venture outside and fend for myself, crossing the busy streets, when it's so much easier to follow the path in front of me? One mall feeds into another, new vistas of glimmering, opalescent walls appearing at every turn. Dramatic cliffs of consumerism beckoning me forward with their endless, traffic-free walking space.

For the longest time, whenever I'd think of my mother, shopping was the first thing to spring to mind. I wonder, now, if it was really the shopping that enticed her or if she simply needed someplace to escape to, and malls in this city were the only option.

I'm reminded of a passage in a book by Aldo Rossi that I read back in architecture school. Rossi writes about how we tend to see the house of our childhood, strangely aged, in the city as it changes around us. If my mother were alive today, I imagine, our condo would have this shade of curtain, that hue of bathroom tile. Some essence of her seems to be in the air around me, her ghostly presence: faint, fading notes of mint and jasmine. As tears cloud my vision, I can almost hear her voice, touched with both worry and disdain. *"Why are you living your life in the past, Jill? You think you'll always be young, but the truth is you're not even young now. Let your father be. He'll be a ghost soon enough, anyway. You have your own life to live."*

When I finally make my way to the hospital, I discover that Ba already has visitors. A man, his wife, their teenage son. These people look vaguely familiar, like distant cousins I must have met eons ago. Then the man looks up at me — startled by my sudden presence — and the skittishness in his eyes makes me recognize him immediately. First Cousin. Of course. The electrician's outfit has been replaced by dress pants and a crisp white shirt, in an attempt to show he's going that extra mile to be respectful, I guess. He looks like a different person, like an office worker, almost.

First Cousin introduces me to his wife and their son, Charles. We all shake hands. His wife wears heavy, glittery makeup meant for a woman half her age. Charles is a lanky kid with a sallow complexion and evasive eyes. After answering my question about which high school he goes to, he returns to perching his butt on the window ledge, playing a game on his phone. Meanwhile, his parents resume standing at Ba's bedside, their weight shifting from one foot to the other as though they're tired and trying to stabilize themselves. Paying respects, in our culture, entails standing until your legs turn rubbery.

"As I was saying" — Ba raises a finger in the air, like he's just getting started — "I've helped so many people in this family."

"Yes, that's true, Uncle," First Cousin says, smiling tensely.

"All the money I lent your siblings —" Ba pauses to hack up phlegm "— for school and this and that. And did anyone ever pay me back?" A gnarled hand waves through the air. Having an audience has perked him up. "Did anyone ever so much as thank me for my advice?"

"Well, I'm here now, Uncle. And I'm thankful."

"What's that? I'm a deaf old man. Speak up!"

"I'm grateful to you."

I try to catch First Cousin's attention while rolling my eyes. Poor guy, forced to put up with all this nonsense. The accumulation of debts that haven't been repaid is my father's favourite topic of conversation. All the financial and emotional support he's given his sisters and their children over the decades. No one ever thanked him, no one expressed proper gratitude, he insists. *That's not true,* I want to scream. *Just look at the circle of people gathered around your bedside, putting up with all your crap.* The cards and half-dead flowers cluttering up his nightstand. Yet my father doesn't get any pleasure from this stuff. Whatever sense of repayment he's looking for, he isn't getting it from this.

And then it occurs to me: maybe Ba actually likes the notion that the scales are tipped against him. He clings to this idea that people are indebted to him, because that debt helps confirm his self-image as a good, generous man, a man who gave freely of his time and resources, never receiving anything in return. And yet, the rub: if he's truly been generous all his life, his acts of generosity wouldn't constitute debts, they'd be gifts. But they're not gifts, for Ba expects to be repaid in full. Which brings me back to my hunch that he wants, more than anything, to feel that people are forever indebted to him.

"Is there anything I can do to make you more comfortable, Uncle?"

A withering look from my father, like it's all too late.

Could it be Ba's own sense of indebtedness that's tormenting him? The tab of morally dubious acts he racked up during those early years, when he was unmarried, unaccountable to anyone. Celeste's harsh words won't fade from my mind.

During architecture school, I made a short film.

For days, I drove around far north of the city to locate the site. I found an abandoned barn, which had been mostly burned down. Its remains were like a shipwreck, fragments of charred wood scattered over the frozen land, half buried by the endless expanse of alabaster snow.

The film begins by focusing on the swaying movement of a few delicate branches, accompanied by the sound of howling wind. A minute later, the camera slowly zooms out to reveal that these branches belong to a sombre-looking clump of dead trees on the horizon. The sound of digging becomes audible, though it isn't clear who's doing the digging. As the camera keeps zooming out, the digging noise gets increasingly violent and the vertical stretch of sky and earth assumes a bruised quality. After a final roar of wild wind, everything falls into silence. Blackness.

The film was my final project for a course. It became part of an installation, in an enclosed, narrow space at the far end of the student gallery. I filled a plexiglass tray with motor oil and placed it on the floor underneath the video projector, which was suspended from the ceiling. The mirror-like surface of the oil reflected the video. This allowed me to talk about the piece as an expression of the antagonism between the countryside and the city, history and modernity.

But the prof, a lithe guy with a shock of snow-white hair, was more interested in what I was trying to convey through the act of violent digging. As he questioned me about what the person in the film was trying to exhume, all the other students in the class stood around, interjecting their own comments and queries from time to time, as is the custom in architecture school. *Was this a statement about how technology — the filmic medium itself — has reshaped and done violence to our lives? Or was it an attempt to break down the barrier between the digger and the increasingly distanced landscape, through the physical act of digging? Yet why was the digger kept out of the camera's frame?*

My upper lip began to sweat. While I was usually agile in these kinds of discussions, for some reason I didn't feel up to it that day.

"I guess it might have something to do with the fact that I'm from Hong Kong," I blurted. "In a metropolis of that scale and density, it's very difficult to have any attachment to place."

"So the digger is seeking ...?" the prof prodded.

"A sense of ... anchorage, I guess?"

This was a pat, sanitized answer. I wasn't sure what the real answer was (and I'm still not), but I felt in the turbulent depths of my gut that it wasn't something I wanted to talk about in public.

To my relief, the prof seemed satisfied and moved on to another student's work.

What I didn't reveal was that I'd actually tried very hard to put myself in the film. The camera perched on a tripod, I'd filmed myself for hours hacking away at the frozen ground with a shovel, until my hands lost all sensation. I took breaks to warm up in my car, only to discover that as flesh defrosts, it aches and hurts more than when it freezes. But it didn't matter how many times I went out to try again. I couldn't break the ice, not even a chip. The ground remained a hard, impenetrable surface.

My sister continues to keep to herself, exuding an air of secrecy that reminds me of Mom, particularly when she was scheming. Although I tell myself I'm just irritable and paranoid from lack of sleep, I soon discover that my suspicion's right on. I overhear Celeste asking Rina to pack all her clothes. It seems that she's bought a plane ticket back to Toronto, leaving tomorrow morning. Unable to believe my ears, I burst into the kitchen, and Celeste backs up so suddenly that she knocks over a box of cereal, sawdust nuggets scattering everywhere. Rina quickly leaves.

"When were you planning to tell *me* about your departure?"

"Look, it's not like I'm doing much good here, anyway."

"What about Ba?"

"What about him? I've said my piece about paying off the Mas, but in the end, you know what? I really don't care. Handle the situation however you see fit! And it's not like either of us can give Ba what he's looking for — whatever that is."

"So this is all going to fall on my shoulders." Just as I always knew it would, in the end.

"Look, Jill, maybe Ba'll die tomorrow. Then we're both off the hook. I just can't —" a gasp, a suppressed sob "— stay here in limbo, waiting until he's ready to die!"

"And I can?"

"Plus …" she begins.

"Plus what?"

She hesitates. "I'm … pregnant."

"You *are*?"

A tiny nod. "I thought I might be, when all this hit. With everything going on with Ba, I didn't have time to get my head around it. But last week, I went to the drugstore and bought a test." A more vigorous nod this time.

That explains all the vomiting.

"Is this what you want? A *baby*?" It's hard for me to imagine Celeste as a mother.

"Eric and I were trying a few years back, but it didn't happen."

"Congrats, then, I guess."

"Thanks."

"So, yeah, okay, I guess I can understand why you want to get home to your husband." I'm surprised to hear these soft words coming from my mouth.

"I do."

"Ba'll be thrilled. He wants grandchildren, you know."

But Celeste's shaking her head, staring glassy-eyed at the floor. "Don't tell him. *Please*. Not yet."

"Why not?"

"I don't know."

I keep right on looking at her. She's not getting off that easily. "He's not going to live much longer. Why wait?"

"I guess I need this to be something I'm doing for myself. Not to please Ba. Can't you understand that?"

"No, I don't understand! Our father's on his deathbed. If you're taking off, the least you can do is give him a bit of happiness before —"

"Please, Jill." Her anguished look paralyzes me, as usual. "You don't have to understand. You just have to keep quiet, okay?"

NINE

I tell myself Terence is right. *Drop it. Crumple up the fucking letter, toss it into the trash.* Or maybe I should keep it as evidence, in case further harassment follows. I picture myself putting on a tailored black dress and sweeping my hair up in a chignon, so the police will know I'm not just some crazy woman — I deserve to be taken seriously.

But Terence's suggestion that I have no real evidence of blackmail has stayed with me. Besides, if you want something done right, you have to do it yourself. That's what Ba's always preached, in any case.

I find a notepad and begin writing in Chinese, the words halting. I'm better at reading than writing, my hand cramping up at my lapses in memory. I dig up the red dictionary in Celeste's desk, the old, elaborate language gradually coming back.

Benjamin,

I got your dad's letter hitting us up for cash. I should inform you that my father recently fell ill — very ill. In fact, he had to have major surgery and remains in a fragile state. To be frank, it is unclear how much longer he'll live, so I am taking over all his affairs.

I must say your father's letter came as a shock. I don't know what to say. I have no idea what your father is talking about. Do you people make a habit of demanding large sums of money from perfect strangers? Perhaps my father knows you from the old days, but to me, you and your folks are nothing more than strangers.

If my father were well enough to read the letter, he'd probably tear it up. End of story. No doubt, that's exactly what I should do. But if you wish to meet so you can explain what the hell this is all about, I'd be willing to give you a half-hour of my time. If you're too busy, no worries! I'm very busy taking care of my dying father.

Contact me by mail at the address on this envelope or by email, which would be preferable, at jillylau321@gmail.com.

Regards,
Jill Lau

Reading it over, I wonder if I've spread it on too thick about my father being on the verge of death. But it can't hurt. Whatever Ba did to them back then, they'd better think twice before harassing and blackmailing a dying old man, unless they want blood on their own consciences. Also, it's a good way to let these people know that my father is out of the picture. They're dealing with me now.

• • •

Once Celeste is back in Toronto, she and I fall back into our old method of communicating through short, seemingly cheery emails.

She sends me a photo of herself turned sideways, T-shirt bunched up to expose her midriff, which, as far as I can see, is as flat as ever. "Eeeek — 11 weeks!"

I reply by sending the link to a popular mommy blog chronicling the humorous mistakes new mothers make in their first year of parenthood.

Celeste writes back: "Yup, I totally get it. My sex life's gonna be non-existent and I'll be fat and sleep-deprived for, like, the rest of my life. My mind will be a ball of mush, but it's like that already, so now at least I'll have an excuse, right? XOX Hugs from Me & the Little One."

Since when does my sister sign emails with "XOX Hugs"? I wonder if she's hormonally out of whack.

No mention of our father at all. It's as though the elation of motherhood and starting anew has pushed her into a blissful state of amnesia.

We talked about parenthood a number of years ago. It was shortly after Celeste had started dating Eric, who, as far as I can tell, comes from a boringly normal, happy family. This worried her, because, like most people from boringly normal, happy families, he wanted to keep the cycle going.

"I wouldn't have a clue how to be a mom," she said.

"I don't think our mother had a clue, either."

"Can hardly blame her. Mom was pretty much raised by a maid."

"And look how well that turned out!"

"Yep, the blind raising the blind. Best to put an end to the madness."

I wonder what's changed my sister's mind now. Some belated, hormonally driven glimmer of optimism?

Or, more cynically, I wonder if she's embracing this pregnancy because it gives her the perfect excuse to get out of taking care of Ba.

The apartment above Terence's yakitori bar looks like it hasn't seen a tenant in years. There are boxes of restaurant supplies stacked along the walls, and grimy footprints on the tiles. Usually, when people say a place has potential, it's a nice way of saying it's a dive. In this case, though, I actually mean it. The floorplate's wider than expected. It'll be a good spot for a sake bar: secluded, out of the way, yet close enough to all the restaurants and night-life on Staunton.

I talk about the beauty of a Zen minimalist aesthetic and ways of warming it up so customers won't find it too austere. I mention the possibility of a pale-grey colour palette, all the gradations in tone that can be found in synthetic stones these days. Terence sees I'm excited by the project and that in turn excites him.

"Before we shake, how long are you planning to stay? Your leave of absence must be up soon."

"Yeah, well, I might be able to get it extended for six months." A mat leave replacement has expressed interest in staying on longer, covering my job. Yesterday, the HR manager emailed me about this possibility and I've been mulling over my response.

"Six months! That's great. I can introduce you to other clients, as well."

And six months will turn into a year or two years or I'll simply never go back. "Let's not get ahead of ourselves."

But it's nice to feel wanted. Terence's demeanour softens. Although he's still talking business — possible clients across the border in Shenzhen, where all the action is these days — his voice has lost all brusqueness and he's moved a step closer. I notice the fullness of his lips, unusual on a man of his age. The faint stubble on his chin stirs an urge to run my fingertips along the grainy texture, though I don't act on this impulse, of course.

"So how are things going with your father? Any more news about the pen pal?"

This snaps me out of my dreamy mood. I tell him about the letter I've sent to Benjamin Ma.

"You really think it's a good idea to meet up? You know nothing about this kid."

"What? You think Benjamin Ma's dangerous? Creepy?"

"I thought you were going to let the whole thing drop."

"He probably won't even write back." I'm surprised by how much this thought disappoints me, my curiosity like a swollen mosquito bite I'll scratch to the point of infection.

"Well," Terence says, after a stiff silence, "it's great that your father's coming home so soon."

When I say nothing, he adds, "Isn't it? Considering that's what he wants."

I stare at some crumbling brickwork, the edges jagged. "The truth is I'm just so sick of my whole life revolving around what my father wants. I'm so tired of constantly dealing with his evasions and lies."

It's a weird feeling to say this aloud. That I've long been aware Ba was stretching the truth. Creating morality tales about the virtue and reward of hard work that Celeste and I were supposed to eat up as easily as peanut butter on crackers. As a kid, I played along simply because that was the role expected of me. And because — more disturbingly — I sensed Ba had come to believe his own fictions, as if it really were possible that a benevolent supervisor could take pity on him and bestow gifts of cash and freedom. He has a very malleable memory, my father. Once he's convinced himself something happened a certain way, the story hardens in his mind like iron, like truth.

"People do what they have to do to survive," Terence says mildly, pulling me back up from my rabbit hole. "Besides, back then, everyone was crooked."

The 1960s were a pretty corrupt time in this city, it's true. Civil servants and government officials were taking backhanders left, right, and centre, and criminal organizations were running pretty much everything. Terence has a point, I suppose. Is trafficking in stolen heirlooms really any worse?

"And hey, it's not like my own family background's lily white, if you know what I mean."

I wait for him to elaborate, but he keeps quiet.

"In any case, your folks did well for themselves," I say.

"As did your father."

Ba's getting released tomorrow. I'm at the hospital, packing up his things in giant shopping bags. All his pale-blue and yellow pyjamas get folded into neat, fluffy squares. Weird how old people cease to dress like adults, reverting to the colours and clothing of infancy. I throw the extra diapers into one of the bags.

"Glad you're coming home?"

"Hmmm." His lips press together, eyes not straying from the TV screen. More gloom and doom about the economy. I flip to a nature show, fluorescent-orange slime spreading in slow motion across a jungle floor.

"You know, Ba, I've been thinking. There are a lot of things we've never talked about. Like your life, when you were younger."

"My life's an open book. What do you want to know?"

"Oh, I don't know." I stare out the window at the flow of tiny cars and tinier people, everyone going about their minuscule, capsulized lives, under the setting sun. As I wonder if Benjamin is ever going to respond, a vertiginous sensation overtakes my gut. "If you have any regrets about stuff you did when you were younger, you could tell me. I'd want to know. If there's anything you want to get off your chest —"

He looks up, coldly. "What are you talking about?"

"I'm just saying. I wouldn't be judgmental."

"Because there's nothing to judge. I've always been an exemplary father, haven't I?" His shoulders stiffen.

"Okay, Ba. Calm down. Yes, of course you've been a good father."

If Nick were here now, he'd be looking at me with that sheen of quiet panic I became so accustomed to, near the end. He no longer got me at all. And that scared the shit out of him.

While I claimed not to care what my father thought, talking trash behind his back, when it came right down to it, I did care, according to Nick. I cared about pleasing my father more than anything in the world. It baffled him how much I cared. He didn't understand how someone I'd moved to the other side of the world to get away from could exert such influence over my life.

Nick had been hoping that once we got back to Toronto, our relationship would return to normal. But instead, the cool disdain my father had directed at him had infected me. That was what Nick shouted at me, some weeks later, after everything between us had become enveloped in sulphurous fog. Maybe he was right, though I never consciously changed my attitude. I don't recall a moment of thinking *I don't love Nick anymore because Ba gave him the thumbs-down*.

When I tried to salvage things — in my hopeless, half-assed way — it was too late. "Sometimes, Jill, you have to make a choice. You're not a little girl, for Christ's sake." Curls sticking to his sweaty forehead, Nick looked anguished that I'd chosen my father over him. But siding with my father was the last thing I wanted to do. I just couldn't break the spell.

A similar sluggish feeling wraps around me now. Why can't I just let it all go, like my sister, and accept that I'm never going to understand this man? Why can't I walk away, get on a fucking plane?

• • •

I check email. Still nothing. Fifteen minutes later, I check again. I even check the spam folder. Just scams offering to help me triple my income and dating services guaranteeing *YOU ARE NOT ALONE* and folks posing as Western Union and other folks promising me an instant facelift through some miracle cream.

That night, I dream about my mother. I'm bad at remembering my dreams. As soon as I awake, the images are already being washed away, like waves lapping over footprints in the sand.

She was young and glamorous, dressed in one of her vivid *qipao*s. That much I remember. I think she was doing madcap things, like a girl in a Godard film: kicking up her heels in bars, waking up with strange men in hotel rooms, impersonating femmes fatales.

I'm not sure whether she was happy, but she seemed very alive, her skin aglow with energy, vitality.

It's not even nostalgia that I'm feeling. It can't be, because I never knew my mom back then, so there's no original memory to idealize. There's only an album full of old photos, seen through the filter of cinematic history. And my mother was likely styling herself after movie stars when she posed for the pictures in the first place.

Funny how I only became interested in her when she was on her deathbed. Just as the possibility of actually knowing her was slipping away, I became preoccupied by these fantasies about how she might have been interesting and cool when she was young. We might have been friends — perhaps that's the crux of the fantasy. But instead, she was just my mom. And not a particularly good mother at that. And then, she was dead.

• • •

Getting my father moved home is no easy task. He clings to my neck while I try to lift him from the wheelchair into the taxi, dragging me down like a bag of bricks. The wheelchair jams up when I attempt to collapse it, and the driver looks none too pleased about having to lift it into his trunk.

Back at the condo, I begin unpacking my father's stuff while the new nurse gets him settled. She's a heavy-set, older woman from the mainland, dressed in a peach cotton uniform that reflects her cheery disposition. Although the homecare agency provided excellent references, Ba doesn't appear to be taking to her at all. Something about her motherly attitude's pissing him off. When she tells him that he should rest and wipes his forehead with a soft cloth, he strikes her hand away and stares at the wall in seething silence. It won't be long before I'll be forced to call the agency and request a replacement.

I can do nothing right either, it seems. As Ba tries to wheel himself around — bumping into furniture, getting stuck in doorways — he barks at me for putting his reading glasses in the wrong place and what on earth happened to his favourite slippers? The purge we did in his absence infuriates him. Worried that he'll sack Rina, I tell him it was all my idea. His bony hands grip the arms of the wheelchair and for a moment it appears he's on the verge of pushing himself up, hurling himself forward to strike me. But his legs are far too weak for that, and he sinks back down, the flare in his eyes extinguished — sad, watery pools.

My assessment of his palliative state was perhaps nothing more than wishful thinking. He's as feisty and impossible as ever. Cheery thought.

By the time dinner's over and Ba's retired to his room, I've reverted to the petulant air of adolescence. My head pounding, I go up to the terrace for a smoke. That's when Terence calls. I jump at the chance to get out of the house.

We meet at his restaurant a half-hour later. Since it's Tuesday, the place isn't too busy. Sitting at the bar, we drink cold sake and watch two stocky, shiny-faced chefs with white bandanas around their foreheads roast yakitori skewers over the smoking grill.

"How was your father's return home?"

"Don't ask."

"That great, huh?"

One of the chefs passes over a plate of skewers and we order more sake.

"Do you ever think about moving back to New York, Terence?"

"Not really. What would I do there? I got out of finance."

"You could do anything. You could open a yakitori bar."

"But I've got that here."

"Yeah, but ..." I guess it doesn't get to him. Or not enough, anyway. Hong Kong's home for him. I know he's not thrilled about living with his mom — she's been crankier than ever since his dad passed away — but Terence accepts his situation. He's okay with it. At heart, he's a good son.

"Why?" he asks. "You thinking of moving to New York?"

Shaking my head, I suddenly feel very tired.

"What's wrong? You're crying."

"It's just the heat from the grill."

As he hands me a napkin with one hand, the other one comes to rest lightly on the small of my back.

"I don't know why I said New York," I say, sniffling. "I could've said Alabama, for God's sake. Right now, it would just be lovely to be anywhere in the world but here."

"Hey. You've had a lot to deal with lately." Terence leans closer, stroking the back of my rib cage — gently, tentatively, like he doesn't want to make me skittish — and it occurs to me that everyone in the restaurant probably assumes we're boyfriend and girlfriend. How easy it would be to slip into those roles. All I'd have to do is nudge a bit closer and turn my chin upward and then we'd be kissing. I wonder what it would feel like to kiss Terence; it'd probably be the most natural thing in the world. Or maybe so natural it'd become cloying, icky — that excess of tenderness I can't handle right now. I'm not sure I want everything between us to tumble into desire, that waterfall of warmth in the belly. And the last thing I need is another reason to stay in Hong Kong. Weirdly, it's easier to cope if all the disparate elements of my life don't come together to form a whole.

So instead, I stiffen. Turning away from him, I bite into a morsel of chicken, a bit pink and raw at the centre.

If Terence feels rebuffed, he doesn't show it at all.

A few more days go by, with no word from Ben or his dad. Whatever. I try to keep busy by focusing on the drawings for Terence's bar. After showing him some sketches that he liked, I've moved on to the next stage. Headphones jammed on, zoning out to some old electronica mix, I'm clicking away on my computer, tearing down walls and positioning new doorways.

Every so often, I come out of my room to check on Ba. Sometimes he's up, glued to the TV. Other times, he's stretched out on the sofa, asleep, his bunioned feet poking out from under the blanket like old turnips. Or his eyes are fixed on the ceiling, as though he's just waiting, in quiet terror, for death to come and ferry him away. When that doesn't happen, he gets bored, fidgety, impatient. He demands that the nurse check his diaper again or fetch a cup of tea.

I think about sending another letter to that post-office mailbox. Examining the photos I took of the dead mouse, I consider preparing some printouts along with a note: "You guys have a sick sense of humour. I think the police would agree."

In the end, though, I hold off. My father has always preached the importance of patience in business dealings. When push comes to shove, the person who cares the least has the most leverage; giving the impression that you're on the verge of walking away can work in your favour. Even if in reality, you're checking email every half-hour.

And then, there it is. Is it? I blink. Blink again. Like I'm beholding a conjurer's trick, an illusory message in my inbox, spam disguised as something important. From BKMa@sina.com. Subject heading: "Meeting."

Elation shoots up my spine, followed by a surge of dread.

Hi Jill,

Let's meet and chat. Tomorrow at the Zoological Gardens, 1:00? I'll be standing by the chimp cage.

B

TEN

The zoo's a fifteen-minute walk, down the escalator and then along Caine Road. I set off, a floppy straw hat shielding my face from the sun but offering no protection from the damp, woolly weight of the air. A nice Starbucks, the AC blasting its arctic chill: that's where I should have suggested we meet. Why am I going out of my way to indulge Benjamin's whims?

All my carefully rehearsed words for him are getting muddled in my head as I focus on trudging along without passing out. The new, pseudo-European bistros give way to the dreary cement buildings I remember from childhood. I wonder whether this kid is just as on edge about meeting me. I certainly hope so. At last, the zoo comes into sight, a scrim of green. I pause under the awning of an empty diner across the street to mop my forehead.

Then I make my way up the concrete stairs that ascend into the thick, wooded wonderland. The sky is canopied by translucent yellow-green leaves that wrap all the itchy, sweet moisture and buzzing insects in a hot embrace.

Terence thinks this kid could be bad news. We chatted about it last night on the phone. Having a guy on my arm, according to Terence, would send the message that I'm not about to be pushed around. It's sweet that he wants to protect me, I guess.

But I don't want to scare Benjamin off. I want him to feel comfortable opening up, and, with Terence staring him down, that wouldn't be likely to happen. The compromise we reached is that Terence can be here in an "undercover" capacity. He'll be sitting on a bench, reading the paper, while I feel the kid out. I wonder if he's here already. The whole thing is so ridiculous it's like we've stepped into an episode of *Law & Order: SVU*.

But maybe not. Maybe Terence has first-hand experience with these things. I have no idea whether he's ever helped his brother out with the nether side of the family business. Do they have a team of musclemen on the payroll? What happens at their gambling dens when folks can't pay up? Do they still even own such places? Or has that earlier phase given way to other, more respectable ventures?

It amazes me how little I know about Terence's life. I've never been to his house or met a single member of his family. This isn't unusual in Hong Kong, though. Condos are small and crowded, even the upscale ones. Friends tend to meet at bars and restaurants, rarely at home. Home is a sealed-off sphere, where any number of eccentricities and secrets can be kept private.

Making my way up into the park, I find myself in a large clearing. Massive cages, interspersed with palm trees, enclose a great deal of activity — swinging, jumping, screeching, shitting. I have to admit that even as a kid, I was never a fan of all this. The histrionic behaviour of the animals unsettles me. It's like they're mimicking the roles we expect them to play.

After walking around for a while, I still can't find the chimps' cage. Does the zoo even have chimpanzees anymore? I'm wandering past the lemurs and orangutans, when I glimpse, through the mesh, a bearded face staring over at me. I walk around to the other side of the enclosure.

But he turns out to be a middle-aged guy, a father. His little girl waddles over in her yellow romper and clutches his leg.

Behind the man, I catch sight of Terence strolling by some massive turtles, snapping pictures.

For several minutes, I continue to pace around and crane my neck. Finally, I sit down on a bench to dislodge a stone from my sandal. A tap on my shoulder, from behind, makes me jump.

"Are you, by any chance, Jill Lau?"

I get up, fumbling to put my shoe back on. "Hi. You must be Benjamin."

We shake hands. Mine's so sweaty I can't tell if his is damp, too. He's older than I expected, closer to thirty than twenty. A trim and toned guy of medium height, dressed in grey trousers and a white button-down shirt. His thick hair has been cut into the shape of a helmet, and I remember my mother's old claim that men from the mainland all have the same bad haircut. I never quite knew what she was talking about until now.

He doesn't take off his sunglasses, giving me the feeling of being observed through one-way glass. I don't take off my glasses, either. His smooth, almost pore-less skin has an impenetrable quality. As he turns to the side, I glimpse a dark-brown splotch at the edge of his left eye, peeking out ever so slightly from beneath the plastic frames. This must be the guy Rina saw.

"So." The guy sits down on the bench.

Tensely, I perch down beside him.

"Sorry to hear about your father's health," he says.

"Are you?"

"Why wouldn't I be? It's a terrible thing to grow old."

His Cantonese comes out with a Guangzhou accent, all the tones slightly trampled on, flat, off-kilter or something. Yet I feel like I'm the one at a disadvantage here, because my Mandarin's crap. While he can accommodate my linguistic handicap, I'm not as dexterous. It's not easy for mainlanders to get into university in Hong Kong. The kids who make it in are very clever, the cream of the cream, excelling in school exams all along the way.

"What are you studying?" I say into the silence. A throwaway question.

"Oh, humanities."

Clearly, his father has told him to play his cards close to his chest. Just as I'm sussing him out, trying to give away as little as possible, he's doing the same. Filing all the data away to report back to his dad later.

I don't buy for a second that Benjamin's majoring in the humanities. He looks too old to be an undergrad and he doesn't seem quirky enough to be a philosophy or history grad student. Med school's more like it. I can picture the lab coat overtop his tidy, professional outfit. There's a hospital right around the corner, which might explain why he chose this spot. Maybe he's on lunch break.

"Well?" he says.

"Yes?"

"You demanded to meet."

"Right. *The letter.*"

Is that the hint of a smirk creeping over his lips?

I try to appear calm, detached. "The thing is, Benjamin — Ben. Can I call you Ben?"

He gives the tiniest of nods.

"Your father's letter asks for payment, as you know. A tidy sum of money. But I'm not at all sure what we're supposed to be paying *for*. Maybe you could help me out here. Enlighten me."

Leaned forward, chin cupped in one hand, he appears to be staring at a monkey. The monkey swings from tree to tree, making wonky faces.

Perhaps he was expecting me to speak through euphemisms and innuendos and cryptic parables, like the Chinese are accustomed to doing in these situations. "I hope you don't mind that I've come right to the point," I say. "In Canada, we're very direct."

"Oh, so you've decided to be Canadian, now?" A tinge of amusement.

"My nationality's hardly the issue here."

"Isn't it, though?"

I don't know what to make of his robotic half-smile. "Look, Ben, I have no clue what you're talking about." Despite my anger, a pleading quality has entered my voice, I'm dismayed to notice. "If my father took your family's heirlooms and sold them on the black market — as your father's letter implies — it was a mad, chaotic time, you have to understand. Everyone was up to that kind of thing. It wasn't only my father."

The guy's lips press together in a colourless squiggle. I can't tell whether he's startled that I've been so forthright or if something else is responsible for his silence.

On the edge of my vision, Terence is moving closer, a blur of dark linen clothing. He must be able to tell I'm tense. Pretending to peer into a cage, he throws an enquiring glance my way.

"The thing about my father," I continue, "is that capitalism has always been in his blood. It *is* his blood, his lifeblood. It's surprising he never got into trouble, back in Guangzhou, before it was okay to admit you're capitalist to the core. But that's my dad for you: he shifts, he adapts."

Ben's air of imperviousness is driving me crazy. Feel free to jump in at any time, I'm tempted to scream.

Instead, I keep going with my monologue: "I understand why your father's pissed off about how my dad got the money to buy his building. I get that part. But why the photo of the Red Guard armband? Ba's never had anything to do with that brat pack. And sending dead mice in the mail?" A volcano of emotion erupts at the back of my throat. "That's just plain gross!"

He leans toward me slightly. "You really don't know anything about what happened back then."

Deliberately, I don't react. It's not a question, after all; it's a statement of fact. For a second, I detect a strange softening in his attitude toward me, a humid cloud of something almost like pity drifting my way. Then, the emotion chills, in a flash.

"Ancestors can't find peace in the afterlife unless they have proper burials. Why don't you tell your father that? Ask him if he's been haunted by any ghosts of little old ladies lately."

"What the fuck are you talking about?"

"You don't need to understand, so long as your old man does." A slender white envelope emerges from his back pocket. He extends it toward me, in a teasing manner, like at any moment he might retract it and I'll have missed my chance.

I pluck it from his hand.

With that, he stands up and leaves.

Screeching fills my ears. Two monkeys are going at it, flinging food and shit at each other with remarkable enthusiasm.

Terence comes over to me, after the guy has disappeared. "You okay?"

I shrug, still dazed with fury.

"Locusts," Terence says. That's what mainlanders are often called here. Butting in line, talking too loudly, waving around their credit cards at Prada and LV.

Yet what disturbs me about Ben, I realize as we're leaving the zoo, isn't that he fits the stereotype of the nouveau riche tourist. He doesn't. It's something harder to pinpoint. What does this kid have to feel so high and mighty about, anyway?

"Did you find out anything useful?"

I hold up the envelope. "He gave me this."

"What is it?"

We slow down, pausing under the shade of a tree. I thrust the envelope at Terence, my nerves a jangling mess. "Open it."

He extracts a white paper, folded in thirds, and shakes it out. As he skims across, his forehead furrows. Silently, he rereads it.

"Well?"

"I have no idea … it's some kind of record, I think."

I snatch the page, impatient.

> October 10, 1967. The county seat experienced a Violent Event. During the day, rebels paraded thirty-six stubborn conservatives and capitalist roaders, and injured twenty-eight individuals (ten permanently) during nighttime. When these activities spread to the communes and villages, 998 were beaten severely. Within this group, fifty-one suffered permanent disabilities, two were killed, and ten others died of causes

It appears to be a photocopy from a book in Chinese. The text before and after the excerpt has been blocked out, a line of black dots from partial, amputated characters trailing off at the end.

If Terence is correct that it's a record, what is it a record *of*? I've never come across anything like this in my life. Who wrote it? Who chronicled this "Violent Event"? And why is it so important for Ba to know about a bunch of strangers being injured to the point of being disabled for life? *What on earth does any of this have to do with my father?*

I fold up the page and put it back inside the envelope. Shove the envelope into my purse. I begin walking, the gravel crunching like broken bones beneath my feet. I feel very remote from myself, my body. Even when Terence grabs me by the arm, I can't shake the sense that I must focus my attention on the smallest, simplest tasks, just in order to keep on moving, breathing.

"Slow down," Terence says. "Does it mean anything to you?"

"Nothing at all."

"Well, I guess you'll have to ask your father, then."

"Like he'd ever tell me anything." I keep on trudging ahead, sweat stinging my pores.

When I get home, the place is eerily quiet. I call out to my father, the nurse, Rina. No one answers. My father's bedroom is empty, the bed neatly made. It's possible that Rina's out shopping and the nurse could have also stepped out on some errand. But Ba? He should be here. Where else could he be?

I wander from room to room. Stillness, emptiness. I've become like a stranger to this condo, no different from the real estate agent who will one day, in the not too distant future, give tours.

Voices from up above, on the rooftop terrace, break my reverie.

At the top of the staircase, I push open the metal grate and step outside into the sticky air. There he is, sitting in his wheelchair at the white table, his back toward me. He must have asked the nurse to carry him up, though she's nowhere to be seen. In her place, a stranger sits. A broad-shouldered guy in a dark, boxy suit, his fleshy forehead shimmering in the heat. One of Ba's old business associates? Instinctively, I stay under the awning and duck behind a cluster of potted trees.

Peering through the leaves, I catch Ba's face in profile while he shifts around. That's when I notice his strained expression — the flash of fear. The man in the suit takes on a menacing quality: he's not Ba's old business friend. He's not a friend at all. Is he some thug

Benjamin's father sent over to press his point? Now the guy's leaning toward my father, his shoulders slouched and meaty. Though I should be frightened, a strange fascination flutters over me, keeping me motionless. If this guy scares the crap out of him, Ba might open up to me.

My foot jostles something.

A clay pot falls over with a crack.

Two heads swivel around, and I step out from behind the leafy curtain.

The guy's expression softens, startled. Or maybe he never looked threatening to begin with; maybe it was all in my imagination. In any case, he ceases to appear thuggish while approaching, a big smile spreading across his face, glasses fogging up. Eddy Chan — *Christ*. How could I have mistaken Eddy for a thug?

Tired and dehydrated, I feel my body going limp. My wish a moment earlier for the threat of violence now seems awful, humiliating. The deranged fantasy of a woman losing her grip.

As I sit down, he and my father resume talking. Ba's reminiscing about the old days, his glory days with Eddy's father.

"You wouldn't believe the original state of that building when your father and I picked it up," Ba says, shaking his head. "We had to knock the whole thing down and start over. That neighbourhood was such a dump back then."

"But you and my dad could see that it had potential."

"Your father wasn't even in Hong Kong yet, was he?" I say, turning toward Eddy.

He colours. "I suppose that's right."

"Mr. Chan was still in Guangzhou, right?" I'm trying to get this straight in my head, once and for all. "Ba returned to Hong Kong first, got back on his feet, then bought the original building. And then your father arrived and they built the new building together. Isn't that what happened?"

Ba laughs, a bit nervously, it seems. "Who cares about who came back first? Samuel Chan and me, we were always a team! We ... worked well together ..." His voice contorts as a coughing fit overtakes him, his eyes watering.

Jumping up, Eddy gently hits my father on the back and rubs in circular motions to ease the congestion. I remain frozen, and Eddy casts me a quizzical look, as though he can't understand why I'm not being a more caring daughter.

But something has turned cold inside me.

"After we moved to Vancouver, my father never found another partner like you," Eddy says, a kiss-ass as ever. "He pretty much gave up trying, went into semi-retirement. Played a lot of golf. Work never inspired him the way it did on this side of the world."

"We had some good times together."

"Indeed, you did."

"Eddy married a nice girl," Ba says to me in a chiding manner.

"That's great. Congratulations. When was the wedding?"

It turns out they got married a few days after Ba collapsed.

"I was planning to attend." Ba continues to stare at me like I've robbed him of some great happiness at the end of his life.

Funny to think that if I'd been a different kind of woman, I might have seen Eddy Chan as prime husband material. We could be married, jointly running the family business, three kids in tow. Ba and Mr. Chan united forever in a shared gene pool, a generation of bratty grandkids.

Alas, it wasn't meant to be.

"How did you and Mr. Chan meet in the first place?" I say to Ba.

"Oh, we were on the same work team in Guangzhou. Both hard workers."

"Did a nice supervisor also grant him a travel permit to return to Hong Kong?" This comes out sounding more incredulous than intended.

Ba erupts in a coughing spasm again.

"Seriously, Ba."

When he doesn't reply, evading my gaze, I look straight at Eddy. Surely, he must be curious about these things, too. "Didn't your father ever talk about this stuff?"

He shakes his head, trying to smile disarmingly.

"Mr. Chan must have been one of the friends you started the peanut oil business with, Ba?"

"Oh, no. We had bigger fish to fry, from the get-go."

A sideline smuggling stolen heirlooms? "Really — like what?"

"Oh …" Ba crosses his arms, reverie fading.

"We should let your father rest," Eddy says.

Rina comes up to the terrace, back from shopping. She asks whether we'd like some tea. While Eddy and my father begin chatting about the state of Hong Kong's economy, I chime in now and then, but what I'm really wondering is whether Ba paid smugglers to get Mr. Chan into Hong Kong, just like he smuggled in First Cousin and the rest of our family. All of it funded by other folks' vanished treasures.

Rina carries up a tray laden with teacups, biscuits, and fruit.

While pouring the tea, I try to steer the conversation back to our building, wanting to probe further into how it got built. But I find myself getting sidetracked when Ba mentions that the economic downturn could work to our advantage.

"True," I muse, "high-end shops are looking to relocate to cheaper areas. And Sheung Wan's actually gotten quite trendy."

Ba leans forward, slurping his tea. "We could charge higher rents, then, couldn't we? Particularly for the ground-floor retail space."

"If it weren't for the fact that the lobby's such an eyesore. We should think about giving it a facelift." Although going into this wasn't my intention, it has been on my mind.

Eddy winks at me. "See, you're a natural. It's easy to learn the ropes."

"You agree with me that the lobby is hideous, then? That fluorescent lighting is terrible."

Eddy's chin teeter-totters back and forth, like he's doing some weighing up of pros and cons. Sodden crumbs flying from his lips, he says, "Sure, it'd be nice to have a swanky lobby, but the area still hasn't quite gentrified to that point. We would sink a lot of money into a reno without being able to recoup it in rent yet. Let's revisit this question in five years, maybe?"

"Oh, I disagree. If we're going to do it, why wait? And if we move on it soon, I'll still be here in Hong Kong to do up the drawings and oversee construction."

He keeps shaking his head.

Ba leans forward and puts a bony hand on my arm. *Simmer down,* the gesture seems to say. "If Eddy thinks we should wait, we'll wait. Save some money for the time being, eh?"

In an instant, Eddy's become the son Ba never had. And in our culture, sons outrank daughters, plain and simple.

As my father and Eddy continue to talk and plan, I recede to my place of silence and invisibility at the edge of the table. Is this how things will always be? Even if I stick around to deal with the business, I'm going to be forced to seek Eddy's approval before Ba will ever back me. And what's going to happen after Ba's dead? I'll have to deal with yet another arrogant man thinking that he's teaching me the ropes?

But as I watch the two of them, their heads bent together in a dark tent, my anger is gradually overpowered by a different feeling. Puzzlement. Déjà vu. Like father, like son. During my childhood, I remember how on the occasional Sunday afternoon when Mr. Chan would drop by for tea to discuss some pressing business matter, my father always seemed to soften in his presence. It jolted me, because it was so unusual to see. Mr. Chan's gaunt features would inflate like an old sail just as he was getting ready to press his point, as though he were addressing a crowd, putting on a bit of a performance. You could tell he was a man who liked attention and was used to being listened to. Yet he never had to say much. Mr. Chan was the one person in the world whom Ba would never oppose or strong-arm. If this man said something should be done a certain way, Ba would just agree, no questions asked. And now, he concedes to Eddy in exactly the way he used to kowtow to his father.

Always that respect, reverence. Why? What history did those two men share? Perhaps the flash of fright I initially perceived on Ba's face in Eddy's presence was not just my imagination playing tricks on me. Eddy's no thug. But there's more to my father's desire to impress and defer to these people.

ELEVEN

Ancestors can't find peace in the afterlife unless they have proper burials, Benjamin had said. *The mini grave in the shoebox, upended all over the floor.* Then he asked whether my father had seen any ghosts of little old ladies lately. What did he mean by that? My father doesn't even believe in ghosts or the afterlife, as far as I know.

And then there's that weird piece of writing. After dinner, after I've retreated to my room, I pull the envelope from my purse and hold it gingerly by the edges. A gulp of Scotch to steady my nerves. I extract the paper and force myself to reread it. Again and again. As if this will somehow enable me to decode some deeper meaning beyond the impersonal language about numbers of people beaten by the "rebels," the good guys. And the extent of injuries inflicted on the "stubborn conservatives" and "capitalist roaders," the bad guys.

Is it a government record of some kind? During the Cultural Revolution, the government kept records to document violence? Ben's cool observation about how little I know continues to taunt me.

If this is a government record, I wonder how Ben or his father gained access. While there's slightly more transparency these days, papers like this are likely kept in some rare books library or government archive. One would have to be a scholar or academic to get at them, I would think.

I examine the columns of text, noticing how clear each character appears, all the lines perfectly uniform, un-smudged. Like the graphic layout of the Chinese novels I occasionally pick up at the airport bookstore.

And it's written in traditional Chinese, rather than in simplified Chinese. Books in Hong Kong continue to be written the old-school way, unlike books published on the mainland, where a simplified writing system was introduced to boost literacy rates.

Something about this niggles at me.

I flip open my laptop. Thanks to touch-sensitive screens, searching for things in Chinese is a lot easier than it used to be; you simply write each character with your fingertip.

I do an internet search on the first two sentences: "October 10, 1967. The county seat experienced a Violent Event."

But nothing relevant comes up, as far as I can see. It's just a hodgepodge of stuff about Martin Luther King and something about a violent uprising in Algeria. Adding "China" to the search terms doesn't help, either.

Although the events of the day have left me drained, I'm too wound up to fall asleep. I try to forget about everything by watching old clips of *The Blue Planet* on YouTube: phosphorescent schools of fish swim through their blue abyss, feasting on plankton.

It's two in the morning and I still can't sleep, thanks to all the yapping coming from Ba's bedroom.

While he can't stand the day nurse, he's taken a strange liking to the night nurse. Strange, for one thing, because he so seldom likes anyone. And strange because this woman isn't at all attractive. Usually, when my father warms up to women, they tend to be young and perky. But the nurse is a squat woman in her sixties with arms like rolling pins and a squarish, merry face and fringe of self-cut hair.

Interestingly, she manages to compensate for what she lacks in looks with her soft demeanour. She acts as though she's young and desirable — giggling girlishly, fussing about my father, but not in a maternal, authoritative way. She runs to fetch his congee and massages his feet and asks little encouraging questions every time Ba launches into yet another story about the old days, almost like she's got a schoolgirl crush. Hard to believe, considering she's changing his diapers and the plastic pouch that connects to what's left of his bowels.

Despite my father's insistence that he's dying, a levity always comes over him upon the night nurse's arrival. It's enough to make me nearly jealous. Ridiculous. She's paid to be nice to him, I remind myself.

Sleep's a hopeless prospect at this point, so I watch another snippet of *The Blue Planet*. As a jellyfish undulates and contracts, an idea swishes into my head.

October 10, 1967. The county seat experienced a Violent Event. This time I do the search in English.

While most of what comes up is the same stuff as earlier, halfway down the screen something new catches my attention.

It's a book, housed on Google Books. *Idealized Rebellion: The Chinese Cultural Revolution in Historical Context*, written by a sociology professor at UCLA, David P. Liu. Up in the left corner of the screen, I see a red book cover with a black-and-white photograph of a clique of Red Guards, smiling grimly. On a sample book page, a couple of sentences appear highlighted in yellow — almost exactly the two sentences I googled.

My pulse thrumming to life, I skim the rest of the page and the following one. It looks like Terence was right; the excerpt does originate from a government report. Or a "county gazetteer," to use the author's term. Quoted passages from various gazetteers are sprinkled throughout the chapter. It seems they were compiled during the era that followed the Cultural Revolution, when the Party began calling for the rehabilitation of "false" and "innocent" victims. The numbers of those injured and killed, according to the author, likely represent underreporting.

My eyes flit about in a frenzy, the bright white screen glowing before me like a solar eclipse, certain recurring words and phrases standing out. *Mass organizations. Armed street battles. Class struggle. Mass violence and killings.*

Originally published in English a decade ago, the book was translated a few years back into Chinese and published by Hong Kong University Press. Benjamin must have come across it at the university bookstore or library. Perhaps history is his area of study, after all.

Many pages have been omitted, since this is only a preview. Fumbling for my credit card, I buy the e-book. Then I try to calm down, so I can read with any degree of concentration.

The book maps levels of violence during the Cultural Revolution, distinguishing among different types of violence and where they tended to occur, whether the countryside or the city. While street battles were an urban phenomenon, the farther you moved outward toward the peripheries, the more creative and unregulated the forms of violence became. Pogroms. Political witch-hunts. Whole families being chased into canyons and off the edges of cliffs.

Graphs and charts convey the numbers of people persecuted, injured, and killed by county, but my tired eyes can't take in these stats.

The author takes for granted that the reader already knows quite a bit about Cultural Revolution history. The book refers to a series of events called the "Great Armed Battles" in the summer of 1968, like whatever happened is common knowledge. But when I think of the summer of '68, I think of students with billowy hair and tie-dyed T-shirts marching through the streets of New York and Paris, chanting about civil rights and Vietnam and worker solidarity and love, not war. Did this side of the world have its own version? The Great Armed Battles. It sounds grandiose. Though students over here take their causes very seriously, if the Red Guards are any indication.

I let the internet guide my compulsive fingertips. Handfuls of other e-books pop up, but as I skim abstracts and previews, the writing's no less academic and mind-numbing. I google several key words and then try additional words to make the search more specific to the Guangzhou region. Historical websites, university websites, articles, more e-books. My eyes skim ahead, jumping around from site to site, too much information firing in nerved-up bursts from retina to brain.

Finally, my tired eyes seize on this preview of an e-book on Amazon:

> October was a bleak month. Since my father's arrest, our house had become eerily quiet. Even my youngest brother was on his best behaviour. Whenever one of us kids would ask our mother about where our father had been taken, she'd try to smile, despite the tears filming her eyes. "His friends in the Party will protect him. Nothing bad will happen to him." As the days wore on, though, her brave front began to crack. One evening, I overheard her sobbing and complaining

about my father to my aunt. "Why did he have to speak his mind? *What good are his principles if his whole family gets labelled as blacks?*"

At school, I lived in constant fear that other students would find out about my father's plight and kick me out of the Red Guards. All my friends were Red Guards — it was considered cool, back in those days. We dressed in faded army uniforms, patched around the knees to give our look an exaggerated proletarian emphasis, leather belts slung low on our hips. We showed off our bright-red armbands in the way that kids these days display their intricate tattoos. Although initially upset about having our hair bobbed, we adapted. If Mao had asked us to shave our heads, we'd have considered it chic.

Since not all students — certainly not the ones labelled as greys and blacks — were allowed to belong to the Red Guards, membership was highly coveted. Mao had created a cult around himself; we revered him like a god, a rock star. Anything he said about class struggle, about revolution, we took as the pure, unquestionable truth.

That Mao had called on us young women to be as tough as men made us adore him all the more. "Women can hold up half the sky" was a popular slogan heard from loudspeakers in the streets, in Mao's very own voice, along with his other sayings about the tumult and glory of class struggle. At last, we girls were going to do our part in making history and revolution! Little did we understand that what

Mao actually meant was that we'd be expected to haul bricks and dig ditches.

Within the Red Guards, girl gangs formed. Although I was never part of a gang, one of my old childhood friends — an overweight girl who used to be teased and called "Fatty" — developed quite a reputation for being as fierce as any boy. Her squat, truck-like body, which had once counted against her, now made her a force to be reckoned with. She was one of the few girls deemed tough enough to accompany the gangs of boys on their house raids. Now when people laughed at her jokes and called her "Fatty," it was with affection and respect.

By the fall of 1966, classes were no longer being held. Many of our teachers had been denounced and humiliated by the Red Guards. The bad students and troublemakers, who'd once been the targets of our teachers' disciplinary action, became their worst tormentors. I saw my math teacher, a thin, hoary-haired man, slapped across the face and kicked to the ground by a boy he'd failed. A posse converged around his fallen body. I'd always done well in math. Although this man was strict, he was a good teacher. Confusion and disgust swelled in my throat as I watched him being beaten, but I quickly suppressed whatever I was feeling. After all, if Mao said this was what we should be doing, who was I to question our great leader? School became like a permanent recess, kids milling through the empty hallways, discussing how to carry out Mao's directives.

By this point, the property had been badly vandalized. Since Mao had called on us to destroy everything that represented the old culture, the tiled roofs and carved eaves of all buildings had been smashed. Antique statues, like the one of Confucius outside the school's temple, had been toppled, hammered to pieces and even urinated upon. In the library, the bookshelves had been ransacked, all the books burned or torn to shreds. From time to time, I'd peek inside. It was like looking into a mass grave, a crematorium of lost learning. But I knew it was reactionary and bourgeois of me to be indulging in such nostalgia.

Although I've long known about the Red Guards, something about this personal account makes that whole period become all too real. It's from a memoir called *Walking Through the Red Curtain*, by Alice Keung-Cartwright. The cover shows Mao's squarish face looking outward with visionary wisdom, a Mona Lisa smile playing on his lips. The image is in colour, but it has a bleached-out, evanescent quality. On Keung-Cartwright's Wikipedia page, I discover that she left China in the late 1970s for England, where she obtained a doctorate in museum studies from University College London. Then she worked as a curator of Chinese art at a museum in the American Midwest for many decades, until her retirement. She died five years ago, after a long battle with cancer.

This erudite old lady used to be a Red Guard? *Really?*

After buying the e-book and downloading it to my tablet, I continue reading:

Although I tried to talk the Maoist talk in order to fit in, in truth I was a shy, bookish girl, who had no understanding of or interest in revolution and resistance. And resistance to what? As far as I could tell, most of the old landlords had already been dispossessed and thoroughly humiliated. I missed the order of sitting in a classroom and learning; I missed the cadence of my teachers' voices as they delivered their lectures on Chinese literature and poetry. Of course, I couldn't admit any of this. Instead, I spent my days just trying to blend in, keeping my eyes down, worries about my poor father never far from my mind. I wished for nothing more than to become invisible.

"Hey, you!" Fatty called out at me one afternoon. She was rushing down the hallway, her cheeks fired up, as though lit from within by a furnace. A group of other Red Guards, both boys and girls, were trailing behind her. "We need you. We're going out on a raid!"

"Oh ... but ... I wouldn't be any good." I'd never been asked to go on a raid before. Although it was supposed to be an honour, there was nothing that appealed to me less.

"Oh, come on. Don't be such a wimp." As Fatty appraised me, her eyes turned grey as slate. "From what I hear, you of all people are due for a lesson in class struggle. How's your dad doing these days? Have they released him yet?"

My mouth dry, I stared at my feet.

"You have to draw a line between yourself and your folks. Now's the perfect time to prove yourself. Get moving — you're coming!"

We piled into a car, a half dozen of us. Since Mao had ordered everyone to support the Red Guards, vehicles were always available for our use. I was pressed against a paunchy, balding man, the instigator of the raid. As he told his story, he was sweating profusely, enveloping us all in his pungent cloud. It was his neighbour he was complaining about. He claimed that she'd collaborated with the Nationalists. Her deceased husband had once been an officer high up in the Kuomintang, according to him. She had buried a statuette of Chiang Kai-shek, the old Nationalist leader, in her backyard, because she couldn't bear to part with it. "These people never learn! They're ox devils to the core."

Everyone in the truck nodded. Mechanically, my head bobbed up and down, too. But even then, I knew in my gut that this man was lying. He despised his neighbour for some other reason that had nothing to do with politics. The Red Guards were being used to settle old grudges.

We arrived at a warren of dingy streets, the dilapidated houses crammed together, their walls little more than plywood slats. As Fatty and her gang rushed ahead and charged through one of the doors, I hung back, hoping to slip away. But I worried that if I vanished, the Red Guards would hold it against me. A cacophony of screams and shattering objects came from within, followed by much laughter. Fatty began taunting the pleading inhabitant, calling her vile, slutty names, like "worn-out shoes." As I stood on the hard mud in the little backyard all by myself, the damp chill worked its way into my bones. I stared at lone blades of grass, dead and straw-like. Then, from inside, I heard someone calling out my name.

The interior of this poor woman's house — if you could call it a house — had been ransacked. The floor was strewn with broken dishes and clothes torn to shreds. A sickly odour encompassing blood, sweat, and unwashed skin — along with something indescribable, like the smell of animal fear itself — turned my stomach. The room was very dim, since the one lamp had been smashed. At first, I thought the dark lump in the middle of the floor was a pile of clothing, until it quivered ever so slightly. An old woman, a blanket pulled over her back. As her face peeked out, her eyes were bright white and bulging. *"Red Guards, have mercy on me! I swear on my life that I have done nothing wrong!"*

Someone yanked the blanket off her. She was half-naked, dressed in a short nightgown, her bare legs covered in bruises and bloody cuts. Evidently, this wasn't the first time that Red Guards had paid her a visit. A whiff of a horrible fecal odour drifted upward. Despite the woman's pitiful pleas, Fatty appeared unmoved, languid amusement playing at her lips. She took off her belt and struck the woman's back with the buckle end. As the woman shrieked and rocked back and forth, Fatty kept on striking her. Her eyes met mine, with a blasé look, as if the whole thing was starting to bore her. And then, to my horror, she handed the belt to me.

"Your turn. Time to prove your allegiance to Mao."

I thought of my father and how he'd bravely taken a stand.

Then I thought of my mother and her claim that his principles were no good to anyone now.

As though in a dream, my body beyond my control, I accepted the belt, surprisingly weightless in my hands. I raised it mid-air.

My victim's shriek felt like it was coming from my own throat.

● ● ●

A little past ten, I awake to the sound of a jackhammer — an army of jackhammers. It's like the vibrations are going straight into my clenched jaw. In this city, new buildings are constantly going up, while the old ones are being renovated. Construction forms a blanket of white noise that most of the time I hardly notice. Except at times like this.

Whatever sleep I've managed to get, it's been light and restless. Dream images of a screaming old lady being whipped and children getting chased off the edges of cliffs are still fading.... Being yanked awake by the jackhammer is actually a mercy.

After pulling on my bathrobe, I step into the hall. The living room's empty. Where's Ba? I don't hear him in his bedroom.

Then the front door opens, as the day nurse wheels him in. Ba's holding a few letters, which I can tell are only bills. He keeps searching through them, as though he's somehow missed one that might magically materialize.

The nurse sighs. "Mail only comes once a day. And what could be so important at your age? You need to rest —"

"Did I ask for your opinion? You work for me. If I tell you to wheel me down to the lobby every ten minutes, you'll do it. Are we clear?"

"I'm just worried about you, sir. It's not good for you to get so worked up."

"Tsk." Ba turns away, bristling.

A few minutes later, she returns with a cup of tea. I ask her to take a fifteen-minute break, go out for a stroll.

"What?" my father demands. Breaks are unheard of in his world.

"I want to have a word with you alone, Ba."

Something about my sleep-deprived, fretful demeanour shuts him up. The nurse grabs her purse and scurries out.

I have to tell him about this latest turn of events. What choice do I have? Ba will be livid that I've been keeping him in the dark and he won't understand that I've only been trying to protect him. But at this point, his wrath is the least of my worries.

"Last week, another letter arrived in the mail. I didn't want to upset you."

"What?" A trembling hand shoots out.

When I return from my bedroom with the letter, Ba has put on the bifocals that hang from a cord around his neck.

I can't wait for him to finish reading it through before I launch in. "Do you have any idea who these people *are*? They want money. They claim that we *owe* them. Is any of this true?"

"Shush." Ba doesn't look up from the page.

I remain silent for about another ten seconds. "Well?"

"They're … they're full of crap. They don't know what they're talking about."

"But you do know this man, Mr. Ma. Who calls himself your old friend from Guangzhou. Who *is* he?"

Ba rolls his eyes, wariness taking over. "It doesn't matter. The point is I don't owe the Mas anything. If anything, they owe *me*."

"But the heirlooms? What's all this business about you taking their heirlooms?"

Images of Red Guards toppling statues and tearing up books and beating up frail old ladies flit before my eyes.

He holds up a hand. *That's enough*, the gesture says.

"But —"

Again, the hand comes up, like a stop sign. His face turns away. "Where's that useless nurse gone to?"

"She's taking a break, Ba. You're stuck with me for another few minutes." I haven't even gotten to what I really want to ask about — the excerpt from the gazetteer. I reach into my pocket, where it's folded up in a tiny square. "And there's something else —"

"Not now," he interrupts. "Wheel me to my room. I need to lie down."

As I help my father into bed, his arms clutch my neck, like a child trying to escape from drowning. He's very careful to avoid my gaze as I adjust the blankets over his body. I'm surprised not to see more anger, if he's the injured party to whom the Mas are somehow indebted, as he claims. Instead, he looks drained. Contrite, almost. This is the closest my father has ever come to appearing on the verge of tears in front of me. It scares the shit out of me.

After breakfast, I return to my tablet and resume reading the memoir:

> Following my participation in the house raid, a shroud of guilt wrapped around me at all times. Sleep became a rare luxury. And even when I was able to fall asleep, my dreams were haunted by that old lady's shrieks and pleas for mercy. I resolved never to take part in a raid again, by keeping a very low profile at school.

Then, to my immense relief, Fatty's power within the Red Guards began to wane. Her father, a high official in the Party, suddenly came under attack; posters denouncing him went up all over the streets of Guangzhou. Suddenly, the shy, awkward girl I'd known in grade school returned. When Fatty walked across the schoolyard now, she kept her eyes down, her face as expressionless as an empty sink. Her mother, also a Party official, was so distraught over her husband's fate that she killed herself by jumping out a twelfth-storey window. Then Fatty disappeared — she simply stopped coming to school. Perhaps she and her siblings had gone into hiding. These stories, these tragedies, were actually rather common at the time.

One afternoon, I came home from school to discover that my own father had been released from detention at last. A shadow of his old self, he refused to talk about anything that had happened. The experience had aged him by fifteen years and stripped twenty-five pounds from his already slender frame. His eyes had an empty look, like they'd been replaced by marbles.

Things were changing within the Red Guards. Initially, membership had been clear cut. The children of Party officials formed the inner circle. Now, however, their parents were coming under attack and being purged, just like Fatty's father. So students labelled as "greys" and even "blacks" began forming their own organizations, claiming to be the new Red Guards. No one knew who the true Red Guards were any-more — everyone was vying for status.

Despite the chaos, the movement remained strong. Travelling to Beijing to see Mao con-tinued to be a rite of passage for all those pro-claiming themselves Red Guards. Since train travel, accommodations, and food were all pro-vided for free, the trip was not just a luxury for those kids whose families could afford it.

I had long been eager to make the pilgrim-age. Now that my father was back at home, my mother encouraged me to go. I sensed that she wanted me away from my school and our neigh-bourhood; perhaps she thought I'd be safer on the road.

The trains were packed, students sitting two to a seat and overflowing into the aisles. The sta-tion in Beijing was a labyrinth of endless lineups, as loudspeakers boomed down instructions about where we should wait to be processed for lodging. My two friends and I were finally assigned to a uni-versity dorm, where the rooms were horribly over-crowded and reeked of unwashed teenage bodies. The toilets were all backed up, stench wafting into the hallways. And there weren't enough blankets to go around, let alone beds. Since it was winter and the dorm was poorly heated, some students were sick and coughing already.

Nevertheless, a feeling of festivity was in the air. Although most of us could barely communi-cate with each other, our dialects all being so dif-ferent, it was interesting to meet kids from all over

China. Without saying anything, we had an affinity; we knew that we were united in a common mission. Our willingness to share food, clothes, and what little else we had went without saying. For the first time since my father's troubles had begun, I felt close to being happy.

One of my friends met a cute boy from Chengdu and ditched us to hang out with him. But I wasn't interested in getting sidetracked with flirtations. My heart and mind belonged to one man alone: Mao.

The first time I saw Mao, the experience was nothing short of otherworldly. We had to get up before dawn to walk for several hours to Tiananmen Square, an endless sea of Red Guards all chanting and raising our little red books, like countless flames against the dark sky. Then we were arranged in rows and told to sit cross-legged on the cold ground for a very long time. My butt turned numb. But the singing all around me kept up my spirits. And then, before I knew it, melodic cries of "Long live Chairman Mao!" were engulfing me and roaring from my own throat. An open car was passing by — *there was Mao; it was actually him, in the flesh.* Waving at us, waving at *me.* Although in retrospect I'm sure that every one of us felt this way, at that instant I was sure that he was making eye contact with me alone. Girls all around me were pricking their fingertips to write their adoration of Mao in blood on handkerchiefs, but I felt above their silly rituals. I had experienced a deeper connection.

When we weren't chasing glimpses of Mao, our time in Beijing was filled with pretty monotonous tasks. We copied wall posters to take back to Guangzhou. We learned Cultural Revolution songs to sing for hours. We were supposed to be undergoing military training, which never happened. The air force officers who came to work with our group were more interested in having us girls do their laundry.

In our spare time, a couple other girls and I explored the city. None of us had been to the capital before; a sense of freedom and adventure flowed through our veins. But the streets had become dangerous, ever since Mao had pushed his revolution into high gear, intent on purging the Party of all potential rivals. Denunciations of high officials had become almost a daily occurrence. Even the president, Liu Shaoqi, had been condemned and knocked from power. Under Mao's command, Rebels had taken control of Shanghai, and he called upon Rebels throughout China to rise up in similar fashion and seize power. Cities everywhere were turning into seats of chaos.

Everyone was game to proclaim themselves "Rebels" and seize power. Emulating how the Red Guards had risen, various mass organizations had popped up, made up of disgruntled factory workers, railway coolies, low-ranking cadres, demobilized soldiers — virtually anyone with some gripe could find a group. Even government workers and shop assistants found Rebel groups to belong to. As these mass organizations mushroomed in membership, some formed loose alliances, yet they often couldn't agree on which leaders to denounce and which ones to protect. All sides claimed to be the true revolutionaries and radicals, while accusing other groups of being "conservatives" and "capitalist roaders." Names like "bourgeois," "revisionist," "class enemy," "rightist," and "fake-leftist" appeared on posters and signs held by the throngs of enthusiastic Rebels out on the streets every day. To prove that they were the true leftists, rival organizations became increasingly aggressive toward each other, breaking out in fights at demonstrations. Struggle sessions became more violent, bloodthirsty. No longer was it simply a matter of seeing some poor guy paraded down the sidewalk wearing a dunce cap, his hair shorn. I saw women being forced to kneel on piles of broken glass for hours, their faces contorted in agony. A young woman made to kowtow repeatedly in front of a crowd raised her head a moment too soon and got struck in the eye by an old lady's cane, a river of blood gushing down her cheek. Apparently, some organizations had started employing ex-convicts to devise especially brutal forms of "class struggle."

Although I found all this violence repulsive, it was dangerous to turn away too quickly. I witnessed a slender girl, her pale, downcast face pinched in disgust, rushing to extricate herself from the crowd that had gathered around a spectacle of violence. A man grabbed her

sapling-thin wrist and began mocking her weak
stomach, calling her an elitist. When she refused
to join in the chorus of denunciations, she was
pulled right into the centre of the crowd to join
the other victims.

My mind's gone numb, unable to process any more of this
absurd misery. Although I try to finish the chapter, the words keep
slipping away and I give up.

Up on the terrace, I smoke cigarette after cigarette, watching
the grey plumes rising and vanishing in the pale, endless sky.

Eventually, I come down and check my email again. But there's
nothing from Ben. I think about emailing him. *I read the contents
of the envelope you gave me, but I'm just not that smart. You're going
to have to help me connect the dots.*

Or is it that I simply can't bear to connect the dots?

I've started to let myself wonder whether Ba was involved in
the rebel movement. A cold, imploring feeling wraps around me.
It sounds like just about everybody got sucked in, in the end.
And much as I hate to admit it, Ba isn't the kind of guy who likes
to sit on the sidelines.

The night nurse slips out of Ba's room and gently closes the door.
Although he's drifted off for now, he'll awake in a few hours and
ask her to heat up a bowl of soup, which will energize him for a
couple more hours of chitchat before he dozes off again. I don't
know how this woman manages to stay alert, night after night,
her mood so bright and buoyant. I don't know how she stands

it. Seven nights a week. When I asked if she'd like an evening off, she said she prefers to keep busy, now that her kids are all grown up.

Most of the time while my father sleeps, she just sits at his bedside and keeps watch over his quivering eyelids. She stirs only at rare moments, like now, when she steps into the living room and stands near the window.

"You can go up to the terrace," I say, from the doorway of the kitchen. "The breeze up there is nice at this time of night."

She turns around, startled. "I should get back to your father."

"He's asleep. Don't worry about him for a minute. Sit, relax."

Hesitantly, she perches on the edge of the sofa, and I drop down beside her. Perhaps I'm intruding on her alone time; perhaps she doesn't want to chat with me at all.

"I hope my father isn't boring you with his old stories?"

She shakes her head. "Your father's a great man."

"I guess Ba's been telling you about how hard he had to work after he returned to Hong Kong?"

"He did amazing things in Guangzhou, too."

I detect the faint accent now. No doubt, it's faded over the years, leaving only a vestige recognizable to the knowing ear. "You and my father seem to get on well together. You're from Guangzhou, aren't you?"

She nods.

"I don't suppose you knew my father back there?"

"No, but I knew men just like him. Brave, fearless men."

The adoration in her face sends shivers over my skin. What did Ba do back then to win this woman's reverence? And do I really want to know?

After a moment, I hear myself say, "You're talking about the days of class struggle, I assume? Things got quite out of control, I understand."

She just keeps looking at me. Neither confirming nor denying anything.

"When the mass organizations rose to power, men like my father must've gotten involved, right?"

"Everyone got involved." A proud sheen passes over her eyes. "I was just a teenager at the time. But there were men in my family like your father. They all fought on the side of the Red Flag."

"The Red Flag?" The name sounds slightly familiar. I think I remember reading something about the Red Flag on one of the historical websites or in an e-book. That memoir?

"Oh, did your father never mention the name of our group? The Red Flag. Everyone I knew supported them. It's terrible — tragic — what happened in the end."

"Oh. And what happened, exactly?"

Anxiety freezes the nurse's face. Perhaps she's realized that in her reminiscing, she has overstepped. "Your father never told you?"

"He did, but I've forgotten what he said."

She's not buying it. "I have to get back." She's already on her feet, flustered, backing into the hall to return to the bedroom. While I may have hired her, Ba is very much her boss.

TWELVE

I awake late, curled up like an overcooked shrimp. Sunlight streams through the thin curtains of my bedroom and a red flag flutters across my brain, a vestige of some fading nightmare. I close my eyes and bury my face in the pillow, but the image won't leave me.

For the rest of the day, I alternate between wasting time on YouTube and reading bits of Keung-Cartwright's memoir. Maybe I'm hoping it'll cast light on Ba's past, or maybe it's just another way of wasting time. Maybe I prefer wasting time over finding out anything substantial.

> Back home in Guangzhou, things were worse than ever. During the four months I'd been away, Guangzhou, like Beijing, had descended into a state of gang warfare and chaos. Both my parents were being held in detention. My grandmother, who was now caring for my younger brothers, refused to answer any of my questions about what

had happened, her face grey as ash. After everything I'd witnessed on the streets of the capital, I shuddered to think about what had gone on here.

For the first time, doubts were starting to creep into my heart. Doubts about Mao. Doubts about whether all the violence and suffering he'd inflicted upon my family really were going to lead to some beautiful, utopian future. Of course, it seems strange now that these doubts hadn't assailed me a long time before — a testament to how brainwashed we all were, back then. And coming out from under Mao's spell was no instantaneous process. I just remember experiencing around that time a blanket of hopelessness upon my shoulders, a heavy awareness that all this upheaval had perhaps been for nothing. As I put my youngest brother to bed at night, it bothered me that his little face looked so tense. Didn't he deserve to have some semblance of a normal childhood?

My school was in shambles. The original contingent of Red Guards, who'd once ruled the halls, had long fractured. I had nothing to do all day, like all the other kids roaming the streets. After months of idleness, my brain was starved for learning, stimulation, *anything*. But all books in our house had been burned. While reading was a dangerous activity, I decided that I no longer cared. I was willing to risk it.

I'd heard that a secret book market had opened on the edge of town. The black market had expanded to encompass all kinds of "decadent" items that Mao had driven underground.

Antiques, art, jewellery. The very kids who'd once gone on rampages as Red Guards were now hocking the loot. It seemed that not everything had been destroyed; hidden reserves were now surfacing. Gangs had formed around these enterprising activities.

The book market was housed in a couple of old trucks, parked down a side street in a run-down neighbourhood. From a distance, I watched a girl around my age climb into the back of one of the trucks and sort through boxes covered in tarp; she chatted with a bearded guy who chain-smoked on the sidewalk. Then she handed him something — money or a pack of smokes — and slipped a couple of books into her satchel.

Acting casual, I approached the truck, like I was a regular customer. The bearded guy glanced me over and indicated that it was all right to take a look.

I lifted the tarp, my eyes feasting on the brightly coloured spines, the familiar, beloved names. Zola. Dickens. Eileen Chang. James. Chekhov. Before the Cultural Revolution, books from all over the world had been published in China. As I ran my perspiring fingertips over their covers — as if I needed to touch them just to ensure they were real — chemical reactions went off in my brain.

I was going to read again.

I had only a tiny amount of money, earned by washing an officer's socks and underwear in Beijing. I thought it wouldn't be enough for anything, but the bookseller turned out to be nice. Perhaps he sensed how desperate I was for my fix.

I chose Shakespeare's *A Midsummer Night's Dream*. Although I could have bought *Macbeth*, I'd had enough of tragedy.

• • •

These days, it's painful to watch Ba eat. Since he can't swallow rice, which globs to the back of his throat, he has a bowl of watery congee instead. Chinese greens are also difficult to manage, so he eats only the fibrous stalks, boiled down to soggy nubs. When it comes to fish, though, he refuses to deprive himself. The sweet, fatty meat of the belly remains his one pleasure. He devours large, dripping hunks, crisscrossed with matchstick-thin slices of ginger and green onion, his teeth still skillful at separating the flesh from the bones. But the smallest bones can't be dislodged and from time to time one gets stuck in his esophagus and he coughs so violently that his shoulders shake like a shack in a rainstorm.

Tonight, we're not having fish, though. Rina's made a casserole of pale-green winter melon, ruffles of black fungus and tiny cubes of pork. Ba isn't impressed; she always messes up the seasoning, in his view.

"So, Ba … I've been thinking more about the Mas' allegation. That you stole their heirlooms."

His eyes remain downcast, staring at a slippery chunk of melon at the edge of his bowl. "I already told you they're full of crap."

I extract from my pocket the envelope Ben gave me and place it on the table. "You're going to want to take a look at this."

When I nudge it closer, he backs away. "Can't you see that I'm eating?"

"It's from Ben. And his father. A photocopy from a book about —"

He slams his cup down on the table. *"I'm done listening to those people."*

Whatever leverage the Mas thought they'd have, they've clearly overestimated the effects of guilt. The flash of remorse I glimpsed on his face the other day has been wiped clean.

"Well, anyway, Ba," I say, as a breathless sensation comes over me, "I realize that it would've been a natural thing for you to do. I mean, all those books were just going to be burned anyway, right? All those vases were on their way to being smashed. So I get it." *I know you, I know how your mind works.* "Why not help all that stuff find its way to the black market? Right?"

When I say "black market," my father's ears perk up, though his expression remains like a boulder. "What would *you* know about the black market?"

I know more than I care to know, thanks to that frigging memoir. I know that a lot of folks were driven more by their entrepreneurial instincts than ideological fervour, in the end.

But I don't want to get sidetracked. "It stands to reason, Ba, that the black market was flourishing. Cities throughout China were in a state of chaos. But not all the loot got destroyed, did it?"

I can tell he's surprised by the degree of certainty in my voice. "Sure," he says, in a noncommittal way. "When times are tough, everything has a street value. I don't deny that."

Now that I've provided the perfect opening, I'm perplexed that my father isn't bragging about how he moved in to corner his piece of the market. He ought to be looking proud. But he just continues poking at the casserole.

"This tastes mushy. I'm telling Rina to make fish tomorrow."

After a long silence, I ask if he'd like more congee.

"*Protein.* The doctor said I need more protein." He holds up between his chopsticks a small, crushed bone with barely any meat hanging on. "How am I supposed to regain my strength with Rina trying to starve me to death?"

"If you want her to buy better cuts of meat, you've got to increase the shopping budget."

"To let her pocket more change?"

Let her keep the change. Let her help herself to the silverware, too. *It's a small price to pay for putting up with the likes of you.*

I decide to try a different angle. "Ever heard of an organization called the Red Flag?"

He puts a morsel of meat into his mouth. He chews for a long time and then spits out the bone.

When I repeat my question, he remains quiet. His face slackens, like old leather. He recognizes the name, that much is clear. The glimmer in his eyes — fear, regret? — sends a shudder through my rib cage.

"Who told you about the Red Flag?"

I don't want to get the night nurse in trouble. "Never mind that. Who were they?"

"It was just a group of guys. We … we tried to take care of our turf. But in the end …"

"Yes? In the end …?"

"Things were rigged against us."

As Ba stares down at his arthritic knuckles, I think about how agile those hands once were. I think about the night nurse's claim that men like my father once carried out acts of bravery.

"What do you mean, Ba?"

He refuses to say anything.

I try again. "The Red Flag got defeated?"

"When's your sister coming back?"

"I told you. Celeste had to return to Toronto. Her husband's there. Her whole life is there."

"Oh, yeah? And what about me?"

"What about you? *I'm* here."

"Both my children ought to be here." He stabs at a piece of melon, having lost all control over the chopsticks. "I've been a good father. Everything I ever did was for you girls. *If nothing else, I've been a good father.*"

I don't know what to say to this. It's as though he thinks fatherhood can offset something bad he once did.

"Maybe I'll call my lawyer," he says. "It's not too late to change my will, you know."

The threat of disinheritance, his last shred of power. Money. Everything always comes down to money, in the end. Celeste doesn't care. Part of me admires her attitude, her ability to walk away without a second thought. Why can't I do the same?

"Don't, Ba. Don't complicate matters. *Please.*" If he favours me in his will, it will wreck my relationship with my sister. What's left of our relationship, anyway.

He keeps on chewing, as if he hasn't even heard. Human relationships mean nothing to this man.

It irks me how slowly he eats, not letting even a stringy fibre go to waste. We've been sitting here for forty-five minutes. And then I feel bad about that surge of resentment in my belly — that screaming wish in my head to let this *please be over, please let him die, God, let him choke on a bone, for all I care, so I can get on with my fucking life.*

Food is money. It's that simple. Just as Ba once treasure-hunted for cans on the verge of expiry to sell on the black market, he's now forcing himself to bank whatever last bit of sustenance he can manage. He can't help it. If the food's there, he'll make use of it. There's something admirable about such a relentless will to survive, I suppose.

Part of me wonders, though, what's the point of this persistent clinging to life? Wouldn't it be better to just let go? Is he just afraid of the unknown, of the black abyss?

"Is there anyone in Guangzhou you'd like me to notify about your condition?"

He looks up, a dribble of soy sauce at the edge of his lips.

"Relatives, I mean. Or old friends." Or old enemies. I sip my tea, scheming. "Isn't there anyone you'd like to talk to on the phone, one last time?"

"You've got to be kidding," he says. "I've got enough useless relatives here."

"What about after you die? Don't you want me to get in touch with people to invite them to your funeral?"

"Funeral? I'm not having a funeral. Why should I give any of those folks a free banquet?"

• • •

By the fall of '67, the Party had had enough. Although Mao had initially stirred up the mass violence to strengthen his political position, the plan was now backfiring. Mao and the Party Centre issued a call for "revolutionary unity," in order to end the violence and lay the ground for united local governments that would be called "revolutionary committees." No easy task lay ahead. Over the past year, people had become used to lawlessness and street justice. And the question of which Rebel organizations would gain representation in the new revolutionary committees was contentious. Excluded groups weren't going to take it lying down.

This was when the worst of the violence occurred. In Guangzhou, armed battles between different factions persisted throughout the summer of '68, the sweltering days that became known as the Great Armed Battles.

I remember coming home one day to find that our apartment building had been attacked. A ladder had been thrust through the bank of windows on the second floor, in a military-style charge. Bullet holes made undulating patterns all over the brick walls. It was the work of the Red Flag. After raiding a military base, they had machine guns at their disposal. All the opposition groups, pitted against the new government, had come together under the banner of the Red Flag.

We were told that we had to move out of our apartment, because the building was no longer safe. Although this was true, the real reason was that fighters on the new government's side wanted to use the top floor as a command post. The entire block was to become a fortress, as families got relocated and shuffled around. My grandmother, my brothers, and I ended up housed in a ground-floor apartment with the children of another parent-less family.

I shared a small room with my two youngest brothers. At night, I pulled them close so they could bury their faces in the crook of my neck to muffle the sounds of shootouts, shattering glass, and cries of surrender. On the worst night, a high school dormitory was set on fire and nine students jumped to their deaths, their screams echoing throughout the entire neighbourhood.

• • •

Through my bedroom window, I can see into the kitchen, on the other side of the courtyard. Under the fluorescent light, Rina is standing at the sink, which is piled high with dishes. While lying on my bed in the dark — dusk falls early in this city, even in summertime — I watch her sturdy arms lift the heavy woks in and out of the suds, steam making her broad forehead shine, her tendrils curl. Even though she's moving, there's an impression of stillness about her, a soft weariness. As if the loneliness of the day — the loneliness of her life — has come to weigh upon her whole body. At last, she can drop her cheery front and let her true feelings out.

Part of me wants to burst into the kitchen and hug her, but I don't, of course. The last thing she needs is me acting like a needy child. It's her own family that she misses.

My father's in the next room. I hear his old Nokia phone opening and closing with soft musical trills like a zippy xylophone as he checks for missed calls that never materialize. The world's forgotten all about him. And shouldn't he find solace in this fact? Whatever he did back in his day, whatever blood he got on his hands for the Red Flag, those days are long over. He should find comfort in memory loss, in his decaying body.

But unfortunately, my father isn't that kind of guy.

At last, he puts the phone aside to strike up conversation with the night nurse. Laughter bubbles up, followed by waves of conspiratorial whispering. I place my ear against the wall, in hopes of catching a snippet about Guangzhou and the Red Flag.

All I manage to make out are fragmented complaints: about my sister's absence, about my own bad attitude, about how much Ba misses his beautiful wife, about the filthy crap-bag he'll have strapped to his gut for the rest of his life.

• • •

At last, it became clear that the Red Flag was losing ammunition. Its fighters were all dead, injured, imprisoned, or exhausted — the fighting had gone on for far too long. Thus it was time to concede defeat. It was time to negotiate.

While the Red Flag was initially promised fair representation in the new government, in truth its representatives didn't last long. No sooner had they been inaugurated than they found themselves being purged, jailed, and tortured. Compared with the other mass alliance, which the new government ultimately favoured, the Red Flag was considered more militant, less moderate. Youthful fervour had no place once the government had decided it wanted seasoned bureaucrats to run the show.

Having been denounced by the Party, the Red Flag quickly lost all political legitimacy. Its cause turned into a lost cause. Rumours were soon being spread about the atrocities that its leaders had supposedly committed: they'd tortured the masses in prisons and dungeons, they'd eaten for dinner the hearts of the prisoners they'd beaten to death. A government-sponsored exhibit recreated these dungeons for public viewing. The show was a blockbuster success.

And so, it was all over. The Red Flag was no more. No more ribboning screams, no more rainstorms of gunfire. Silence reigned over our neighbourhood and surrounding precincts, as though a shroud had settled over Guangzhou. Although the factional fighting was rumoured to be continuing in the countryside, a tenuous calm had taken hold here.

We had a new government to rebuild our schools and homes and get the blood cleaned off the streets. Life was supposedly going to return to normal.

No wonder Ba didn't want to talk about the Red Flag. His comrades had suffered and died, dishonoured, the ideals they'd all fought for erased from history. What an odd moment to be standing there, bewildered, in the wake of such colossal failure. And Ba's bad knee, bad back … For the first time, I wonder whether all those old injuries might have originated from back then.

Or were my father's injuries of another kind, the kind that leaves subtler traces? Survivor's guilt. The dubious blessing of knowing that you, for some odd reason, were one of the lucky ones who had made it out alive. His absolute refusal to look back comes, perhaps, from an ever-present awareness of what lies behind. A faint red stain, always visible, like his own shadow, on the periphery of his vision.

THIRTEEN

After another sleepless night, I phone Celeste. In the background, I hear the CBC rising and falling in her living room; my life in Toronto feels very far away. For a moment, I contemplate telling her about everything that's happened since her departure. Why should she be allowed to walk away and leave me burdened with all this crap?

But she sounds groggy, unfocused. It's late in the day over there and pregnant women are supposed to go to bed early. I decide to spare her, get right to the point. "I need Second and Third Aunts' addresses."

"Oh. Why?"

"Ba's not going to reveal anything on his own. So I'm helping him out. Second and Third Aunts were there with him, in Guangzhou. They could be a real resource."

"Okay, do whatever you need to do. Just know that I'm done trying to fix Ba. Leave me out of it."

"Fine."

"Well, I'd suggest you start with Third Aunt, then," she says. "Second Aunt's husband despises Ba."

"Why is that?"

"I don't know exactly."

Second Aunt's husband's bad class background made life difficult for that wing of the family, back then. I wonder whether that has something to do with his ill feeling toward my father. Was Ba involved in persecuting men like him?

No point going into any of this with Celeste, who has more important things on her mind, like parenting books and meetings with her midwife. I scrawl Third Aunt's address in red pen on my inner wrist.

A little after ten, I set out. The line for the minibus is already trailing down the street, so I decide to walk to the subway. It's Sunday, maids' day off. All the Filipina girls are dolled up in their glossy lipstick and tight jeans, while the Indonesian ladies stick to long, black skirts and bright headscarves, even in this heat. For the rest of the day, they'll indulge in makeshift picnics, wherever they can find a few feet of empty pavement, paint each other's toenails, braid hair, giggle, gossip. I hope that Rina has her own clique.

On the blue line, I go several stops east. A little prune-faced lady runs her trundle buggy right over my foot as she gets off the train. No apology, not even a timid glance back. Old people in this city are very bold and self-entitled. They talk loudly, and they don't hesitate to tell off strangers. Then they reprimand schoolchildren on the street for being too noisy. Ba's right up there with the best of them.

I get off at Quarry Bay. I don't usually have reason to come to this part of the city. Exiting on King's Road, I walk past the public housing projects, built some forty or fifty years back. Despite their orange, turquoise, and cinnabar facades, they appear dingy, as if made of old Lego, remnants of another time. Quarry Bay's an industrial neighbourhood, or it used to be, in any case. With skyrocketing rents in Central and Causeway Bay, businesses have been relocating wherever they can, so the area now has its share of mirrored office towers, mixed in with dry-goods stores and fruit stands. The sickly sweet scent of overripe mango wafts by, making me nauseous.

My aunt lives in block D of the public housing complex across the street from a funeral home, a massive white-stucco hull. There's no guard on duty, so I walk right through the entrance into a courtyard, which doubles as a parking lot. The horizontal security bars across apartment windows are laden with air-drying panties and bras in pastel colours, and clotheslines are stretched outside the windows where shirts, dresses, and nightgowns dangle on hangers. Although this kind of display is commonplace in our overcrowded city, I still feel unsettled whenever I look up and see several storeys of strangers' intimate, worn-out garments hanging out in the open, like some enormous lost and found.

To avoid the lineup for the elevator, I take the stairs up to the third floor, enduring the hot fug of the stairwell.

Before knocking, I try to formulate what I'm going to say. No brilliant strategy comes to mind.

The door creaks open. The aroma of something deep fried and spicy wafts forth on the un-air-conditioned air. Uncle squints down at me through his glasses, clearly surprised. He's a tall, stooped man in a crumpled, pale-blue shirt, tucked into grey jogging pants. His comb-over has thinned to a threadbare sheet, neatly oiled down.

"I happened to be in the neighbourhood. Thought I'd drop by to say hello, if that's okay?"

"Of course, of course." Yet he freezes up, looking perplexed, before shuffling aside.

The living room doubles as a dining room. It also serves as someone's bedroom, sheets folded up at the edge of the sofa. The furniture's all faded Ikea fare, too many pieces crammed into the small space, the air glittering with dust swirls. A large calendar, with a photo of a windswept beach, hangs above the TV, offering a tantalizing glimpse of wide, open space. A little shrine sits in the corner, laid out with black-and-white photographs of our ancestors. In the not too distant future, Ba's photo will be there, too.

"Does Second Cousin still live with you?"

Uncle nods. "She just started work as a paralegal."

"You must be proud."

He doesn't say anything, still looking at me quizzically. I can hardly blame him. I'm not like my sister, who used to wish that she'd been born into this side of the family. Dropping by for an impromptu visit would be more her thing.

"Is my aunt around?"

"She's at the market." Uncle pats the air to indicate I should sit, wait. "How's your father doing? Your aunt went to see him, last week. I sent along a thermos of soup. He wasn't in the greatest mood, so she didn't stay long."

"I'm sorry I missed her. Ba's never in the greatest mood these days. But he always appreciates your soup."

Uncle's a great believer in herbal remedies. If I were to look in these cupboards, I bet I'd find a few bottles of tonic wine with bits of snake entrails floating around in them.

My eyes drift toward a framed picture on the side table. It shows a family dinner, everyone huddled together and smiling in that typical family picture way. First Cousin sits between his mother and Second Aunt. From the youthful look of their faces, it must have been taken shortly after they'd been reunited. First Cousin looks exhausted and rather shell-shocked, as if he can't believe they're actually all together, in their little apartment at the edge of Kowloon.

"Ba appreciated that First Cousin came by the hospital, even if he didn't show it."

"It's my son's own fault. He waited far too long."

"I had no idea that he and Ba had had a falling-out. The whole thing seems pretty silly, if you ask me."

But Uncle shakes his head, his mild temperament clouding over. "My son is to blame for the way things soured. Your father's a difficult man; everyone knows it. It wouldn't have killed my boy to indulge him. Go over to the building and change a few light bulbs, that's what I told him! Rewire a fan. What's the big deal?"

"No, he had the right idea. You have to set limits with Ba. Otherwise, he'll just take, take, *take* from you." Agitation surges up my throat. "And even then, your debt will never be paid." The room blurs and I fumble in my purse for a non-existent tissue. I wipe at my eyes with the back of my hand instead.

Uncle, looking embarrassed, goes to fetch a glass of water and handkerchief.

It steadies me, the bracing coldness in my mouth. "Sorry, I don't mean to be such a mess here."

"Can't be easy living with your father, now that he's in so much pain."

"It's more than that — someone from the old days has it in for Ba." I pull the two photographs and Mr. Ma's letter from my purse and fan them out on the coffee table. Pulling out my phone, I retrieve the photos of the soiled lobby floor, trying to give the bizarre events of these past weeks some semblance of coherence.

Uncle doesn't interrupt. He just sits there, letting my increasingly hysterical words wash over him.

"You say the kid's name is Benjamin Ma?" he says, at last.

I nod. "Ba might've been involved in a smuggling scheme. He ripped off their family heirlooms. When he was part of the Red Flag, he might've —"

"The Ma family," he interrupts. "Ma Wing-Cheong. I believe he's your Mr. Ma. Benjamin's father."

"So ... you know him?"

"Everyone knew everyone back then. Our neighbourhood in Guangzhou was that kind of place."

"Well, who *is* he?"

Uncle's thoughts seem to have drifted a thousand miles away. "Regardless of what people thought of your father, I've always respected the man, because everything he ever did was for his sisters. Without your father around to take care of her, my wife would have never become my wife. She would've starved to death during the war. Or been reduced to a maid. Or worse." Anguish quivers at his jawline. "There are people in this life who are able to make things happen. Your father is one of them. I've always been grateful to have him on our side."

"But the Ma family didn't have Ba on their side."

The door opens and my aunt waddles in, her arms weighed down with plastic bags bursting with leafy greens. Even in this weather, she's got on a tangerine cardigan that fits her little round torso like a teapot cozy. Uncle and I get up to help her with the bags.

Her eyes turn watery as they settle upon me, every muscle in her body tensing up. She thinks I've come to give her the news that Ba has died.

Putting a hand on her arm, I shake my head. Ba's still alive — alive and kicking. I realize, as her face clears, how much her entire sense of well-being depends on him being able to look after her.

After we've put away the groceries, the three of us sit down at the kitchen table.

"A letter arrived from Ma Wing-Cheong," Uncle says, extending his hand.

I pass over the sheet of paper, which he shows to my aunt.

She reads it. A shadow creeps over her eyelids. The letter trembles as she places it face down.

As Uncle reaches for her hand, she recoils. She stares at a blurry brown stain on the Formica surface.

"I think we owe Jill an explanation," he says.

"Those people have some nerve to ask us for money, after all these years. After they did nothing to help my brother. And *now* they want to act like we're family?"

"Family?" I say, confused.

Third Aunt keeps silent, sullen.

"What did Ba do to them?"

"Oh, the Mas." A pinched, disgusted expression comes over my aunt's face. "It was a bad time for everybody. We *all* suffered. Not just the Mas."

"Don't get so worked up," Uncle says. "It isn't good for you. Maybe you should lie down."

"Why? So as soon as I turn my back, you can start talking trash about my brother? After all he's done for us?"

Uncle shoots me a helpless glance.

"I'm sorry I've upset you, Auntie," I say. "But what's this about the Mas being family?"

"Don't. *Don't talk to me about the Mas.*"

Oppressive silence fills the room, as I stare at the wall covered in nicks and cracks.

"The Mas aren't going away," I say at last. "Won't you please help me, Auntie?"

"I think you should leave now."

I stand up, my knees unsteady.

"No, it's all right," Uncle says, patting the air.

When my aunt continues to stare ahead, making no effort to convince me to stay, I let myself out.

I walk through the neighbourhood, past all the mom-and-pop grocery shops and noodle restaurants, toward more public housing buildings up ahead. Although I could duck into an air-conditioned coffee shop, I force myself to endure the humidity. "We *all* suffered. Not just the Mas." Sweat prickles my forehead and back. I think about what Uncle told me, about how my aunt came very close to becoming a maid or worse. If it weren't for my father's enterprising spirit, she could have been forced to do unspeakable things.

We *all* suffered. The look on her face as she spoke: eyelids trembling with sadness, drunk on self-pity. A plea for sympathy. More than a plea, a command. The claim that she suffered, too — as much, if not more than the Mas — was her way of shoving a rag into my mouth.

I've seen that look before, countless times. The family resemblance between my aunt and father was never greater than at that moment. They have the same pug-like nose, the same mournful, self-righteous eyes. As if the skull of the same miserable ancestor were peeking out from both their faces.

The suffering card. All those years Ba spent sweeping sidewalks, cleaning gutters, the days blurring into one long dust storm of a wasted life. *You don't know true suffering, not like* I *do. You don't know a thing. I was justified in doing whatever I had to, in order to survive.*

"And *now* they want to act like we're family?" I think about how my aunt's face contorted as she said that word. *Family.*

The Mas are our family?

The truth settles upon me like the weight of the sticky air.

The letter makes more sense from that perspective. How easily Mr. Ma asked for financial help. Because that's what family members do: they help each other out in times of need. I wonder how they're related, which far-off branch of the family tree they occupy.

If only my aunt had remained at the market a little longer. Uncle seemed willing enough to talk to me, as though these things have been weighing on his conscience for decades.

• • •

On the subway home, I see on my phone that I've received an email from Ben:

> Have you given your father the envelope yet? It should refresh his memory. From time to time, these old-timers need a refresher in history.
>
> Need I remind you about my father's losses from the stock-market crash? If you plan to make financial restitution, the time to act is now.

These people can't seriously believe that I'm going to shell out money without knowing any details at all. Even if we are somehow related.

I write back:

> Ben, I must confess that I'm still puzzled about what happened between our families. Too many blanks remain for me to pull out my chequebook just yet.
>
> That said, I'd be interested in meeting with your father face to face. I realize it may not be easy for him to write about what happened back then. It might be easier to clear the air if we were to meet in person. I'd be happy to extend an apology on behalf of my father for whatever part of your family's suffering we've been responsible for, and to make restitution for the lost heirlooms. This, in my view, would be the best way to "settle the books once and for all," to borrow your father's phrase.

What do you think? If you send me your
father's address in Guangzhou, I will arrange to
travel there in the next few days.

A few hours later, I get a reply:

What makes you think my father has any desire
to see you?? His life is hard enough, with all the
terrible memories that dealing with you people
has stirred up.

I write back:

I will consider $$ compensation after your
father and I have met in person.

• • •

I phone Uncle the next morning, at around the same time I
dropped by the day before. I'm hoping that my aunt goes to the
market every day at roughly this time.

"Are you alone? Can you talk?"

"Well … that depends on what you want to talk about."

"I realize you don't want to upset Auntie. Fine. That's why you
should talk to me alone."

"Oh, Jill. Just let it go."

"I'm *not* going to let it go. Expect to see more of me until I get
some answers!"

There's a stiff pause, followed by uneasy chuckling. "What?
You're just going to barge into my house whenever you want?"

"If necessary. I'll be nice, of course. I'll show up with pastries
and pies."

"Your aunt's diabetic," he says. "She can't have sweets."

"The Mas are related to us."

"I ... I don't know what you're talking about."

"There are other folks I could go to for answers," I say. "Like First Cousin, for instance. Celeste tells me he lives two floors above you. But I don't want to upset more people than I have to. We all lead stressful enough lives."

He coughs, and I continue. "Or I could head straight across the border to Guangzhou. Track down this Mr. Ma character myself."

"That wouldn't be such a good idea."

"That's why it'd be better if you just talked to me."

"I have to go — your aunt's coming in now."

Click.

It's late. I'm up on the terrace, on the phone with Terence. A new levity has entered his voice, because he's a free man. At last, he's pulled the plug on his relationship with Julianne. Or rather, thanks to his neglect for the past month, she's pulled the plug, which works for him. Less guilt, less blowback.

"So, mission accomplished. You're feeling okay about being single again?"

"More than okay." He laughs.

I'm happy that Terence can move on with his life. Is that all that this feeling is? This warmth rushing over my skin? Best not to overthink it.

"Now we can go back to talking about your problems," he says.

And I have problems galore.

But according to Terence, I've been going about things all wrong. "Let your uncle come to you, when he's ready. You can't rush these things. And I think you're out of your mind for wanting to meet this Ma guy in person. He could be batshit crazy!"

"I don't care if he is. As long as he tells me what happened."

"But … why? Why is it so important to you?"

I stare at the black, formless mountain. "If Ba did something bad to start his business — if it's *blood money* I'm going to inherit — I want to know. Wouldn't you want to know?" And then I remember I'm talking to Terence. His family knows a thing or two about blood money.

"Anyone who devotes his life to making money is going to have some sketchy money in the mix."

"And that doesn't bother you?"

"Did I say that?"

There's more I want to ask. About how he deals with his own baggage. Yet I can't seem to find the words.

"Ever wonder why I got out of the financial sector, Jill?" He gives a bit of a chuckle. "But I don't pretend to be any saint here."

I hold back on telling him that he's been pretty saintly toward me throughout this whole ordeal. Don't want to embarrass the guy.

"Want to hear a story my old man used to tell me, when I was a little boy?"

"Go on."

"My grandfather, as a young man, was walking through a field one day with two friends. This was around where Shenzhen is today. Back then, it was all just villages and farmland. They came across an airplane that had crashed to the ground. The pilot was dead. All the passengers, too. My granddad and his friends were shocked, horrified. While looking through the pilot's satchel for his ID, my grandfather discovered a bag of gold ingots, tucked beneath the seat."

"What did they do?"

"They kept the gold, of course. Split it three ways. That's how my granddad managed to buy his first restaurant."

"*Right.* Or so your father told you."

"Yup. There never was any gold, of course. There never was any plane. I later discovered that my cousin had been told a similar story by his father about where their money came from."

"So, what are you saying?" I know what he's saying — that my father, like his own, is a crook — but for some reason I need him to actually say it.

Yet Terence is too tactful for that. "Fathers like to yap on about their sad, impoverished pasts. Overcome through twenty-hour workdays. Plus the occasional stroke of luck, of course."

"Like discovering a bag of gold bars. Make-believe gold bars, that is."

"Just because their origins are make-believe doesn't make their value any less real."

I'm not as patient as Terence. I manage to wait two days. Then, in a burst of tumultuous nerves, I call up Uncle and announce I'm going to Guangzhou tomorrow. Lies spring from my lips spontaneously, thoughtlessly. I claim that Mr. Ma has agreed to meet me, because I've offered him a good deal of money in compensation for whatever my father did to their family.

When Uncle says he doesn't think that's a good idea, that I have no idea what I'll be getting myself into, I demand that he sit down with me. Reluctantly, he agrees to meet at a Pacific Coffee near his apartment, the next morning.

I arrive ten minutes early. Although the little, round tables and overstuffed red armchairs are the same as at Pacific Coffees in Central, the café is four times as large and mostly empty. Sitting by the window with my gigantic mug, I wonder if Uncle's even going to show up.

He wanders in a little after ten, his shirt more crumpled than usual, the wispy remains of his hair catching static, as though he forgot the oil altogether. I ask him if he'd like a coffee, but he declines.

"Thanks for coming," I say.

"You didn't give me much choice, did you?"

"These things are important to me."

"Why?" Uncharacteristic hostility flares across his face. "Why do you have to go stirring everything up?"

I hold his gaze. "It's important because I need to understand my father. And if he's done something awful to the Ma family, it's up to me to make amends."

"You think it's that simple, do you?"

"Just tell me. Let me decide for myself."

Looking reluctant, he picks at a loose thread coming unravelled at the bottom of his shirt. "If you really want to understand what happened between your father and the Mas, there are some things you first have to understand about what your father was up against. What has he told you about his life in Guangzhou?"

"Not much. He's talked about working as a street sweeper."

"That came later. I'm talking about the early days, before all the madness and struggle sessions, before the endless pressure to write self-criticisms."

When I keep silent, he continues. "Your father wanted to start a peanut oil company. There were lots of restaurants in our part of the city — this was before the Communists forced them all out of business — so your dad thought there'd be a good market for peanut oil. And he was right. But to get a company started, he needed capital."

"Didn't he team up with a few other guys?"

"In the end. He and his buddies scraped together enough cash to start a very small operation, a one-room shop. But that wasn't what your father originally had in mind. He'd been dreaming big, you see. His initial plan for raising money was to turn to the richest members of his family." Uncle looks up, letting his words sink in.

"The Ma family."

A nod. "They're related by marriage. Ma Wing-Cheong, your Mr. Ma, would've been just a boy at the time. His father was married to your father's aunt."

I feel a slap of astonishment. We're related more closely to the Mas than I'd guessed.

"Anyway, the Mas were one of the wealthier families in our neck of the woods. They owned a lot of property. They lived in a big house with a beautiful garden, where the elders used to meditate."

"Ba thought these people would help him out?"

He gives a weary grimace. "I'm afraid he overestimated the bonds of family. The Mas didn't know him. To them, he was a scrappy little guy from Hong Kong, talking big, asking for a handout, while trying to call it an investment. They didn't want anything to do with him."

"And ...?"

"And your father, as you can imagine, was very bitter. Eventually, though, he and a couple friends managed to scrape together enough to get started on their own. The peanut oil shop did all right for a couple years. And then the Communists took over. The shop, like so many other businesses, died a quick death. The years that followed were very tough on everybody."

Uncle talks about how Ba struggled to get by. For a while, he worked cleaning the streets, as part of a work unit. The problem was that he couldn't resist dabbling in schemes on the side. Trading in food-ration tickets and other coupons with fluctuating values. The authorities called this activity "scalping" and it was not legal. Ba was caught and sent as a conscript labourer to a brickyard for several months. Upon his release, his work unit refused to take him back, so he was forced to return to the brickyard, because·it was the only place where he could find work and shelter. Then he tried to escape to Hong Kong by hiding in the freezer car of a freight train. Before the train got far, he was discovered and sent to another labour camp. After his release, Ba managed, over time, to work his way back into the good graces of his work-unit supervisor. By that point, he'd learned his lesson and stuck to sweeping the streets.

"More than once, during those long years, your father went to the Mas and asked for help. But by then, they had their own problems. During the Land Reform movement of the '50s, they progressively lost their land. Ma Wing-Cheong's father was persecuted. Because he was mild mannered, he managed to escape the worst of the violence directed at landlords and held on to a bit of property, where the family lived in a much smaller house. Nevertheless, your father must've felt they still had it in their power to do *something* to help him. He went to their house, bearing the gift of peanut oil from his old stash, all that remained of his defunct business. 'Won't you please help me get back on my feet?' he asked the elder Mr. Ma. 'I could work for you, sir. I could clean your house and tend your garden.' But Mr. Ma pointed outside and said, 'That tiny plot is no garden. Our old garden now belongs to somebody else.'"

"In other words, he ignored my father's plea," I say. How desperate Ba must have been to humble himself and ask for their help, time and time again. "What did Ba do when they turned him down?"

"What could he do? Life went on. Your father continued sweeping the streets."

"Until the Cultural Revolution broke out."

"Yeah, that changed things." Uncle massages the crook of his neck, staring out the window at the empty pavement.

"Changed things how?"

"It's difficult to understand, unless you've lived through it. What it's like to go from years of mindless, meaningless toil to being told it's okay to rebel. In fact, Mao wants you to rebel. Rise up against your elders and superiors and smash all the old heirlooms and other signs of class privilege and remake society as some beautiful, egalitarian place. Purge the old landlords and other ox-ghosts and snake-demons. Down with the lot — let's stomp on their heads. The vision — the struggle — entered people's blood like a drug."

"Did Ba … get involved?"

"We all did. The mass organizations were everywhere, asking folks to join up. Things got increasingly violent, especially toward the end."

The Great Armed Battles. I think of the scenes of street-fighting and chaos in Keung-Cartwright's memoir. A grey, buzzing sensation fills my head. "So he took part in the looting and violence?"

"After so many years of keeping it bottled inside, he had a lot of anger to let out."

"I guess that's when Mr. Ma's heirlooms got … what, wrecked?"

Uncle doesn't deny this.

"Or Ba stole them? Is that what happened?"

His face tightens, his lips thinning, vanishing. "Heirlooms had other uses, you see. By that point, an organization called the Red Flag had risen to power."

"Yeah, I read about the Red Flag online."

"Then you know that they'd managed to unite many other groups in a mass coalition. Your father and me and most other guys in our circle became part of the Red Flag. Your dad, as you know, is a gutsy, resourceful guy. He was good at making weapons, stealing supplies, doing whatever else needed to be done. But it was more than just street-fighting. There was a good deal of pressure on everybody to show revolutionary zeal. To prove that we were the true radicals — better than the other groups we somehow ended up being pitted against. Struggle sessions against those from bad class backgrounds became part of the daily circus."

Uncle waits for me to connect the dots, like he can't bear to say anything more.

I'm not quite connecting them. "Okay …?"

"The discovery of old treasures, hidden away. *That's what I'm talking about.*"

I still don't get it.

He sighs, and reluctantly continues. "The treasures played a key role in the dramas of denunciation we were all expected to take part in. The hidden valuables were supposed to be 'proof' that the landlords were up to their old tricks, hoarding their wealth, rotten to the core, incapable of being reformed."

"These old treasures would often be discovered?"

"They weren't truly discovered — the whole thing was rigged from the get-go! This is how things would unfold: someone 'discovers' heirlooms buried away somewhere — literally buried under tombstones, sometimes, for we were not above digging up graves." He lets out a muted laugh, shot through with shame.

It's hard for me to imagine this gentle man going on a rampage, tearing up gravesites. And yet, this is what he's telling me, what he's confessing. "What would happen next?"

"The landlord or landlord's descendant would get rounded up and brought on stage and the accusations and humiliations and kicking and punching would begin. All because of some old jewellery in a coffin. Your father, I have to say, was very good at getting into the spirit of things."

"I see." But what do I see? I see only a napkin I've crushed into a ball, gradually unfurling, as if in slow motion. "Ba made the Mas a target?"

"I guess he felt it was payback."

"I see." Part of me wants to leave it at that. Leave these euphemisms intact. How Ba "got into the spirit of things." But for some odd, masochistic reason, I need details. "What exactly did Ba do to them?"

In the bright, artificial lighting, Uncle's skin looks like an elephant's hide. "You sure you really want to know?"

I nod.

"He dug up Ma Wing-Cheong's grandmother's grave. He found something inside — some gold bracelets or jade earrings, I can't remember. People did that, back then. They buried valuables with their loved ones, so they could take the riches to the next world."

The package sent to my father's building. Suddenly, I understand its perverse symbolism. The joss stick, the dirt, the funeral paraphernalia, the tiny, stiffened rodent's body.

But no treasures, no jewellery.

Because they'd already been stolen, the grave left torn apart. Ben's great-grandmother's spirit left without a resting place. So that's what he meant when he asked whether Ba had been haunted by any ghosts of little old ladies.

"Following the discovery, Ma Wing-Cheong's father was attacked at a struggle session."

"What happened …?"

"He received such a vicious beating that he never recovered. He limped with a cane for the rest of his life."

FOURTEEN

My father's asleep on the sofa. I examine the hollows under his cheekbones, the thin, colourless mouth collapsed in on itself. His fragile eyelids clench up every few seconds, as if trying to block out a searing image. Never a restful face.

Now I have some idea why.

I open my laptop and begin scanning all the historical websites I was reading before. Then, seizing my tablet, I return to the e-books, to Keung-Cartwright's memoir. I don't even know what it is I'm looking for — some fact or image that might disprove the story Uncle told me? Or is it confirmation I'm actually seeking? Or is this turn to the internet just a tic? Maybe it's an online support group I'm searching for — Children of Fathers Who Have Done Very Bad Things.

My father's short temper and manic outbursts. His tendency to grab attention by suddenly telling people off — the poor nurses at the hospital who just wanted him to take his frigging meds. His flair for mockery. It all takes on a darker hue, now that I know what I know. I can picture how he would have been at the struggle sessions, "getting into the spirit of things," revving it up. Pointing fingers as the best way to protect himself from being pointed at, his tongue the only weapon he needed. Others would have done the punching and kicking for him.

Or maybe this is just what I need to tell myself. Maybe he enjoyed making his victims shriek as much as anybody.

In any case, this is a man who's done terrible things. The realization assails me like the flash of the sun, the incandescent afterimage impossible to escape from. I wonder if I should wake him up — scream in his face, demand answers — but a woozy sensation overtakes me, cut through by sheer exhaustion.

Later that day, I open my laptop and search for the words.

Dear Ben,

But what to write? If it's an apology I owe these people, words of the right magnitude are nowhere to be found.

Grave robbing.

A beating that left a man crippled.

Sorry doesn't cut it. Nowhere even close.

Ba's up, watching TV. It's one of those historical Chinese soap operas with emperors and concubines in bejewelled headdresses and majestic robes, gazing at each other through sultry, scheming expressions. Every so often, things erupt into a kung fu battle when the court comes under attack.

The nurse blinks, struggling to stay awake. I ask if she'd mind walking down to Marks & Spencer for the oat biscuits my father likes.

At the commercial break, I mute the volume. "Ba, remember how we were talking a while back about whether you had any regrets about stuff you did when you were younger?"

He looks at me blankly. "And what did I say?"

"Nothing."

"Right. Because I don't have any."

"Well, I've been thinking." I'm perched on the edge of the sofa, my butt teetering like it might lose balance at any second. "*I* have regrets."

"Oh?"

He doesn't appear all that interested, but I press on. "When I was a kid, I used to steal things."

This gets his attention. "Like what?"

"Oh, little things. Candy, coloured pens. A lot of kids did it, I suppose."

"But we always gave you money. You got all those little red envelopes of cash at Chinese New Year."

"Yeah."

"Why steal, then?"

"The thrill of taking something for free, I guess. Plus, I knew you and Mom wouldn't approve. So that made the thrill doubly delicious."

Ba glares at me, the fire in his eyes fading to dull confusion. "Why are you telling me this now?"

"I don't know. I just want you to know, I guess."

I could go further in confessing my sins. I could tell him about how my shoplifting adventures escalated to lipsticks and eyeliners by the time I got to high school. The only thing that compelled me to stop was that one of my friends got caught by a security guard, who threatened to call the police. Then, fast-forwarding to my university days, I could mention all the drugs I did. And there was that prof I had an affair with. A short, stout guy with wild composer hair and a Napoleon complex that made him surprisingly good in bed. At one point, he was talking about leaving his wife and kids. Thank God he didn't. Definitely not my proudest moment.

"Did you ever steal anything, Ba? Or do something you felt ashamed of?"

After a long time of staring at the soundless TV, he says, "Why are you asking me this? What is it you want me to say?"

When I don't reply, he adds, "Where did that damn nurse go?"

"What is it you need, Ba?"

His chin juts out, hostility mixed with humiliation. "If you must know, somebody needs to change my diaper."

By the late afternoon, I'm so antsy I need to take a walk. After buying a loaf of bread at the bakery, I continue along Robinson Road. The clang of hammers and the shrill screams of swirling blades seem to have increased in volume over the years, but perhaps I'm simply getting old, conjuring some gentler, quieter version of this street that was always just a childhood daydream.

A bald hunchback staggers onto the sidewalk, pushing a wheelbarrow. His shirt is off, his shrunken chest and sagging belly exposed like a deflated balloon. He's got to be well into his seventies, far too old for construction work. He crouches down to pick up some broken tiles, and he stares at the shards as if trying to piece together the puzzle of his life.

Five dollars a month.

My father's wage at his first job, as a boy.

He's told me this so many times, but only now, as I watch this old man — his bow legs misshapen by so many decades of labour — does the meagreness of that existence hit me. My father could have become this poor old man. If he'd stayed in Guangzhou and accepted his lot, no doubt that's exactly what would have become of him. Instead, through some dark cunning, he became another kind of old man: a rich, miserable old man. The chip on his shoulder, from knowing how poor he once was, has never left him.

Fragments of philosophy edge their way into my mind, in a confused way: *historical materialism, rebellion, negation, freedom ... muck of ages.*

During my last year in undergrad, I read *The German Ideology.* Although I don't recall much about the big ideas running through the book, certain idiosyncratic phrases — like "muck of ages" — have stayed with me. Marx is talking about how the proletariat must overthrow the ruling class through revolution, and in so doing shuck off the "muck of ages," as though the entire distorted division of labour that's given rise to inequality since tribal times might simply be washed away, like so much mucky mud. That's the image that came to mind for me, at least. Marx probably intended something far grander.

But wouldn't it feel lovely to fling off all that crap of socialization or false consciousness or whatever it is? And be born anew?

That's the feeling that Mao must have tapped into. After decades of simmering in so much unspoken frustration, people were ready for something new, something *revolutionary*. Folks like my father, folks like Keung-Cartwright, they all wanted to be born anew, with dewy, clean skin.

How devastated — how cheated — they must have felt, as it became apparent that no shimmering utopia was on the horizon. The city was still the same old city, its walls now mottled with bullet holes, its statues all smashed.

And my father. With blood on his hands. What on earth became of him?

I wonder, yet again, about how he managed to escape from Guangzhou. While so many of his friends in the Red Flag perished, Ba, phoenix-like, returned to Hong Kong and rebuilt his life from nothing. Were the profits from the heirloom-smuggling scheme funding the Red Flag's campaign? And after the Red Flag's downfall, did those profits somehow buy my father's escape?

"There are people in this life who are able to make things happen," Uncle had said. "Your father is one of them."

As I head toward the overpass, the dust begins to clear.

Outside a sleek tower, which is enclosed by a fence of gilded arrows, stands a security guard dressed like a French soldier, a *kepi* on his head. In the courtyard, a massive white tent is going up for some gala event; it's filled with laughter, cigarette smoke, moving bodies, the hum of conversation. The air is tinged with the sweet scent of hibiscus trees. The silhouettes of the workers will soon be replaced by the silhouettes of glamorously dressed guests.

What determines who remains a labourer and who becomes a guest? How can all these people be present on the same street, their lives so separate and self-contained?

I feel like I have no idea what I'm doing here, either. I'm floating somewhere between the damp sidewalk and the grey, clotted sky.

As I'm brushing my teeth to get ready for bed, some other lava-like emotion, more complex than guilt, stirs in my stomach. Much as I'm sickened by what happened to the Mas, there's a part of me that thinks — is this too awful to admit? — they might have deserved it a little.

Let's just say I can see where Ba was coming from. Considering everything he'd gone through — their refusal to help him financially, the collapse of his fledgling business, the brickyard, his failed escape, the labour camp, all those bleak years of cleaning streets — he'd have had to be a saint not to feel a drop of vengefulness, wouldn't he? The Mas could have done something to help him, couldn't they? Instead, they turned him away, time after time. To them, he was just a poor, embarrassing cousin.

• • •

Unable to fall asleep, I turn back to Keung-Cartwright's memoir:

> Attendance at school became mandatory again.
> A new kind of propaganda team arrived to get
> things in order. Under the supervision of these
> stern bureaucrats, we students had to sweep up
> the smashed bricks and tiles from the hallways
> and clear out the mountain of singed books from
> the library.
>
> Once that had been completed, there was
> little for us to do. We had no textbooks. The
> few teachers who hadn't been targeted and vic-
> timized were too terrified to teach us anything
> — no one knew what the new regime would
> sanction. All day we did nothing but take turns
> reading aloud articles by Mao and editorials
> from the *People's Daily*. And thanks to the pro-
> paganda team, we had a new set of Maoist songs
> to learn, as well as these absurd "loyalty dances"
> that involved twisting our bodies while waving
> around little red books.
>
> Little did we know how easy we had it.
> Perhaps for a moment I almost believed that life
> would return to something resembling normal.
> But Mao had other plans up his sleeve. While I
> and my classmates struggled to stay awake at our
> desks, we'd already been slated to be sent away to
> the countryside for "re-education." According to
> Mao's master plan, we were going to be turned
> into a hardy populace of peasants.

• • •

"Sir keep asking where your sister," Rina says the next morning, as I walk groggily into the kitchen. "I tell him she not here, she back in Canada, but he say, '*No*. Her flight arrive tonight! Cook big fish, enough for three people.'" She smiles, at first meekly and then conspiratorially, when I release a sigh.

"He's confused again," I say, "having a bad day. His memory's become like a sieve."

"A sieve?"

I shake my head, too tired to explain anything, the air heavy against my face. A monsoon is coming. I can feel it in the pressure between my ears.

"Don't worry, ma'am. I watch out for him." There's a hint of suppressed merriment in Rina's bright, clean-scrubbed expression as she returns to the kitchen. Secretly, she relishes her gain in power.

She probably thinks I don't notice these things. Her little attempts to bully my father have been growing bolder in recent days. Yesterday evening, through the walls of my bedroom, I overheard Rina asking him for the keys to the cabinet where my mother's old vases and dishes are stored.

"Why?" Ba said.

"I need bowl for mixing. Sir, I told you already, the old one broke! You don't want to give me money for new one, *fine*. But I need bowl from cabinet — otherwise, what else I make casserole from?"

To my surprise, my father handed the keys over.

While Rina is busy cooking something, I look inside the cabinet. All my mother's ornate dishes and fake antique vases have been examined and reorganized. If I were to search Rina's bedroom, I suspect I'd find a thing or two stashed beneath her bed.

But this would pose other problems: I'd be forced to sack her and be left scrambling to find a replacement on short notice. Still, it makes my blood boil. She's supposed to be one of the good ones, yet even the good ones prove untrustworthy in the end.

On the other hand, who can fault her, I suppose? Rina probably sees herself as simply taking the bonus that Ba would never give her on his own. She has to look out for herself, especially with Ba on his deathbed; her next employer could be even worse. Hong Kong's labour laws aren't kind to these women.

Now Rina peeks out the doorway of the kitchen and when she sees me, a timid air surrounds her. "Your father ... he all right? No more letter?" she whispers.

"Nothing for you to worry about. I already told you that."

Ba's propped up in his wheelchair before the TV, even though it's switched off. He knows that we're talking about him and has taken on the look of a sullen child. Fumbling with his phone, he tries to look like he has an important call to make.

"Did you call that tenant back?" he says over his shoulder.

He must have overheard me on the phone yesterday. The super at Ba's building was telling me about all the tenants who have been complaining about this and that, demanding that various things be fixed. With everything else going on, I've been falling behind on my landlord duties.

"Which tenant, Ba?"

He looks uncertain. "The one who ... needs the repair."

"That doesn't narrow things. The whole building's falling apart."

"Well ..." He scratches his head. "Fine. I'll do it myself."

His phone clicks open with the familiar little musical trills, but he makes no call.

• • •

Dear Ben,

I don't quite know how to say this. Recently, I've become aware that you and I are related. In view of everything that unfolded between our two families all those years ago, I think it would be good if your father and I could meet and talk things through face to face.

I understand that your family suffered, due in part to my father's actions. Like many folks, it seems he got caught up in the chaotic spirit of the times, which obscured his judgment. I would like to offer our apology and some form of compensation for what your family went through.

At the same time, I'm interested in hearing your father's side of the story and whether he has any regrets about how his family treated my father, when he was penniless and desperate.

As I've said before, I would like to make a trip to Guangzhou. Please send me your father's address and suggest a time when it would be convenient to meet.

Regards,
Jill Lau

An hour later, there's still no reply to my email. That's okay; I'm prepared to be patient. Since I am, by nature, such a patient person.

"Your sister …" Ba rubs his eyes.

"She's back in Canada, like Rina told you."

The tea towel is still tied around his neck like a bib, stained with yellow remnants of breakfast. "Her flight is arriving tonight."

"*No, Ba.*"

He looks perplexed, disheartened, then disgusted by his inability to refute me with more certainty. "I … I had a dream last night."

"Yeah? What did you dream about?"

"Your mother. She asked me to bring the family together, before I die." He gives me a sidelong glance, gauging whether his words are evoking pity. "You have to call your sister. Tell her to take the next flight out."

Frustration bubbles up inside me, hot and formless. Why can't he just be grateful that one of his daughters has put her life on hold to be at his side? "I can't make her come, Ba. If you want to talk to Celeste, *you* call her." *And if you're so eager to have her here, maybe you should have been nicer so she wouldn't have left in the first place. Maybe you should have been nicer to a lot of people. But then you'd be an entirely different person.*

"Oh …" He toys with the crumbs speckling the table. His gaze drifts out the window to the mountain, which is shrouded in mist.

"Ba, we have to talk," I say.

"About?"

"The Red Flag. Your involvement in the Red Flag."

His head recedes into his neck and shoulders, like a turtle getting ready to go to sleep.

"Come on, Ba." *I need to hear it from you. I need you to confess your sins.*

His chin flops downward, eyes at half-mast.

When I shake him, he pushes my hand away. "I'm tired — let me rest."

Rhythmic snores soon gurgle up his throat. If he's faking, he's doing a damn good job.

A few minutes later, his eyes blink open. He looks at me as though all has been forgotten. "Your sister is coming tonight."

• • •

We were told that we could bring no more than one suitcase and a bedroll. We were going to be heading north up to the mountains the following week for a grand adventure. This was announced to us by the head of our school's propaganda team, a portly man with a shiny, red face. The way he said "grand adventure" — with a glint of ironic merriment in his eye — left no doubt what he was actually talking about. Yet we students were so wretchedly bored that we almost didn't care what lay ahead. If we had no choice but to go live with the peasants, at least it might be more interesting than being chained to our desks, doing nothing.

On the appointed day, we were loaded into trucks at the crack of dawn. Packed in like sardines, the only place to sit was on our suitcases. For many hours, the trucks drove along one dusty, bumpy road after another, the blazing sun pulling me into what felt like a light dream.

It was my first time being so far outside the city. Some of the villages we passed had an idyllic look — at least, from a distance — and I remember thinking that maybe this wasn't going to be so bad. Maybe Mao was right, after all. If Mao believed I'd become a better person by returning to my primitive, authentic origins, who was I to doubt his wisdom?

Toward dusk, sleepy and dehydrated, I could see the lush Nanling Mountains coming into focus against the ashen sky.

Upon climbing out of the trucks, we found ourselves being reorganized in groups of eight, four boys and four girls in each. I was happy to see that I'd been placed with my old friend Ling, a thin girl with an offbeat sense of humour. "Adventure of our lives, my ass," she whispered in my ear. "I'd rather be digging ditches." The other kids in our group I barely knew.

A chubby local official made a short speech, then introduced a team of peasants, who were supposed to be our hosts. A grubby-faced woman missing several teeth approached our group, speaking energetically in some dialect no one could understand. Her gestures seemed to indicate that we should follow her.

We walked for a couple hours over uneven terrain through the inky shadows, night falling quickly. If it weren't for Ling's sweaty fingers clutching mine, I would have tripped many times. We were going upward on a slight incline, toward the foothills. At last, we arrived at our destination, which, in the dark, appeared to be nothing more than a cluster of huts. Later, I'd learn that the name of the place was Lechang.

Not until the following morning was I able to get a proper look at our dwelling, a crude wooden cabin. Electricity was non-existent, so except for the trickle of sunlight through our one tiny window, we were in the dark. Not that there was much to see. A wall divided the cabin; boys on one side, girls on the other. Ling and I shared a bed, a wood platform covered in a sprinkling of hay.

There was nothing resembling modern technology here. Forget phones and cars — even wheelbarrows were hard to come by. We soon learned from the gap-toothed woman who'd been our guide that we were not to receive any special treatment. According to Mao's directive, we were to be treated the same as all the other peasants and learn by doing. This was part of his program known as "Thought Reform Through Labour." Thus, our daily activities consisted primarily of three tasks: gathering and chopping a never-ending supply of wood for fuel, hauling massive buckets of water attached to long wooden poles slung over our aching shoulders, and collecting and transporting goat manure to serve as fertilizer for the fields.

This last activity was by far the most loathsome. The baskets used to carry the cakes of poop were awkward to balance on our backs — bits of the wetter excrement kept flying onto my bare neck and arms. The smell, mixed with the smell of my own sweat, was disgusting. As Ling and I were trudging uphill one day, she in front, her basket fell off her shoulders and pulled her entire body downward. Both of us ended up covered in poop, our legs buckled beneath us at painful angles. Our leader up ahead didn't even seem to notice that we'd fallen behind. A hiccup of high laughter came up from Ling's throat. I expected some witty comment about our shit-covered plight, but she remained quiet as we stood up gingerly. Her cheeks were wet, with more than just sweat. I realized that what I'd mistaken for a hysterical laugh had actually been a sob.

Not surprisingly, my skin began to erupt in strange patterns of rashes, with pustules here and there. But that was the least of my worries, compared with the nausea and diarrhea sending fiery waves through my insides. Most days, I was so weak and dizzy it was as though I were seeing my life reflected on the surface of gently rippling water. The only thing that anchored my sense of reality was the occasional echo of gunfire in the distance. Here in the backwoods, the fighting amongst Rebel factions was continuing on. I found myself praying that some Rebel group would invade our village and put an end to our misery.

It turned out that the more dangerous threat was the rain. It rained for days, like some angry deity was pissing down all his wrath on our pathetic human efforts. All the firewood became useless. One of the cabins collapsed. I awoke every morning to the sight of several inches of water on our bedroom floor, the platform on which Ling and I slept like a little endangered island. Ling and I clung to each other's damp skin, neither of us wanting to get out of bed first. At some point, we'd virtually stopped talking, as though language itself had lost all meaning, our system of communication reduced to primitive gestures and touch.

And then, just when we thought things couldn't get any worse, the Wu River flooded. Torrents of brown water flowing down the mountain carried branches, whole trees, garbage, fragments of dwellings, busted tables, and dead animals. People, too. The waterlogged, grey bodies were as lifeless as bags of sand. The dead babies were the worst to see. They haunt my nightmares to this day.

• • •

"Well, what do you think is going to happen, if you manage to meet up with this Mr. Ma person?" Terence asks.

We're at a flooring shop in Wan Chai. I'm running my fingers along a sample of synthetic wood, which looks fairly natural, until I notice the whorls are a bit too perfect.

"I'm going to talk to him, of course."

"And say?"

"I'll apologize for everything that happened to Mr. Ma's father, I guess." The beating, the ransacked ancestral grave. And who knows what other horrors. "Then maybe he'll apologize, too, for the fact that his family didn't do anything to help my father."

"Then you'll hug and make up?"

"Maybe."

"And then you'll write him a big, fat cheque."

"Hey. I'm not trying to buy his forgiveness. I'm looking to genuinely make amends here."

Terence holds up a floorboard sample.

"Too teaky," I say. "It looks jaundiced."

"I thought you liked teak."

"Only in Danish Modern stuff. Nothing else. It won't work as the floor of a bar."

He holds up another sample, and I shake my head.

"Too brownish. The tone looks muddy, mucky." The muck of ages. A dirty, flooding river, an endless stream of diarrhea.

"I don't know, Jill. I'm not sure you're going to get this truth and reconciliation experience you're hoping for." He paces a bit, looking pensive. "I'm not sure that you're seeing the full picture."

"What are you talking about?"

"Well, if the dead mouse and the remark in the letter about vanished treasures refer to what happened to the grandmother's grave, then we're still unclear about how your father got the money to get back on his feet upon returning to Hong Kong. Right?"

"It seems likely, as I've said before, that Ba was trafficking in stolen heirlooms. Not necessarily the Mas' heirlooms. But other people's."

"Did your uncle say anything to suggest that?"

"Not explicitly."

"And nothing that Ben or his father have said points in that direction, either."

"But it's been implied." Uncertainty stirs in my gut.

"You're assuming a lot," Terence says. "And you still have no idea how your father managed to escape from Guangzhou."

"That's why I need to meet with Mr. Ma and get some answers." Exasperated, I head to a different section of the store to look at tiles.

A few minutes later, Terence joins me. "If you hear from Mr. Ma and he agrees to meet, I don't think you should go out there alone. It isn't safe. I'll come with you, okay?"

"That's sweet of you. But Guangzhou in August? It's not going to be fun. The city will be a giant sweaty armpit."

"I'm not looking for a fun vacation."

"Anyway, who knows whether I'll even hear back." The thought depresses me, making me antsier than ever. The more I learn about everything that happened back then, the heavier the load of goat poop on my own back. I want to get this thing over with; I want to *move on*.

I stumble upon a tile with an interesting tone. Slate-like, but not too grey. In the light, it almost looks whitish. I hold it up. "This, we might be able to work with."

"You don't find it a bit cold?"

"There's something comforting about an austere environment."

"I'm not sure that most people would agree with you there."

"So I'll be the only customer in your bar, then."

A twitch of a smile plays across his lips. "Works for me."

If you ask me — and I've had some time to think about it now — what Ba did was actually pretty remarkable. Gutsy, Uncle called him. My father was one of the guys improvising weapons from kitchenware and insecticide, dreaming up sabotage missions, maybe. And God knows what else. While it's horrifying, I have to admit there's a part of me that finds the whole thing strangely thrilling.

After a lifetime of seeing him as this dried-out old man, with no interest in this world other than making money, it's refreshing to think he once had another side. There's something humanizing about knowing he felt passion in his blood. His years of hardship must have taken their toll and in the end, there was only so much he could take — he united with the masses in an upsurge of fury against his oppressors. I find myself fascinated by the spectre of this troubled young man, this other man, this man I can't at all recognize. My father, before he was my father. When the spark of life still sent tingles through his flesh. Despite the tragic outcome of his deeds, despite the errors in judgment he made along the way, I actually find it easier to feel some compassion and love for this man now.

And yet, awful images jut into my imagination. A boisterous crowd closing in around some poor guy, fallen to his knees, something dangerously close to festivity in the air. As the shouting gets louder, about to give way to the release of violence, I see my father's face at the hot centre of the group. What is he doing? I want to look away, but can't bear to. Who is he? Who is this man of sharp words and devastating, wiry strength?

By the time I'm heading home from the tile shop, school's out. The faces of little girls on the street catch my attention: eyes bright, complexions flushed and petal-like, unformed bodies hidden within shapeless royal-blue dresses, their school uniforms. The older ones cluster together, already aware there's strength in numbers, while the littlest ones clasp the hands of their nannies and mothers. As I scan the sidewalk, I'm vaguely aware that I'm searching for a small face that was once very familiar.

And then I can feel my father picking me up, his shoulders a solid perch from which I'm tall as a giant and can see everything, the tops of people's heads like so many grassy hilltops. How certain I am of my own strength, how beautifully naive. Nothing will ever go wrong, not with Ba's warm body there beneath me.

The taxi seems to be lurching and careening as it winds up the mountain. My body, limp as a rag doll, sways with each abrupt movement. I drank too much at the Captain's Bar, where Terence invited me to meet him for a drink (I've been seeing a lot of him today). One drink turned into multiple drinks, countless drinks.... It's been a long time since I've reached this state where the red and yellow car lights leave behind a glittery, slow-motion trail.

Terence, on the seat beside me, is also quite intoxicated. When he noticed I was drinking more than usual, he picked up his pace accordingly, because that's the kind of gentlemanly guy he is. As we round a bend, my body is flung against him and I let my head drop onto his shoulder. He smells of some slightly spicy cologne that makes me think of chai latte mixed with cognac and a hint of salty sweat. Weirdly, the combination is rather appealing. I bury my nose in the crevice of his neck and start giggling while he strokes the back of my head like I'm a small, sleepy child.

"Where to now?" I ask. "What time is it? Is Blue Bar still open?"

"Only for another fifteen minutes." But I can feel in the tautness of his arms that he, too, is reluctant to call it a night.

"Where are we going, then?"

"The cab's dropping you at home so you can drink a jug of water and hit the sack."

"But — but — but I don't wanna go home." Ba will probably be up, watching TV or chatting with the night nurse. I'll have to hold my breath and stand up straight and try to act normal. I'll have to endure the twinkle in his eye as he fantasizes that I've been out on a date with some nice young man who just might anchor me to Hong Kong forever. Worse yet, I'll have to smile and placate my father, even now that I know what I know. And maybe I won't be able to do it this time; maybe I won't manage to keep up the pathetic charade.

"No, Terence, I mean it. Please, *please* can you take me anywhere but home?"

He hesitates. "My mom's away at a spa in Bali. If you want, you can come over for one last drink, I guess?"

"Yup, sounds good." I've always been curious to see where he lives.

The next thing I know, we're on Robinson Road, continuing to where the street curves upward and a sharp cut-off takes us onto a smaller secluded road.

As he holds open the car door, I stumble out onto the sidewalk in front of a posh high-rise. A white marble facade, bearing the name "Serene Vista" in fancy silver lettering, greets me.

In the elevator going up to the thirtieth floor, a new awkwardness comes over us.

I don't know what I was expecting. Not this, that's for sure. When Terence opens the door to his unit, I'm met by an elegant interior in cream and oyster tones straight out of *Architectural Digest*. While the place is more traditional than what I'd normally go for — there's piping on the sofas and too many little throw pillows here and there — it's a far cry from the glitzy, cluttered den of an erstwhile crime family I'd been envisioning. The only vestige of that past is a large aquarium, with three narrow, iron-coloured fish that have a prehistoric look moving around in dark swishes. Although I have no idea what these fish are called, they're here for feng shui purposes; that much I know, at least. It doesn't matter how rich she is or how many charity boards she sits on, Terence's mother is just as superstitious as the garishly dressed gangster's wife she surely was in her youth.

He looks embarrassed when he sees me observing the fish.

"Nice place you've got here," I say. "Did your mom decorate it herself?"

"You've got to be joking. I brought in a professional, of course. We moved here last year."

"Your brother and his family took over the old place?"

He nods.

That's the apartment laden with family history, the secrets of his childhood.

While Terence fixes us drinks — vodka tonics, which I suspect he's watering down for my benefit — I wander out to the balcony and light a cigarette. On the other side of the glistening black water, West Kowloon's skyline is as perfect as a postcard, all the skyscrapers flashing blindingly. Text-message-short ads appear vertically along the length of the ICC tower, before the white pixels explode and regroup as bunnies and daisies.

Terence comes out with the drinks. I reach for mine, but my perception of distance is way off and I end up splashing vodka tonic all over his chest. And then, I'm not quite sure what happens next; I guess I lean forward to mop up the mess and somehow we end up kissing. His lips feel soft yet firm, surprised yet not altogether surprised, as they open fully to mine and our tongues swish together in that strange, creaturely dance. He tastes of orange juice — he must have had a gulp in the kitchen — and the flavour is wonderfully bracing, awakening. He pulls away and looks at me for several seconds, searching my eyes, like he's a paramedic checking for my vitals. And then we're pulling at each other's clothes and more vodka tonic's sloshing everywhere and my glass falls to the ground like a water bomb.

Stepping around the crystal fragments and puddling mess, I let Terence guide me inside and pull me down onto the sofa, onto a nest of those fussy little pillows.

FIFTEEN

Three days have gone by since I awoke on Terence's couch, my eyelids stuck shut with the gummy remains of my contact lenses. Curled into a fetal position, I rolled onto the floor — that much I remember, at least. Dawn was pouring through the wall of glass as I staggered to the bathroom and managed to dislodge the gelatinous disks from my eyeballs, everything blurring over in an underwater haze. My head pounded. I stared at myself in the mirror, the events of the previous night rebounding across my tired expression. I downed a mouthful of water, then spat it up, remembering that you're not supposed to drink from the tap in this godforsaken, polluted city.

I realized that Terence must have gotten up during the night. A slender white toothbrush and tiny vial of toothpaste wrapped in cellophane, the kind they give you on long flights, had been left out for me beside the sink, along with a plush, white facecloth. While I scrubbed at my teeth, a disconcerting pang of warmth flowed through my gut. There was something endearing about the thought of Terence collecting free toothbrushes on planes.

The warmth faded; maybe he made a habit of doing this because he frequently had impromptu female guests.

Then, for a long moment, I stood perfectly still in the living room, entranced by his sleeping face. He looked so different like that. Very trusting and child-like, his lips open slightly, emitting strange, soft gurgles and susurrations. When I fumbled around in the shadows for my bra, he began to stir and his eyes opened in a single sweep — gazing at me in that unflinching, unnerving way he had the night before. The next thing I knew he was on his feet, pulling me by the hand into his bedroom.

As we began exploring each other's bodies for the second time, it occurred to me that I didn't remember much from the night before, everything a drunken blur. But this, *this* I was going to remember. The contours of his stomach, the grassy sprinkling of hair below his navel, thickening downward. The tiny, strawberry-shaped birthmark peeking up through the thicket. My lips, my skin rising to meet his, the flesh guided by its own impulses and desires.... Although I thought I'd forgotten how to do this, the whole thing felt oddly, wondrously familiar, like we were already old lovers reuniting after a long, cold winter apart.

Nevertheless, there was a flash of awkwardness when I awoke midmorning. He was up already, his head on the pillow, just watching me sleep. It's a bit unsettling when you open your eyes and the first thing you see is another person looking at you intently. As he nuzzled his lips against my ear and murmured something about making a killer omelette, I suddenly remembered Ba — *he'll be worried out of his skull.* If I didn't get home immediately, he'd call the police. If he hadn't already. Pulling my dress over my head — inside-out, I would later realize — I stammered something about getting in touch later in the day.

As it turned out, my panic was all for nothing. Ba was still asleep when I arrived home; he must have gone to bed very late.

For the rest of the day, I sat around and got nothing accomplished, faint images of strawberry-shaped birthmarks floating around the edges of my brain. I didn't know whether to feel elated or grossed out or cautiously optimistic. One thing was for certain, though: nothing between Terence and me would ever be the same again.

At nightfall, a text message arrived: Hope u made it home safely?

I wrote back: Affirmative. BTW, I think my panties are wedged into your mom's couch.

He replied a few minutes later: Very nice. I like black stretch lace. I'm sleeping with them on my pillow tonight.

To that, I had no response. This swerve our relationship had taken left me panicked, unmoored. Erotic banter had never been part of our repertoire. A big part of me already missed the comfortable predictability of the old us.

Saved by the weather. Never in my life have I been so grateful for a monsoon. It's been raining cats and dogs for the past two days. Meeting up with Terence for a drink and awkward chat isn't an option any more than is leaving the house. The windows are constantly sluiced with the deluge, while the wind wails and knocks down trees; the street below has become a turbulent ocean. The city issues a red alert. Rina improvises peculiar dishes out of tinned goods: sweet and sour tuna with pineapple chunks and a dollop of ketchup, hard-boiled eggs sprinkled with curry powder, dried Chinese sausage stewed with chickpeas.

The lights flicker, the internet is touch and go. I worry that Ben's reply to my email has somehow gotten lost, stuck in the bottleneck.

The storm's particularly bad for Ba. He slumps with his elbows on the table, his hands covering his eyes. I wonder what he's thinking about, what evanescent memories he's trying to cling to or banish forever. I think about everything that Keung-Cartwright suffered, as her belief in the Maoist rhetoric met a swift death, her body breaking down under the weight of so much goat shit, her own bowels flooding with diarrhea. Dead, drowned babies all around her, Mother Nature taking revenge. I wonder whether my father also experienced progressive disillusionment, as all the beautiful ideals of the revolution fell away. Perhaps he woke up one day, his skin covered in shit, in blood, his comrades in the Red Flag dead around him.

. . .

The rain ended at last. After so many days of grey wetness, the sensation of dryness on my skin was a shock, a vibrant awakening. But there was suddenly so much work to be done — clearing away debris, repairing and rebuilding cabins — that no one had time to rejoice or even reflect upon the crisis from which we'd barely escaped alive.

To the peasants, perhaps it wasn't even a crisis, merely the passing of the seasons. Though I noticed in the following days that they became increasingly superstitious, barring certain women from helping with the preparation of food. I discovered that they were menstruating, when my own period arrived and I, too, was shunned from the outdoor stove.

One afternoon, a couple of trucks arrived. It had been so long since I'd seen trucks that their presence seemed otherworldly, unreal. The half-dozen men were relief workers, here to help us undo the damage of the storm. To my surprise, one of the younger guys pulled me aside; he had kind eyes and a stout, rather neckless body. He introduced himself as Jin. "I have news of your father," he whispered. It turned out that our fathers had been old childhood friends. And now my father was ill, very ill, Jin said. Jin had seen him languishing in a labour camp about seventy kilometres away. His illness was very serious — his body had been paralyzed, leaving him bedridden. He probably didn't have long left. The news left me shaken. While I'd known that my father had been sent to a work camp, I had had no idea that his health had deteriorated. Jin offered to drive me to visit him in two days' time.

Surprisingly, none of the peasants tried to stop my departure. I'd assumed that I was their prisoner, but it turned out that my status was more ambiguous. It's possible the peasants were glad to see me go because I wasn't capable of pulling my weight. Or maybe they held me and the other city girls responsible for breaking taboos and provoking the storm. They might have thought that Jin was my sweetheart. Whatever the case, they didn't object when they saw me slip into his truck.

During the long drive, I drifted off. When I awoke, it was late afternoon and we were on a crude road, high up in the mountains, hemmed in by dense, endless trees.

At last we got out of the truck at a clearing and Jin led me through the hot, oppressive air to a sad-looking group of dilapidated cabins. The camps up here had sustained devastating damage from the rain. But the biggest shock was the inhabitants themselves. Men were milling around, carrying buckets of mud and baskets of bricks. They all had pure white hair that contrasted sharply with their sun-baked faces. Some still had the eyes of young men, though their skin had coarsened to the look of terracotta and their legs were thin as tongs. No one was speaking, not even the folks supposedly in charge. In fact, it wasn't entirely clear who was in charge or what anybody was supposed to be doing. Silence pervaded the air — like everyone had become voiceless ghosts. One or two prisoners looked at me inquisitively as Jin and I passed by, but for the most part, we were ignored. Not even the sight of a young woman was enough to catch these men's attention and restore them to the land of the living.

Jin took me to a cabin where all the sick people had been left stretched out on mats. A damp, bitter, fungal smell was all around me, impossible to escape. And then, I recognized my father. His eyes were what gave him away — the expression around them, the way his brow furrowed like a caterpillar. He tried to sit up, but couldn't. When I crouched down beside him, he clutched my wrist. Since his face was partly paralyzed, he was prevented from smiling fully, one corner of his mouth drooping downward. Nothing of the stern father I'd known as a child remained in this face.

Unable to speak, I hugged his thin shoulders, tears running down my cheeks.

As he struggled to say something, I moved my head closer. Moisture glassed the surface of his imploring eyes. "Many … bad … things …"

"Bad things?"

"I did …"

"Oh, Ba. It's okay, just rest."

But my father shook his head, something frenzied and maniacal taking over his gaze, causing me to back away.

He was haunted by old memories, maybe. I knew that when he'd been in power, he'd participated in purges, like all officials, and probably sent a certain number of folks off for execution, over the years. Or maybe more mundane sins were disturbing him. He'd had a falling-out with his brother and never managed to make amends.

"You must … leave."

"Leave now? But I just got here." I stroked his thin, weathered hand.

"Leave … China." He looked directly at me, as if to emphasize his seriousness, his lucidity. "Get out … if you can …"

This was the first time my father had ever said such things to me. I felt like a little girl again, my head all muddled. No matter how turbulent things got on the political front, he'd always remained patriotic to the core.

"But where'll I go?"

He didn't even try to answer. He'd given his directive — the rest was for me to figure out. As his eyes fell shut, he looked like he was drifting away from this world.

I place my tablet face down and rub at my eyes, rubbing away the tears. I tell myself to pull it together. But I can't help thinking about my own father, bad deeds weighing upon his soul at the end of his life, too. Two hollowed-out men, reduced to husks, wanting only for it all to end.

At a little after five in the morning, while I'm eating wedges of toast and honey — an early bird breakfast or insomnia snack, depending on how you look at it — I notice a new message on my phone. *Ben.* I blink, assuming my eyes are playing tricks on me.

The email is very short. No greeting, no salutation, nothing.

> 26 Main St.
> Lianhua
> Shiqi
> Panyu

At last, Ben's father's address …? Can it really be?

Lianhua translates into something like "lily pond." I wonder if it's the name of some village? As I read the address over and over, Panyu causes a slight ripple in my memory. "The house in Panyu." Why does this phrase pop into my head? I can't be certain, but I think Ba or one of my aunts might have mentioned it at some point during my childhood. When Ba's parents and sisters were forced to leave Hong Kong during the Japanese occupation, they found refuge with relatives on the outskirts of Guangzhou. I have a hunch the area might have been called Panyu.

If so, it's possible that several relatives lived there, including the Ma family. Didn't Uncle say they used to have a house with a stunning garden, where the old folks once meditated? Although they lost that property, perhaps Mr. Ma stayed on in the vicinity.

Perhaps the place has sentimental meaning; perhaps over time he managed to reclaim a piece of his inheritance. Perhaps he simply had nowhere else to go.

I can't believe I actually have his address in hand.

The rain's letting up, ever so slightly, the sky losing opacity. A wisp of pink dawn peeks through for the first time in days.

SIXTEEN

The internet tells me there are trains leaving for Guangzhou at 7:25 and 8:15. In this weather, who knows whether they'll be running, but sitting here in the dark is only making me antsy.

After a quick shower, I pull a simple black dress over my head. I rake my hair up into a bun without drying it, and pop in my contacts. My face looks gaunt and ghostly in the sallow light. It's my father's challenging expression I see staring back.

I've never been to Guangzhou before. According to the train schedule, it's only a couple hours away. A day trip should do it. Just to be on the safe side, I throw a toothbrush and extra contacts into my shoulder bag, along with my makeup bag and a change of underwear. I scrawl a note for Rina and Ba, claiming I've gone to meet a potential client in Shenzhen.

As I step into the hall and lock the door, my keys drop to the floor with a clatter, and I feel like there's something I'm forgetting to do. When nothing comes to mind, I take the elevator down, the uncertain sensation clinging like the clammy film all over my skin.

By the time I get to the lobby, the rain's coming down heavily again. Setting out is pointless, so I retreat upstairs and make a pot of tea. I stare out the kitchen window, just waiting, watching the mountain blur into a wild green slurry. At some point, Ba awakes and is wheeled into the dining room. I tell him that as soon as the weather lets up, I'll be heading to Shenzhen for the day. He doesn't reply, as if he hasn't even heard. A moment later, though, he says, "Wear rubber boots. You're going to need them."

Online, I learn that Panyu is larger than I thought. It used to be a county-level city in its own right, before turning into a district of Guangzhou. These days, it seems to be an outlying area that's half suburb, half hinterland, encompassing hundreds of towns and villages. Shiqi is one such town, with a train station named after it. I can't find anything at all about Lianhua. I wonder if it's just a cluster of cottages in the backwoods.

It's early afternoon by the time the rain lets up. I grab my bag and head out, eager to make up for lost time.

Several taxis speed past, already occupied. I open my umbrella only to discover that the nylon's torn loose; not getting much protection from the drizzle, I wait for the minibus to take me to the subway. Then I catch the red line to Tsim Sha Tsui and transfer lines, walking so quickly on the rain-slicked travellator that I slip, my calf grazing the metal ridges. At Hung Hom, I have no clue where the connection to the rail station is; I've never travelled by train to China before. Making my way up to street level, I follow signs that lead to a glassed-in terminal, filled with scaffolding and the roar of construction. At the counter, I'm told that the next train doesn't leave until 2:32, forty minutes from now. After buying a ticket, I join the line of other damp, bedraggled folks waiting to have their bags x-rayed.

After a moment of hesitation, I phone Terence.

"Hey …?" He sounds groggy as he picks up.

"You'll never guess where I'm headed."

As I keep talking, his tone brightens. "So the Ma kid finally came through for you."

"Yep. Curiosity got the better of him."

"Right, curiosity." He mutters something about money under his breath. "You really shouldn't be headed out there alone. Didn't your uncle say the father's not to be trusted?"

"Oh, please. Mr. Ma's a frail old man." Is he? I have no idea how old he is, I suddenly realize.

"Wait for me. I'll come with you."

My silence stretches out longer than it should. "It's okay.... This is something I need to do on my own." It's nice of Terence to worry about me, though. More than nice, I'll be honest. But after everything that's just happened between us, the last thing I need is a flurry of desire and self-doubt distracting me. Just thinking about the whole thing is making my palms sweat, my heart pound.

"Well ..."

"Don't worry. I'll be fine, Terence."

"Let me know how you're making out over there, okay?"

A flutter of warmth, something like anticipation, maybe, comes over my skin. "Perhaps we should go away on a real trip, some other time," I say.

"Yeah? That'd be fun."

I've surprised him — I've surprised myself — but his excitement sounds very genuine. "I'd like to get away for a few days," I say, "after all this business with the Ma family's been settled."

"Well, where do you have in mind?"

"Dunno."

"Shanghai, Beijing, Taipei?"

"I've been to Shanghai a couple times. But I've never been to Beijing."

"Really?"

I laugh. "I know. Crazy, isn't it?"

"You've been to Tokyo, St. Petersburg, and Istanbul, but you've never been to Beijing. You'd be surprised. It's a pretty sophisticated city these days."

"Yeah?"

"There's that titanium dome opera house, shaped like an egg. We could go see a performance."

"Cool, Beijing it is."

"I know a boutique hotel you'd like."

The line's started to move so we say our goodbyes, an unfamiliar tension in the halting laughter between us. The planes of our relationship have shifted forever, leaving everything unstable, about to crack, or cleave into some new formation.

I cut around the line for customs, using my Chinese identity card to swipe through an automated turnstile, touch my thumb to a sensor, and glance up into the camera. This card allows me to travel into China without a visa or passport. The characters at the top roughly translate as "Return to the Motherland," which has always struck me as a ridiculous name for the card. But now it seems oddly appropriate for what I'm about to embark on.

The train's full. Although the rain hasn't stopped entirely, people are glad just to be able to leave their apartments, get on with business. I end up sitting across from a ruddy British guy, who barely looks up from his thick financial report.

Through the drizzly window, the city speeds by. Soon we're passing through shipping yards full of massive cement storage buildings. Then we're zooming through the New Territories, colonies of pale mint and pink towers on one side, rolling hillsides on the other. Brown waterways, shimmering lakes. Lower-scale, suburban dwellings with a pseudo-Spanish colonial look. At the end of the MTR line, we skirt around Shenzhen, a mix of metallic skyscrapers and luxury shopping malls juxtaposed with derelict, makeshift housing right along the rail tracks. And then we pass patches of lush farmland, speckled with folks in rice-picker hats. The idyll doesn't last for more than a few seconds before we're barrelling past lumberyards and bulldozers and cranes and the rebar skeletons of gigantic buildings about to be born from the earth. Remnants of villages pop up here and there, the old terracotta roofs like a child's drawing of ocean waves. I think about the crashed plane Terence's grandfather supposedly found in a field around here, the gold bars tucked under the pilot's corpse. Now, at last, the land itself is worth gold.

I imagine how the landscape must have looked back when my father took the train in the opposite direction after so many years of bleakness; the excitement — the elation — he must have felt, knowing he was on the brink of a new life, a second chance. Now that I have some sense of what he endured, I feel a strange connection to this land. But as my gaze loses focus, everything blurring into a haze of stippled colour and light, an uneasy feeling catches hold of me. The source of the money that allowed Ba to make a fresh start in Hong Kong remains a blind spot. I'm still not clear about whether his involvement with the Red Flag played a role. Did his comrades within the organization somehow help him find a way out before it was too late? But most of his comrades had ended up dead.

Maybe it doesn't matter; maybe none of it matters. Like Terence, I should poke fun at the myth without scrutinizing it too closely. And maybe he's right — there's dirty money mixed in with every family fortune and isn't that just a part of life, really? Especially in a country as vast as this one, where boys like my father, born in the muck and ruins of history, fought their way up by their bleeding elbows with only their street smarts and seventh-grade educations to rely on. My sister's so quick to judge Ba, but where would any of us be if he hadn't lived by his wits? He saved his sisters from homelessness and prostitution, for Christ's sake. Surely, that counts for something. And where would this country be if it weren't for feisty little guys like our father, doing whatever they could to get a toehold in the business world?

I keep my eyes focused on the pale horizon as we pass a junkyard and a dirt road and a cluster of ramshackle houses with only scrap metal for roofing. Soon we're speeding toward Guangzhou, an endless wall of identical beige and grey towers veiled by layers of smog.

Guangzhou East station is a welter of sweaty bodies. Fortunately, my "Return to the Motherland" card enables me to bypass customs again. Once the high-speed rail line has been built, this trip will be reduced to twenty minutes, allowing people who live in Guangzhou to work in Hong Kong and vice versa. What I'm doing might become nothing more than a daily commute.

Ba often complains that people in Hong Kong no longer walk fast enough. The pace of economic growth in a city, according to him, can be gauged by the speed people walk on the sidewalk. When he was younger, everyone was on the go in Hong Kong, stopping for nothing, hungry for the next big opportunity. Not so anymore. Ba is endlessly bothered by the city's slackening pace, its people's disturbing tendency to stroll. What happened to the old Hong Kong spirit?

It migrated to China.

As I try to find my way out of the train station through a succession of retail areas and food courts, I'm aware of nothing so much as the surge of hot, moving bodies, coming from all directions, weaving every which way. It's all I can do to keep moving forward, though I have no clue where I'm going. At some point, I catch sight of an ATM and withdraw a stack of yuan.

Past a McDonald's is a shadowy underpass, where a crowd snakes around a taxi queue. The line appears to be moving quickly, blue, green, and yellow taxis stretching back as far as the eye can see, across four lanes of traffic. As you near the front, you're expected to be aggressive and dart through the packed cabs and exhaust-filled air. I don't know whether their different colours indicate they service different regions of the city. When my turn comes, I wave at whichever driver looks my way and walk all too gingerly along the edge of the traffic, until a door is thrown open.

The car is old and reeks of cigarettes. Or maybe the nicotine smell makes the interior seem outdated, the scent of a bygone era. That and the inadequate air-conditioning system. Barely a breeze flows back through the thick metal bars that protect the driver from his passengers, like we're in a cop car. The guy hardly turns around, so I don't get more than a glimpse of his broad, pock-marked complexion. Through the bars, I see his meaty fingers gripping the wheel.

"Where to, lady?"

"Well, this is the thing. Where I'm going is … probably a bit far." As I'm fumbling to find the words in Mandarin, I'm fumbling with my phone to pull up Ben's email with the address. Nothing comes up. Then I remember that Gmail's blocked here. Fuck. I dig in my purse for a pen and paper, and I try to write out the address from memory.

"Panyu?" The guy chuckles. He also has a weird accent; Mandarin is definitely not his native tongue. He keeps staring at the paper. Thank God that in this country of so many dialects, we at least share a common written language. But he's shaking his head. "I don't go there."

"Well, look …" I try switching to Cantonese, but he shakes his head, so I go back to my pidgin Mandarin. "Money? I'll pay double. Just get me there, okay?"

He keeps driving, contemplating my offer. We get stuck in standstill traffic by a park across from a colossal formation of hotels and office towers. It's almost five o'clock; rush hour's just beginning.

"You a tourist, lady? You got no directions?" He gestures at my phone.

It occurs to me now that this guy has no idea how to get to my destination. In a city of this magnitude, no cabbie's going to be familiar with every little village in the backwaters. "Don't you have a GPS?"

Again, he points at my phone. The expectation seems to be that I am to provide our navigation system.

I try to pull up Google Maps. It's blocked, all blocked. Turning to an unfamiliar search engine, I find myself getting nowhere.

In the absence of a plan, the guy continues driving random routes, racking up the toll. His phone comes out and he starts yakking away in some dialect I've never heard in my life; he may as well be making the sound of a lawnmower.

The city lurches by, looking similar to the central business districts of other Asian cities I've visited over the years: the wide sidewalks, the eight-lane streets that make you feel like you're on a highway at all times, the mammoth towers with massive setbacks, reminiscent of Soviet city planning. Buildings have more generous floorplates and are less densely packed than in Hong Kong, where the mountainous regions keep buildable land scarce and very expensive. But aside from the fact that everything's larger and more spread out here, not much seems different. Prada, LV, Versace — these cities have all the same high-end boutiques. The glitzy homogeneity feels depressing after a while.

On the internet, I fail to find anything — this lily pond village doesn't show up anywhere. A vise tightens around my temples.

"So?" the driver barks over his shoulder. He's getting bored of driving me nowhere. "I drop you at the museum, yeah?"

"No, we're not going to the fucking museum!"

We're entering a dingier neighbourhood. Rain begins to patter the windshield, turning the cement buildings into wavering grey blotches. Suddenly, the driver pulls the car over.

"Here. You get out, miss."

"What the hell? I'm not ready to get out."

"No. My shift's over. You pay, you get out." He points at the meter.

I'm too exhausted to argue, anyway. And maybe I'll have better luck with another taxi driver, who just happens to have grown up in my ancestors' frigging village. I hand over some cash and step out into the humid drizzle.

As I open my umbrella, a spoke snaps loose, nearly getting my eye. I jam the whole thing into a garbage bin and step under a shop awning.

Some of these old buildings are actually rather beautiful, I notice, staring across the street. Despite decades of neglect, despite layers of accumulated dirt and broken windows, they retain an air of decrepit elegance: high, arched doorways flanked by neoclassical pillars, large balconies with ornate railings in filigreed designs, something art nouveau–like about the sensuous curves and ornamental detailing. Once-impressive facades now reduced to slabs of worn-down cement. These buildings were probably the homes of the wealthy merchants this city was known for back in its heyday, before the Communists took over and chopped up all this lovely property into apartments and rooming houses. I guess the neighbourhood never recovered. Some shopfronts are being used to store oil tanks and lumber, while others are hardware stores and vegetable stands. A fat man lazes in the back of his rickshaw, naked belly exposed like an overripe melon, letting the rain wash away the day's grime. When he catches me watching him, his face takes on a toothy, demented grin.

I wonder where Ba used to live. How little I know about all his years in this city. All I remember him saying is that he lodged in the cheapest place possible, in order to save the bulk of the profits from the peanut oil shop for his sisters' upkeep. The girls continued to go to school, while boarding with relatives. Little did anyone know that those were the good days, compared with what was coming next.

The air, laden with dust and the smell of ashes, triggers emotion in my sinuses; I feel like I might start tearing up at any second. The stunted feeling of this place. Its left-behind quality.

I cross the street and continue walking. A kid on a green tricycle nearly knocks me over as he darts out of nowhere and arcs back in the same direction. I watch the back of his head, glossy as a chestnut, grow smaller and smaller, while I stare down the shadowy, cobblestone lane, laundry lines strewn with brightly coloured T-shirts connecting the old buildings. And then the kid on the trike is pedalling back toward me, fast and a little reckless, but very determined. As though the body has memory, I feel the wind on my chest, the cool metal handlebars of the trike at my kindergarten, the seat jittering beneath me … and I see Ba's proud face a blur at the corner of my vision.

As the boy nears, he slows down. He's older than I first thought, close to eight maybe, too big to be on a tricycle. A grey sweater vest, meant for a man, hangs off his thin frame. He takes in my sleeveless dress and suede shoulder bag and delicate sandals. I'm not from the neighbourhood, that much is clear. Curiosity and admiration flicker across his expression, followed by something darker, like deference, like fear. When I try to smile, he turns and takes off.

I continue to walk in no particular direction. After a while, I find myself examining the cement and stone walls, searching for old bullet holes and other signs of the past, of urban warfare. Some sign that the Red Flag was once here, that my father was here.

But of course, there's nothing.

My damp sandals squish and chafe against my heels. Looking around for a café, I can only find a fluorescent-lit noodle shop, where the air is even hotter than outside. After buying a bottle of water, I leave.

By the time I've managed to find a taxi, the rain is coming down mercilessly again. I'm so tired and hungry that my sense of failure only registers in a dull way. It's hopeless — I give up on trying to find the village. At least I know that all taxi drivers in this city know how to get me back to the train station. When we get stuck in standstill traffic a few blocks from it, I decide to duck into one of the restaurants across the street so I can at least have a decent meal before going home. But the place I dart into — shaking water from my hair like a shaggy dog — turns out to be the lobby of a hotel. High ceilings, mahogany herringbone floor. Mauve blossoms arc from low, rectangular vases. Dim light pools here and there from skillfully designed crevices and elegant lamps shaded in ivory cylinders. As I walk toward the reception desk — as if in a trance, unable to stop myself from being drawn into this place of muted opulence and refuge — a girl in a Grace Kelly suit approaches to offer a small glass of iced green tea. "Welcome to The Estuary," she says, before slipping away.

A slightly older woman, her hair swept up in a chignon that accentuates the becoming roundness of her face, greets me at the desk. "Elena Wang, Manager of Front-End Operations," her nametag reads. In English, I tell her I don't have a reservation. Replying in a light British accent, she reassures me they have a room available. One of the best rooms in the hotel, on the top floor. By Canadian standards, the price is high, but it's about half of what I'd have to pay for a hotel of this grade in Hong Kong.

Elena accepts my credit card with her manicured hands. And is this my first time in Guangzhou? Do I have any luggage to be brought upstairs? But when she senses I'm not in the mood to talk about the circumstances that have brought me here, dusty and wet and with only the clothes on my back, her inquisitiveness recedes instantly.

My room, on the twenty-fifth floor, is as tastefully designed as the lobby and surprisingly spacious, with a walk-in closet and large bathtub shaped like a slender egg. With a press of a button, I raise the diaphanous shades and the city stretches out before me: a sea of towers that vanish into more towers, fading at last into the grey horizon. It's impossible to make out individual neighbourhoods, if they even exist anymore.

After looking out at it all for a long while, I call room service and order steak frites and a glass of Bordeaux. While waiting for the food to arrive, I draw a bath. The warm water makes me drowsy as I watch my knees rise above the surface like small deserted islands.

When I awake, I don't know where I am. The sky is black. The constellation of stars confuses me, until I realize they're only lights from the office towers.

A dream is slipping away … Terence and I were on vacation in some old European city, Paris or Barcelona, maybe. Kissing in the street and gazing into each other's eyes over carafes of sangria at sidewalk cafés and doing other such trite, romantic things. And then, just like that, he was no longer there. A fist of panic went through my gut. I began wandering the hot, crowded streets, looking for him, sweat dripping into my eyes.

As I hug my knees to my chest, the air-conditioning chills my clammy body, despite the plush hotel bathrobe wrapped around me.

Glancing at my phone, I see that Terence has texted several times. My first impulse is to call him and vent about the wild goose chase, but my battery's dangerously low.

It's past ten. The problem with having napped for so long is that now I won't be able to sleep for hours. After flipping through all the television stations and only finding an old Harrison Ford flick, I get up and wash my face. I apply a bit of concealer under my eyes, pat on some powder, and slick on an old burgundy lipstick that I happen to find at the bottom of my makeup bag. What else is there to do except sit at a bar, drinking away the failures of the day?

I head downstairs, not planning to stray far. There's a lounge right off the lobby.

On second thought, I pause at the reception desk to ask for a phone charger. Elena winks at me while I wait for her to finish helping an older American couple. Large-boned folks in khaki shorts and golf shirts, here on a post-retirement tour of China. Guidebook in hand, the woman is asking Elena to write out in Chinese the address of some museum they plan to visit by taxi the following morning.

"We don't speak anything other than English, so please, pretty please, will ya jot down directions, too?"

"Not to worry." Elena hands over her card. "If you encounter any problems, just ask the taxi driver to call me at this number."

Why didn't I think of it sooner? There are benefits to staying at a hotel of this quality. Renewed hope and adrenalin shoot into my blood.

When my turn comes, I pass over my slip of paper with Mr. Ma's address. "I … I need to get there tomorrow. It's off the beaten track, I know."

Elena is already typing away, pulling up websites and maps.

"Is it possible to hire a driver to take me?" I ask. "Someone who speaks English, preferably."

"Yes, our hotel has cars at its service." Continuing to type, she murmurs, "This is quite far away. I'll have to ask one of the other staff to double-check these directions. I'm not from Guangzhou, you see."

"Oh, where are you from?"

"Malaysia. Though I was educated in London, where I worked for many years. The Estuary hotel originates from London." She casts me a sympathetic, homesick look, as if to convey that she senses I, too, am less than thrilled with this city. "And where are you visiting us from, if I may ask?"

"Canada. Toronto."

"Oh? How nice."

She's waiting for me to add that I'm originally from Hong Kong or some other part of Asia. When I remain silent, she continues smoothly, "So this trip you want to make tomorrow morning. What time would you like the car to be ready for you?"

We decide it would be best for me to depart after rush hour, at ten o'clock. I remember to ask Elena for a charger; she hands me a portable one that I plug into my phone right away.

At the bar, I chat with Mike from Glasgow, here in Guangzhou for a tech conference. He has a merry, mischievous disposition that matches his thicket of ginger hair, and something about his eager perch on the edge of the barstool makes me think of a fox terrier. He's already rather drunk, it appears. I realize at some point during my first drink that he's mistaken me for a call girl, thanks to my dark lipstick and upswept hair and the giddiness in my chest that's making me more outgoing than usual. When I inform him that I have no hourly rate — not for the services he's interested in — he doesn't appear all that embarrassed and makes it clear he's just as happy to flirt with and get down the pants of a middle-aged architect.

If this were to have happened even a week ago, I wonder whether I might have actually considered it, just to break my long spell of celibacy. The thought jars me, almost as much as the realization that I no longer feel single at all. Terence is on my mind. I want to get this business with Mr. Ma over with so I can get back to Hong Kong and tear off Terence's clothes.

After allowing Mike to buy me one more drink, I excuse myself, explaining that I have to turn in. I'm meeting a big client tomorrow, I say; somebody I've been chasing for a very long time.

SEVENTEEN

W hen I come down the next morning, Elena greets me brightly. I check out, settle my bill. Stepping out from behind the counter, she tells me that my car's waiting at the rear of the hotel, where there's less traffic.

She guides me past a clothing shop and the grand entrance of a ballroom. "How have you enjoyed your stay?"

"It's been fabulous." Remembering the upcoming trip to Beijing, I ask whether The Estuary has a hotel there.

"The Beijing location's especially beautiful, a stone's throw from the imperial palace."

I picture Terence and me taking long bubble baths together, drinking champagne.

The car awaiting me in the valet area is a black Mercedes. The driver, William, seems to know Elena personally; she assures me that I'll be in very good hands. They confer in Mandarin to ensure that he's clear on how to get to my destination. Meanwhile, I get settled in the spacious, cream-leather interior, which is air-conditioned to just the right degree of crispness.

How much easier things are this time around. William quickly navigates our way out of the downtown and onto a multi-lane tollway. Then we're speeding past condo towers and clusters of trees, which soon give way to a vast expanse of pale-grey sky bisected by electrical towers, the skyline receding to a faint, jagged stain in the distance.

We cross a body of water. Trucks barrel past. Periodically, the sky-lines of other commercial centres glimmer into view and disappear.

Excitement twists up through my gut, catching me off guard. Even the air feels different out here — aquiver with possibility, opportunity. How flat the land appears; denuded, almost. As though all the secrets of its past have surfaced and been swept away. Yet, a second later, I see office towers and convention centres and bizarre, ostentatious works of architecture, like apparitions in the distance, as cryptic as Stonehenge on a misty day. We come off that first highway and pass through a toll booth onto another one.

I snap a picture out the window and text it to Terence: ALMOST THERE!!

After we've been driving about a half-hour, the car comes off the second tollway. We pass more towers, no different from the ones in the heart of Guangzhou. Then we enter a less-populated, greener area, where the towers are only half as tall. Billboards highlight the square footage of condos, impressive compared with the shoeboxes people inhabit back in Hong Kong. Six or seven giant statues — silhouettes of men and women in bright, primary colours — are frozen mid-stride as they cross the earth, towering above the treetops between two condominium clusters. The Great Leap Forward comes to mind, though I doubt that's what the artist was striving for. Or perhaps people out here still believe in that old Maoist rhetoric? Perhaps they're still eager to make that great leap, once and for all? I think of how disen-chanted Keung-Cartwright became, her sunburned skin covered in mysterious rashes, her poor father imploring her to leave the country. Did most people come to feel that way, in the end?

After another cut-off, the roads narrow, no towers in sight. Verdant fields stretch out in all directions. Workers bend down in gleaming white T-shirts, tending to some low-growing crop. As we turn onto an even narrower road, the view changes to old cement bunkers surrounded by heaps of tires and junk, royal-blue dump trucks parked here and there. A short distance onward, a sidewalk appears out of nowhere and the buildings become newer, graced with balconies and shops on the ground floors.

Terence texts back: U there yet?? Call me if u run into trouble

I'm not sure what he thinks he can do to come to my rescue if Mr. Ma turns out to be a crazed old man. Or a serial killer.

Another text from Terence: Sure u wanna do this alone??

But an offbeat feeling of invincibility has entered my blood.

William wends the car through a maze of increasingly run-down streets and alleyways. Then we come to an abrupt stop.

We're in front of a row of houses: old brick boxes, scuffed and discoloured to whiteness in patches, tiny pane-less windows on the upper floors. They're fortress-like dwellings, in the style of traditional Chinese houses, though far shabbier and more modest in scale than what such houses typically bring to mind.

"Are we here?"

Nodding, William gestures outside. "It's one of these. Or maybe down one of the alleys. You want me to come with you, ma'am?"

The hesitancy in his voice is not lost on me. "I think you'd better stay with the car."

As I step outside, the heat slams against my face. Although the rain has cleared, moisture still hangs in the air, more oppressive than ever. A murky body of water stretches out on the other side of the road — the lily pond this village was originally named after, maybe? Yet there are no half-drowned lilies afloat. Shored up by a high stone border, surrounded by palm trees, all uniform in height and newly planted, by the looks of it, this so-called pond appears as artificial as the brand-new, four-storey building that stretches along its opposite side. Ornate verandahs run the length of each floor, pagoda-like structures jutting up from both ends, a clumsy nod to tradition.

I wander down the block to where the houses end. A great, dusty expanse lies beyond, reminding me of a desert, though it's really just a dirt field. A street appears in the distance, mirage-like, a confounding turquoise China Mobile sign looming in the distance.

Backtracking, I search for numbers. Not all of these houses even have them. Twenty-one, twenty-three, twenty-four, twenty-seven ... No number twenty-six. Beside number twenty-seven, however, is an unmarked brick house. The wooden, padlocked door bears a red poster of two fierce warriors, their shields and robes embossed with dragons and other supernatural creatures, the grimaces distorting their bearded faces to such an extreme degree they look positively demonic. Gods of the doorway. Doors of the adjacent houses bear similar images, along with red banners covered in Chinese proverbs. I try to remember what gave rise to this ritual, this superstition. All that comes to mind is some myth about two bloodthirsty generals who once helped an emperor to ward off evil spirits. Somehow, they became seen as gods, guardians of entranceways.

Although this house is very old and dusty, somebody's made some effort to maintain it. In addition to the newish poster of the doorway gods, there are signs of repair on the side of the house, I discover when I explore around the corner. Cracks in the bricks have been patched with cement smears.

I find myself standing in a narrow cobblestone alley that cuts off the main road, between houses. Following the path, I head past a crumbling wall around a small courtyard next door to the unnumbered house. In that yard I glimpse a sloped terracotta roof lushly carpeted with bright-green moss, earthy-damp and heady smelling. A gnarled old treetop towers over the wall, dead wisteria vines snaking up and encircling its main branches. I see waist-high weeds and wildflowers and a pile of decayed scrap wood. I wonder whether the courtyard of the adjacent house — number twenty-six? — is just as messy and wild; the wall is too high for me to see over.

Continuing down the lane, I trip and nearly fall into a stone hole, a crude well, where an inch of water, just as green as the water in the pond, stagnates.

More houses stretch back down the alley. Some of them are clearly inhabited: voices and a baby's cry ribbon through the air, the familiar savoury odours of Cantonese dishes wafting out kitchen windows. Braised oxtail, white radish. Must be nearing lunchtime. An amber chicken waddles around in someone's backyard — perhaps very close to getting its head chopped off and turning into a main course. In an open doorway, a small child in overalls plays with a battered toy truck, while two doors down, a whiskery old man dozes in an armchair, his bony feet in a pail of water.

As I keep walking, snapping pictures with my phone, something takes flight in my belly. I have an impulse to kick off my sandals and prance along these stippled cobblestones barefoot, like a child myself. While making my way farther into this warren of semi-abandoned, semi-enchanted dwellings, I nearly forget why I'm here, my imagination drifting to a time I can't remember, a time before I was even born. I picture my grandparents and aunts seeking refuge here during the war: raising chickens, growing vegetables in one of these bedraggled little plots, eking out whatever existence they could manage — much like this hodgepodge of salt-of-the-earth types. And then Ba arrived, after his parents had both died. In a world flung into the chaos of war, this village was the one place on earth where he thought his sisters might be safe.

What would have happened if they'd never left? If Ba had stayed here with his sisters — rather than starting the peanut oil business, rather than moving heaven and earth to return to Hong Kong — he would have never met my mother and I would have never been born. In my place, there'd be another daughter: a truly good, truly pious daughter, perhaps. A dumpling-cute baby clutched against each hip, chickens clucking at her callused heels.

But for better or for worse, I am not that woman.

At some point, I become aware of people's hostile stares; they don't like the way I'm strolling around, looking at everything, taking pictures, peering into their homes. A bald old man, dressed in nothing but baggy shorts, comes to his doorway, hands on hips, and puts on his fiercest scowl, his thin, shrunken chest expanding like an accordion. Perhaps he sees me as the very evil spirit the doorway gods are meant to fend off. I put my phone away and shove on.

On the ground, in the narrow space between two houses, lies an open plastic cylinder, about the size of a Coke can, bearing a hand-drawn label of a skull and crossbones. Ferns meander up the walls, amidst scraps of tiles and broken bricks, an old lipstick, a dried-out flip-flop. A flash of furtive movement catches my eye — I jump back, shivering. A furry creature darts into the canister, which quivers as its delicious poison is consumed.

Another mouse flashes across my mind. The joss stick, the scrap of quilt, the soil scattered all over our lobby floor.

The happiness I felt a moment earlier fades. The child playing in the doorway now appears grubby and malnourished, and a smell like warm urine wafts up from a puddle abuzz with flies. I want to find Mr. Ma and get this ordeal over with, so I can get back inside my cool car and be driven home.

Down the lane, I pass a bunch of young men in yellow T-shirts, standing around, chatting, some of them pushing wheelbarrows.

Amidst the crumbling remains of this village, a new building is going up, a small apartment building, by the looks of it. A stout guy in a hard hat gives me an oily once-over, and I take the opportunity to ask whether a man by the name of Ma Wing-Cheong lives in the neighbourhood. The guy shrugs and adds that he's not from around here. Next, I try to talk to an old lady in a faded housedress, but she just shakes her head and makes agitated motions around her head, as if shooing away a persistent wasp.

I've come to the last house at the end of the lane. Glancing up at the second floor, I see a large balcony with curved cement balusters, shaded by a corrugated tin roof. The place looks better maintained than most. In the shadows, behind a cloud of white blossoms along the railing, a male face is staring down at me. My neck cramps up from craning backward. The man backs away.

Not knowing what else to do, I begin to make my way back toward the main road.

When I pause to take off a sandal and dislodge a pebble, I become aware of a blurry presence at the edge of my vision. But it's just an old man, traipsing behind at some distance.

So this is it. Hot, tired, and desperately thirsty, I sit down on the uneven front steps of this house with no number, this house that might be number twenty-six. Across the street, the Merc awaits me, mockingly grand, hearse-like.

That old man, again. He's paused at the corner beside me. As his straw hat tilts back, his face is illuminated by the sun: high cheekbones, small pointed chin, sepia skin, watchful eyes, a hint of amusement flickering at their edges. He's the guy who was watching me from the balcony at the end of the laneway, I'm sure of it. He's younger than I initially thought; in his sixties, perhaps. But he walks with a limp, the weight of his slight body supported by a cane. This makes him appear, at first glance, more like a man of Ba's generation.

I get up, venture a few steps nearer. "Do you, by any chance, know a man named Ma Wing-Cheong?"

He smiles without moving his lips much, mulling the question over. Finally, he replies in Cantonese, "You could say that I know the guy."

"I've come a long way to see him. Would you be willing to take me to him?"

The hat drops back down, covering his eyes. "You're looking right at him."

I freeze up, barely able to stammer a greeting.

He maintains his calm, amused countenance. "I was wondering when you were going to show up, Jill. Took you long enough."

This convoluted introduction makes it feel inappropriate to extend a hand, with a belated "Nice to meet you." But social niceties are the last thing on Mr. Ma's mind.

Turning his back, he heads a few steps down the lane, pausing in front of the high wall around the courtyard of the unnumbered house. I don't realize that I'm expected to follow until he throws a quizzical glance over the shoulder.

"This is where you live? Number twenty-six?" I call out at the back of his head. When this man wants to, he can walk surprisingly fast, despite the limp.

"Nope. I'm at the end of the lane."

"Then why did your son send me this address?"

No answer.

We're skirting the courtyard wall. He pushes aside a battered crate, piled high with junk, revealing a jagged opening in the bricks, maybe two feet tall and just as wide. After shoving his cane through the hole, he gets down on his haunches and then stretches out on his stomach and slithers through like a snake. I prove far less agile, embarrassingly so. My knees and elbows get scraped — they burn, like I'm dragging myself over sandpaper —

and the hem of my dress catches on something with a shock of tension. On the other side of the wall is a morass of scratchy, thorny weeds. It's like pushing my way into the middle of a coarse hairball. At last, I somehow manage to stand up, shaking fuzz and spores from my hair and arms.

Mr. Ma calmly leans against his cane, barely having broken a sweat.

We're in a small, overgrown garden. The tangle of weeds is not as bad as it first seemed; it runs mainly along the walls. I step forward into the clearing in the middle of the courtyard, and I notice how the earth slopes in gentle undulations, how the sunlight wavers in watery veils. Wisteria vines wind up around the trunk of an old tree and although most of it is desiccated, a handful of feathery white blossoms hang down from the branches. A rusty pot sits on top of a large stone tablet once used for grinding spices, and pale-green mould creeps lacily along the bricks everywhere. I feel certain I've been here before, even though I know that's impossible. Perhaps I visited this place in a grainy dream.

"This is the house where Ba's family lived, during the war." I plan to ask this as a question, but it doesn't come out that way.

Mr. Ma just looks at me. Finally, he gives a nearly imperceptible nod.

"Ba wanted his sisters here. Where they'd be safe. That must count for something!" The defensive edge in my voice makes me cringe. Why do I care so much about convincing him that my father's not a terrible person?

But the man's turned his back on me again. The door at the rear of the house is unlocked. I follow him inside.

It's a dark, dank space, sharp with the smell of mildew. Although the ceiling's high enough, a claustrophobic feeling closes in. Weak light trickles in through the small, high windows.

We walk through a moon-shaped doorway into a larger room that's even darker and more vault-like, without any windows at all. A scraping sound makes me jump: fire flares at the edge of my vision. My neck stiffens and my body prepares to run as a pale-orange glow fills the room, shadows dancing on the walls.

They're just candles. He's lit a few candles.

My eyes adjusting, I see the walls are made of the same crumbling brick as the exterior, whitish with dust. And the floor, uneven beneath my feet, consists of the same. I decide I shouldn't move around too much, lest I trip. Wood rafters cut across the ceiling. Old clay casks and pieces of clunky furniture have been piled up along the walls. Chairs are precariously stacked on top of each other, tables turned on their sides, a credenza stretched out like a coffin. In the corner, a ladder disappears into a void in the ceiling. I guess the old folks, or anyone with bad knees, must have slept on the ground floor. This could be the very room where my grandparents died.

"Who owns this house?"

"I believe it passed down to a bunch of cousins on your father's side. Who knows? He might even be entitled to a cut. Not that it's worth a hill of beans. But you never know, maybe one of these days some developer will come along and buy up all these lots, for a song. I wouldn't mind unloading my place."

"What happened to the big house? The house with the beautiful garden, where your ancestors used to meditate?"

"That was on the other side of the pond. Got demolished years ago. You saw what's there now?" He gives a hollow cackle. "Of course, by that point, it'd long been taken away from us. Somebody else reaped the profits."

Everything the Mas lost. I wonder why Mr. Ma stayed on after his family had become pariahs. Maybe he had nowhere else to go. And by some good fortune, his family managed to hold on to the small house with the pretty balcony at the end of the laneway. And over time, his father would have surely recovered from the beating that Ba incited, wouldn't he? Maybe he eventually regained his reputation in the community, to some extent at least.

But Mr. Ma, like his old man, walks with a limp. I can't bear to ask. I want to believe it was polio or something. He had polio as a kid, that must be it.

Mr. Ma has moved toward a low table off to one side of the room. As I inch closer, I see it's covered with various wooden and stone carvings, little bowls and statues, all broken and pieced back together with certain parts missing. My host stands in front of the table, looking down at a warrior missing his head. A tusk, hanging on a string from a rafter, has lost its pointed tip. There are also musical instruments — small cymbals and gong-chimes attached to repaired wooden frames. These things have been laid out with some care, atop an embroidered cloth. Someone has gone to quite a bit of effort to salvage them. He's lit some incense, which sweetly masks the mildewy air.

"These things got smashed during the Cultural Revolution?"

"That's right, the good old Red Guards. But later, folks secretly brought these remains to my father. They didn't know what else to do with them. Although they claimed they'd renounced the past, deep down they still believed in the power of these old relics, the old rituals. So my father hid the stuff, buried it for safekeeping."

A flask comes out of his pocket. He pours a shot of clear liquid into a clay teacup and holds it out at me. When I shake my head, he shrugs and throws it back in one gulp.

He pulls a tattered purple robe, embroidered with the yin-yang symbol, from a dusty box. As Mr. Ma slips it over his shoulders, something strange comes over him. His joints seem to loosen and he sways, as if in a trance. Pouring more liquid into his cup, he uses his fingers to flick generous drops of it into the far corners of the room. His face has turned slack, devoid of expression; he leans his head back, his mouth slightly ajar, and shakes the wide sleeves of his robe like he's a marionette being jerked to life. A moment later, he seizes a stone tablet and slams it down on the table, as though a spirit has taken possession of his body.

I'm frozen to my spot. While he continues this strange, disjointed perambulation — half dance, half stagger in a drunken stupor — his head rolls back and I catch the dark merriment in his eyes. He's enjoying freaking me out. He's having fun with this parody of the old rituals. But then, his pleasure fades to a flat expression. I suspect that the drunkenness is real enough, that this is not entirely an attempt to play-act the role of the shaman. That flask he keeps in his pocket gets good use throughout the day, I'm sure.

A low, raspy chanting fills the room: "Spirit-soul, spirit-soul, you've had your fun, now time to go home! A pretty girl from the north will guide you through the black forest and massage your feet if you get tired! If you are thirsty, I have this liquor for you! Don't stop to talk to any strangers along the way, spirit-soul, for they will only tell false stories about you and kick you to the ground! So hurry along now, spirit-soul, and be gone! And never return to this wretched place!"

The hand still clutching the tablet draws a wide circle in the air, before he collapses to his knees, all his energy spent.

I don't know what to say, what to do, in the silence that follows. Mr. Ma remains perfectly still for the longest time, staring ahead at nothing. At last, he hoists himself up, resting his hands on his knees. All signs of mirth and mockery have been wiped from his face.

"I … I'm sorry about how your family suffered," I manage to say.

"Your father denounced my father. *Nothing was ever the same after that.*"

"I … I know …?"

He looks at the broken tablet in his hand.

How clumsy, how inadequate my apology sounds. How unaccustomed I am to saying sorry in my mother tongue. When I was growing up, apologies were never expected of me. As a child, you simply endured your punishment, and that was that. No words were expected of you, the deeper humility of silence all that mattered. As I remain silent now.

"So, listen," I finally say. Actions, not words, are what count, in the end. "You mentioned wanting to sell your house so you can move someplace nicer, newer. We could help you out with that. There are plenty of new condos in this district. We could help you buy one, if you want."

His head tilts back, his eyes thin as slits. He puts the broken object down.

"And of course we'd be happy to help your son with his school expenses," I continue. "Ben seems like a nice, hard-working fellow. I'm sure he'll go far in life." More stupid truisms fall from my lips, my tone just as pleading as it was with Ben at the zoo.

Without saying anything — without giving any indication of how my proposition strikes him at all — he stretches an arm above his head, using the other to support his weight on the cane. After this slight exertion, his face remains listless, as if he's ready to take a long nap.

Something about his languorous air starts to bother me. My sensation of guilt — so strong a moment earlier — crosses over into a different feeling, equally potent. I remember how easily these people turned their backs on my father, when he came to them in desperation, in need. Here I am going out of my way to make amends, and this guy can't even dignify my offer with a response?

"Your family could have helped my father, you know. There's a reason why he hated you guys, you must realize."

"Oh, your father didn't need anybody's help. He had his own plans."

"What's that supposed to mean?"

Mr. Ma picks up the incense holder and carries it across the room to where another table has been arranged. A small shrine. The red, rectangular tablet anchored to the wall appears newly made, gold lettering down its centre: "The Lau family and its ancestors live here." A couple words of blessings adorn the upper corners. The usual plates of oranges and tangerines, piled in small pyramids, have been presented as offerings on a frayed runner, along with a smattering of tiny ceramic bowls that perhaps contain a splash of Mr. Ma's precious wine. He lights a handful of red incense sticks and candles. Their glow illuminates an adjacent vase of yellow, tattered flowers. Framed black-and-white photographs crowd around, the faces pale and eerily serious. I point at an old man with near-set eyes and a grizzled chin, asking whether he was my grandfather.

Mr. Ma shakes his head. "There weren't any photos of him. Or if there were, they got left behind in Hong Kong."

Beside the shrine, I notice a loose photograph of my father, placed atop an album. I've never seen him look so young, his hair so black and glossy. Yet this is the same face I've always known: the steely, appraising gaze, the determined lines around the mouth. A cocky smile, the smile of youth. He's leaning against a brick wall — perhaps outside his peanut oil shop? I turn the picture over, but there's no date. When I ask Mr. Ma, he just shrugs, like it isn't important.

Despite his attempt to appear not overly interested, I sense the anticipation in his bones as I pick up the album. He clearly placed the picture of Ba on top deliberately, in order to attract my attention. How carefully everything has been laid out, each ruined object weighted with meaning, each new object procured to stand in for missing pieces of the past. Mr. Ma has gone to some trouble to curate this strange exhibit.

Feeling uneasy, I flip open the album and separate the pages, which are stuck together in the humidity. The album, like the ancestral tablet, seems new. Along with more black-and-white photographs, it contains old newspaper articles that Mr. Ma must have saved from way back when. Clippings that cover the Great Armed Battles, the mounting violence, the tragedies, the deaths. Once again, I can't help but marvel at everything that Ba lived through. His youthful, misguided sense of heroism.

"It's amazing the risks those guys took," I muse aloud.

Mr. Ma's hands remain clasped around the incense holder, billows of smoke occluding his expression. He stays quiet.

As I keep flipping through and skimming the articles, a grainy image catches my attention. I stare at it, unable to get my head around its uncanny familiarity.

There are two pictures of the same man. They've been arranged side by side on opposite pages, like a diptych. In the first one, he's young, in his early twenties. Tall and limber, dressed in a crumpled white shirt and trousers, he half smiles, half squints into the camera with a lingering trace of adolescent self-consciousness. In the adjacent picture — the newspaper clipping — the same man is decades older, his face fuller and stern, no longer good-looking. He's wearing a boxy military jacket. The black ink gives his face a smudgy quality. But I recognize him, nevertheless.

It's Mr. Chan. Ba's old business partner.

As I begin reading the article, my confusion only intensifies. The article refers to the man by a different name — Sun Yun-Wing. Why would Mr. Chan change his name? *Is* this guy Mr. Chan? He was old by the time I knew him and I was only a young girl. Do I even have a clear memory of what he looked like? How can I be certain that this is him?

I keep reading. It appears that this man — whoever he is — rose to a position of some political prominence. The article talks about how in the final days of the Great Armed Battles, he distinguished himself as a brave fighter on the conservative side. After

Mao's call for unity and the formation of new local governments, this guy — Sun Yun-Wing — managed to achieve the top leadership position in Guangzhou. He was put in charge of the new revolutionary committee. While the young heroes of the Red Flag suffered defeat, this man and his cronies landed on their feet.

It doesn't make any sense.

Ba fought for the Red Flag, so how could he later end up in business with the opposition leader? My brain has seized up, incapable of processing anything. My eyes dart back and forth between the two pictures, searching for further evidence — but evidence of what?

I look up at Mr. Ma, who appears to be thoroughly enjoying my discomfort.

"Something on your mind, kiddo? You look like you've seen a ghost."

I cough, my throat sore. The pollution is really getting to me. "It's just … I think I might know this man."

"I bet you do."

"How …?"

"That's a conversation you should have with your father."

Even if I dared, Ba would never give me any answers.

"There's an old saying," Mr. Ma continues. "A boat can't always sail with the wind; an army can't always win battles."

"Okay …" I shrug, not even caring at this point if he thinks me dim-witted. "The point of this saying is?"

"Be prepared for setbacks. Men of your father's generation understood this truth all too well. And sometimes they took it further, realizing it was more than just a matter of needing to sail against the wind. Sometimes a lifeboat is what you really need."

I still have no idea what the fuck he's talking about. I wait for him to elaborate, but I'm met only with cool silence.

After throwing back one last drink, he turns and trudges through the moon door, his back now slouched, like a tired actor who's taken his final bow and wants to go home. I stand in the room alone for a minute, before following him out. The courtyard is empty by the time I get there. It takes me a while to fight my way through the weeds and slither on my belly through the hole in the wall. By the time I'm on the other side, Mr. Ma is nothing more than a grey blotch vanishing down the laneway in the shimmering heat.

EIGHTEEN

U pon returning home, I find I have no one to talk to. Immediately, I phone Terence to discuss the situation, but Mr. Ma's weird behaviour doesn't strike him as anything more than the outcome of too much drink. "It only shows the guy never had any real leverage to begin with."

And the newspaper clipping with Mr. Chan's — or Sun Yun-Wing's — picture? Terence has his doubts. "The memory of an eleven-year-old girl's hardly infallible. And even if you remember the guy correctly, what does that prove? Except that your father, like any astute businessman, was good at making friends in high places?"

I can't answer these questions. But Terence doesn't even seem that interested. When we meet at Blue Bar the following evening, he has other things on his mind. Plying me with martini after martini, he slides closer on the shimmery, silver-blue sofa, until our thighs are touching.

"You think it's sheer coincidence that my father ended up in business with Mr. Chan?" I murmur.

"What's that?" He leans his ear closer.

"Oh, nothing." The aggressive beat of the music makes me feel like I'm running, lost in my own frantic, pounding heart.

Terence reminds me about that cool hotel in Beijing he wants us to stay at, designed by some big-shot architect. "What do you say? Want to get away next weekend?"

A dirty weekend is the last thing on my mind.

Could Chan and my father have had some sort of secret arrangement that sprang from the old days? I recall my father's disdain for anyone who'd jump into shark-filled waters. Befriending someone with power constituted the only sound plan of escape, in his eyes. Could Chan have pulled strings to allow Ba to move back to Hong Kong? If so, something must have been in it for Chan. Ba returned to Hong Kong and established the business that Chan later reaped half the profits from. That, at the very least, would have been his payoff.

Money. Everything about my father's life does, after all, come down to money, in the end.

A deflated feeling sucks at my stomach. My image of his younger self — a hot-headed, heroic man, led astray by naive political convictions — has been overturned yet again.

"So ...? Next weekend?"

Suddenly, I can't believe that I slept with Terence. It unsettles me how he's looking at me with a sheen of hope and neediness in his eyes, as if coming to this point has been his fantasy for years.

"I think I need to be alone for a bit," I say, pushing away from him.

His face freezes over, though not entirely, like a very thin sheet of ice, still watery in patches.

I fumble for words. "I just ... I ... I need some space."

"Fine," he says. "No one's pressuring you into anything."

Yet Terence doesn't sound fine. Dejection mutes his voice, making him sound like a crestfallen child.

• • •

Rather than going on a romantic getaway, I stay at home, day after day, enduring overcooked meals with Ba.

"I came across some old letterhead with the original name of your company the other day. It got me thinking. How did you and Mr. Chan meet in the first place?"

"Why are you asking me this again?"

"I'm just curious."

"Everybody knew everybody back in those days."

I try a different tack. "I wonder why Mr. Chan was so eager to move away to Vancouver?"

"The smog here was irritating his asthma, I guess."

Will I never get any further than these pat replies?

My eyes migrate to the TV. More coverage of the anticorruption campaign in China; another high official has come under attack. Although the volume is low, the news anchor's tinny voice pierces the room, recounting a slew of bribery and graft charges.

When Ba sees me watching the screen, his gaze curls sideways. "Another bad apple got what he had coming."

How can things be so black and white to him, of all people?

"Don't you ever worry about history —"

"Not at all," he interrupts.

"But —"

"You worry too much, Yuk Chu. Things are good now."

Back in my room, I fling myself onto the bed. I return to Keung-Cartwright's memoir, skimming ahead with manic speed, skipping sections to get to the end. It's as though, in my desperation, I'm hoping her story might somehow cast light on Ba's.

The Cultural Revolution's over now, the iron curtain gradually lifting. Keung-Cartwright finds herself living in London, enrolled at university.

> I decided to pursue studies abroad. My father's frail, anguished face in the labour camp, as he implored me to leave China, never faded from my memory. Although I didn't really believe that anything would come of this dying wish, this pipe dream, I kept putting in applications. Through an amazing combination of good luck, hard work, and my mother's behind-the-scenes lobbying of her old political connections, I found myself the recipient of one of the few international scholarships available to Chinese students; the following year, I would commence in the art history program at University College London. I could hardly believe that after so many years of misery and misfortune, things were finally looking up.
>
> London was a beautiful, enchanted city, I was surprised to discover. Due to a lifetime of being indoctrinated against the West, I'd been expecting a wasteland of graffiti, squalor, and louche behaviour — strip clubs and squats on every corner. But that was not the London that folded me into her embrace.
>
> The year was 1978. Mao was now dead and dramatic changes were in the air. During the first year of my degree, I lived at a residence owned by the Chinese embassy, so I remained under a certain degree of government surveillance and control. Nevertheless, the increased freedom I

had — to stroll the streets at leisure, to peruse bookstores, to wander past the countless treasures and masterpieces in the British Museum — filled me with a sensation nothing short of heady.

How devastating and unreal it now seemed that I, not so long ago, had been a Red Guard and participated in the destruction of such precious artifacts and artworks. The screams of that poor old lady whom Fatty and I had whipped. Shame filled me to the brim, flashbacks and nightmares leaving me drenched in sweat. I couldn't believe that girl had been me. A large part of the reason I was drawn to the field of art history and ultimately a curatorial career, I think, was that I needed to atone for the sins of my entire generation.

And yet, as the years sped by and my English improved, as I grew more comfortable wearing short skirts and putting on mascara, it was all too easy to forget the past and slip into the skin of this new person completely. I'd desperately wanted a new identity and now I had one. Sometimes, if strangers asked about my nationality, I would pretend to be Korean or Japanese. It was just easier that way. For many decades, I never talked about my past, not even with the men I dated or my eventual husband. It was too painful and that old me was dead, anyway. What would be the point of digging up all that sorrow and heartache?

Funny how one's entire sense of identity can be so quickly stripped away, replaced. My father must have had a similar sense of rebirth, I imagine. His past — all the terrible things he'd done, the horrors he'd lived through — suddenly dissolving, like fragments of a nightmare. That man wasn't *him*. Couldn't have been *him*. For Ba was here in Hong Kong now, a new man, rushing past mirrored skyscrapers, briefcase in hand, eager to close the next big deal.

He let go of that other life, that bad life.

But now that I know what I know, I can't let it go.

I burst into the dining room, where my father is sitting in his wheelchair, a newspaper stretched out on the table before him, giant magnifying glass in hand.

"Look, Ba, I have to tell you something. I went to Guangzhou."

"Why on earth …?"

Something like shadows seem to be floating around the edge of the room, all swimmy and grey, but they're not shadows, they're more like cobwebs or strands of something that's there and yet not really there, ever so slightly disrupting my field of vision. I blink hard, though nothing changes.

"I met with Mr. Ma. He told me … everything."

"Everything?"

"He told me that Mr. Chan, your old partner, used to be someone else. He had a different name back then. He was a political leader." The words shoot from my quivering lips. "*I don't understand.*"

The magnifying glass remains frozen in my father's hand as he peers through it at me. Like *I'm* the enigma.

I repeat myself, even less coherent this time.

Every muscle of his face clenches up. For a second, this face almost looks young, oddly young, revitalized by anger.

"Don't you see?" he says finally. "There *is* nothing to understand. *Understanding*" — mockery taints his voice — "didn't factor into our decisions."

Something in the air seems to pulse between us.

"You see … how shall I put this?"

Now it's pleading that I detect. As though he really does care about making me understand. Or at least, he wants to compel me to be nicer to him, to take pity on him.

"It's a terrible thing to be hungry all the time," he says. "To not know where your next meal is coming from."

For some reason, his words don't move me nearly as much as they once did. I've been fed this line all my life.

"I know that times were tough," I say. "I know that you needed a lifeboat."

"A lifeboat?"

I'm still not exactly sure what Mr. Ma meant by this, but I can guess. "You were trying to escape. You needed an exit strategy. The travel permit that enabled you to return to Hong Kong. And the start-up capital that allowed you to build your business in record time."

"I got that through hard work."

And you had a little help along the way.

Where did that nest egg come from? Did Chan have a rainy-day stash? A foreign bank account? And what did my father do for Chan in return? "Your fate was somehow tied up with Mr. Chan's," I say, frantic now. Why won't he just tell me? "The two of you had some kind of deal going?"

Ba turns back to the smudged newsprint. "You understand nothing."

I phone Eddy Chan. His cell keeps going to voice mail. I call his office. His secretary tells me he's out of town and refuses to give me a contact number. Eddy and his new wife are off enjoying a belated honeymoon, not to be disturbed by business. I tell her it's more of a personal matter, but she won't budge. He'll be back in two and a half weeks and I can talk to him then.

Celeste offers a more sympathetic ear when we chat on the phone. I report that I've discovered the source of the photos and the dead mouse. "Ba was involved in some nasty business in Guangzhou. He went on a rampage, with a bunch of other radicals, and tore up an old lady's grave. Which led to a man being denounced and beaten and crippled."

"Slow down, Jill. I don't quite follow."

Thoughts ping-ponging about my brain, I find it hard to explain what I myself still can't comprehend. "Oh, forget it." Besides, my sister doesn't sound all that interested, fatigue weighing down her voice.

"Are you sure?" she asks.

"Let's just say that our father did some very bad things. I'm not sure what, exactly. And to tell you the truth, I'm not sure I want to know. Let's just leave it at that."

After a long moment, Celeste says, "Well, I have some good news. The baby's developing well. If all goes according to plan, I'll be able to give birth at home."

When it comes to talking about the baby, she's more upbeat than she's been in years — in her whole life, maybe. Her mind is on midwives, breast pumps, strollers, organic baby food. The kid's kicking up a storm, keeping her up at all hours. But she doesn't mind, because this is all a labour of love. The train wreck of our own family seems to have faded completely from her mind.

"Hey, Jill," she asks as the baby talk peters out, "are you doing all right?"

I'm not used to my sister asking me this. It's always been the other way around. "Sure, I guess? Why?"

"You seem distracted, tired. Maybe you should throw in the towel. Just get on a plane and come home. Like I've been telling you for weeks."

"But who'll take care of Ba?"

"He's got his nurses. Plus, Rina's there. You hire a property management company to handle Ba's building."

"It would be only a matter of time before the company started mismanaging, skimming."

"That's exactly what Ba would say!"

"Well, the apple doesn't fall far from the tree, I guess." I'm in no mood to argue. If Celeste wants to think I'm no different from Ba, so be it.

But her tone is soft; conciliatory, almost. "Just come home, please. Who cares if the property manager skims? It would be a small price to pay for your mental health."

I can't believe my sister is talking to me about mental health.

"I'm just saying that you don't have to be a martyr, Jill. Unless, for some odd reason, you want to be."

I shift funds around; I write out two cheques. One to Benjamin Ma for his university expenses, in the amount requested. And the other to his father for a significantly larger figure — enough to buy a condo and then some. I mail the cheques to the post-office mailbox.

The cheque to Ben is withdrawn within a few days. But a week later, then ten days later, the one to Mr. Ma remains untouched. I wonder if Ben hasn't passed it along yet. I email him to enquire, but never hear back.

I sleep a lot. I dodge Terence's phone calls. All the chores I'm supposed to be doing — collecting rent, hiring repairmen, preparing paperwork for our accountant — get pushed to the next day. And the next day. And then the next week. The mere thought of setting foot in Ba's building fills me with dread. Writing out cheques, accepting cheques, depositing cheques into our bank accounts. My palms sweat and my knuckles cramp up at the thought of touching those degraded slips of paper. Worse still is touching real money, the stacks of bills Ba keeps in the safe in his bedroom. Whenever possible, he likes to pay for things the old-fashioned way. But these days, my flesh cringes even when I'm forced to dole out a few bills to Rina for groceries. *Take it*, I want to scream and throw the whole wad in her astonished face. I want nothing more than to divest myself of these polluted funds that have been paying for the food sustaining my body and all the taxis I've been taking around town and my decadent cocktails and dinners out at the day's end. That overpriced hotel room in Guangzhou. In exchange for putting my life on hold, I've been allowing myself these ever more indulgent luxuries, as though they're just little things that don't count, or as though they're nothing more than a fair day's wage. How easily I've slipped into enjoying Ba's money — using, possessing, controlling it, like it's my own, the company credit card never far from my fingertips. Yet now I never want to touch any of it again.

I give in, succumbing to inertia, the pull of gravity against the crumpled sheets. It's noon — the bedroom is flooded with fiery sunlight — and I'm still just skimming the surface of consciousness, drifting in and out of some shadowy dream. I'm at the airport and a team of security guards are chasing me down, trying to prevent me from catching my flight. And then, I dream that I'm right here, in my childhood bedroom, which has been converted into a tiny, self-contained apartment, a kitchenette where the closet used to be. I throw open the window and light a cigarette. Each time I exhale a ring of smoke, I notice myself shrinking a little more, the floor gradually rising up to eye level.

I drag myself out of bed to take a cold shower. Still, the feeling of being asleep stays with me. How do I know that I'm really awake? I peer into the glass at my puffy eyelids and the sepia sun-spots darkening by the day across my cheekbones.

I think about Celeste's concerned words. Maybe she's right, maybe I *am* going over the edge. The thought almost strikes me as funny.

Then Terence calls me from a landline, so I don't recognize the number and pick up. He, too, is worried about me. Very worried, he emphasizes, his plaintive tone sending shivers of guilt through me. Reluctantly, I agree to meet for tea at one of our old haunts, if only to reassure him that I'm okay. But everything about the city feels off-kilter, as I sink down in the back seat of the taxi, the shimmery, reflective surfaces of all the skyscrapers looming over me like monstrous holograms.

The scones taste stale and dry, the tea tepid, so I switch to a glass of Merlot.

At some point, I say out of the blue, "Sorry, Terence."

"Sorry? For what?"

"Oh, you know."

His lips tense up, trying to hold his disappointment at bay. "Nothing's been decided yet. You asked for some space and I'm giving you some space. Take as much space as you want!"

"I'm not sure that'll help. I think, maybe, I'm just one of those people meant to be alone in life."

"That's such bullshit." He won't stop looking at me, holding me accountable for the hurt in his eyes.

"I'm trying to let you off the hook gracefully —"

"And I'm not letting you."

Before I can say another word, Terence hijacks the conversation by prattling on non-stop about all the new types of sake he's been sampling. Soon he'll throw a tasting party for his friends, once the bar's open for business.

"That's nice," I say. "Unfortunately, I'll probably have left by then."

"What? You're going back to Toronto?"

"I've been thinking about it."

"What are you going to do back in Toronto? Go back to your old job?"

"I guess so." I emailed Carlos yesterday, and he was overjoyed to hear from me. The temp filling in for me has found a permanent position, so I can resume work as early as October if I want to. There I'll be at my old cubicle overlooking the grey-blue waves of Lake Ontario, like nothing ever happened.

"You prefer your life in Canada?"

"Things are just simpler over there."

A sigh comes out of his nostrils, like he doesn't trust himself to speak.

"What's on your mind, Terence?"

"All those towers going up along the waterfront are built and owned by Chinese money. You do know that, don't you?"

"What would you know about Toronto real estate?"

"I don't have to know anything. All I have to do is flip through the *Standard*."

The paper is filled with ads for condos in Toronto, Vancouver, Melbourne, and London, right beside the ads for immigration services and private schools overseas. For folks who can afford it, getting that second passport and home in a foreign location is still an appealing contingency plan — just in case things take an unpleasant turn under Communist rule. And Canadian real estate's a safe place to park money.

"I get it, I really do," I say.

"You get what, Jill?"

"In going back to Toronto, I'm not really getting away … China's everywhere." Something like regret — or even shame — stirs at the back of my throat, constricting my ability to breathe for a dizzying moment. My refuge has been ripped away from me, exposed as a dream, an illusion. There is nowhere far removed from my people and our wretched history. "We're everywhere," I whisper, horrified.

"Then why leave?" Frustration quivers in Terence's voice. "If you can't escape yourself, why keep running?"

To this, I have no reply, beyond a sigh of pure exhaustion. I excuse myself to go to the washroom and splash water on my face, but the cold doesn't revive me at all.

The phone call comes early in the morning. I sleep right through it and don't discover the voice mail until noon. It's Eddy Chan, back from his honeymoon, sounding all too chipper. I call him back and tell him we need to meet up ASAP, but he has a dinner engagement that evening and an appointment with his personal trainer right before. When he suggests later in the week, I tell him nope, it has to be today. I'll meet him at his gym and we can talk in the taxi on his way to dinner. Although he doesn't sound keen, I conclude the call so quickly he doesn't have a chance to back out.

I wait for him in the lobby of California Fitness, a little after seven. He's more stylishly dressed than usual. Marriage appears to agree with him. While Eddy will never be a good-looking guy, he has it within his grasp, as he ages, to look distinguished.

We step outside onto the crowded sidewalk.

"Sorry, I'm in a hurry," he says, heading in the direction of the nearest taxi stand outside Landmark. The message seems to be: if I want to follow him, fine, he can't stop me, and maybe we'll chat a little along the way.

I don't waste time asking about his honeymoon. "I just came back from Guangzhou. What do you know about your father's political career?"

This gets his attention. He slows down, glancing back sharply. "What political career? Ba was just a businessman."

But I sense from his hesitancy that he has some idea of what I'm getting at. "Don't give me that crap, Eddy."

"What? Our fathers had a business together. Mine did the accounting."

"I'm talking about back in Guangzhou."

"What would I know about those days? I wasn't even born then."

"You must know something. Everyone was political back then. Life revolved around Mao, the Red Guards, the mass organizations." I watch him carefully, searching for any minute changes in expression.

A tall woman in a black cocktail dress knocks into me and roughly shoulders her way past. People don't like it when you slow down and impede the flow of traffic. Grabbing Eddy's arm, I pull him down an alleyway. "How did your dad end up in Hong Kong, anyway?"

Eddy's started lightly sweating. "Well … your father returned first, right?"

"Ba came back and bought the property where their building later went up. Your father must have arrived a couple years after mine, from what I gather."

"Right."

As I keep staring at him, the rivulets become more noticeable, trickling down the sides of his face, pooling in his collar. Under the well-cut jacket, his shirt's probably already soaked. What a mess he'll be for the dinner party. Too fucking bad. I feel like a bully, having cornered a snivelly kid in the schoolyard. Much as it sickens me, the feeling is also kind of intoxicating.

"My father wanted a fresh start in Hong Kong, okay? That's the sense I always got. Everyone's entitled to a fresh start, aren't they?"

"Depends. What was he trying to escape from?"

"I have no idea."

"Oh, come on. You must have suspicions."

"Well …"

I grab his arm, leaning in. "*I'm not going to let this go.*"

He shakes me off like a spooked horse, then his eyes swing back at me. "My uncle once said something," he whispers.

"Yeah, about?"

"About how my dad had been in a labour camp."

"A labour camp?"

I think of the camp where Keung-Cartwright's father spent his final days, surrounded by white-haired ghosts. So many once-formidable men reduced to that.

"What was your old man doing in a labour camp, Eddy? His old political allies sold him out?"

"How on earth would I know?"

I'm overcome with that same confusing thrill of excitement that swept over me upon first seeing Eddy and my father up on the rooftop terrace together. How sure I was that he was a thug, here to set my father straight. The startled, fearful sheen in Ba's eyes that I later convinced myself I'd only imagined. Nope, that fear was real enough. Ba looked like he'd been visited by an intruder, for he associated Eddy with Mr. Chan — an intrusion from the past. But at the same time, it was a visit from an old friend, or an ally of sorts.

Eddy turned out to be no thug. That wish for violent confrontation was coming not from Eddy, but from me, all along. I can see that now. I am the one quite willing to draw blood, if that's what it takes to extract the truth.

"You're his son, for fuck's sake. Don't you know your own father at all?"

This makes Eddy flinch.

"Well, what happened? *How did your father get out of the fucking camp?*"

"Look, Jill, someone paid a crapload of money, okay? At least, that's the impression I got from my uncle." He mops at his forehead, exasperation creeping over his face.

"My father …?" It surprises me how calmly I say this, barely even making it a question. As if in my heart, I already know.

"Who else could it have been?"

How seamlessly Ba arranged for First Cousin to be smuggled into Hong Kong, followed by the rest of our family. That job was a walk in the park compared with what he'd pulled off before.

"And how did our fathers …?"

"I don't pretend to know how things played out exactly, Jill. But like your own father, my father was a resourceful man, always planning for the worst-case scenario. He must've known he wasn't protected from being purged. In fact, his high position would have made him all the more vulnerable. The winds of power change direction very quickly, you know."

"So what my father offered was an insurance policy, right?"

Only a man of Ba's underhanded skills would be capable of pulling it off. In the worst-case outcome — if he ended up in a labour camp — Chan wanted to know that he had a trusted friend on the outside, who'd stop at nothing to get him out. His lifeboat.

Keung-Cartwright managed to sneak into her father's camp without too much difficulty, in the disorder that followed the storm. The camps were not always so well guarded, in the end. Ba must have hired someone to go in, pass along bribes, get Chan out, and smuggle him across the border to Hong Kong. And so, Chan's freedom was secured, along with a whole new identity, a new life.

But some furtive thought keeps scurrying across my brain, stealthy as a rat. "Our fathers had a secret deal going. You scratch my back, I'll scratch yours. The funds that allowed my father to get back on his feet in Hong Kong must have been channelled to him by your father. I get all that. What I don't understand, though, is how these two men got in bed together in the first place."

"Their paths must have somehow crossed in Guangzhou."

"Fine. But two guys from opposite sides of the political divide? They seem unlikely allies."

A small, wry smile flickers over Eddy's lips. "My father was never averse to working with his enemies, if you want the truth. In the end, I think he saw these political distinctions as pretty arbitrary. Your father was probably just as practical."

"Practical? Is that what you call it?"

"Well" — he colours at my tone — "I'm just saying, it's a bit like when you're a kid in gym class. Who gets to be on which team? The teacher just assigns you by pointing and giving you a number."

"And loyalties to your team members don't last beyond the duration of the game."

"Something like that. And then, next time, new teams are assigned. New team captains. What really matters isn't the game, but rather the game behind the game."

The game behind the game.

Did my father sell out his friends in the Red Flag in order to help Chan consolidate power under the new regime? What acts of sabotage took place behind the scenes to ensure that the Red Flag wouldn't be a problem any longer? Did Ba play some role? Was this what it took to cement his bond with Chan?

"In any case, I don't understand why you're dredging up all this stuff, Jill. This is ancient history!"

"Not that ancient."

As Eddy tosses me a brittle smile, a surprising wave of something like sympathy — or self-pity — surges over me. He and I are not so different, in the end, much as it pains me to admit. Me and Eddy. Bound by the need to protect our family legacies, our blood money.

"Everything's different now, Jill. Our fathers suffered so that we wouldn't have to. That's what matters, isn't it? Shouldn't we just be grateful for that?"

Is it really that simple? Maybe for some people, it is. How I envy his ability to ensconce himself in this wilful oblivion, as though his biggest worry is that his wife will be mad because he's late for dinner.

He turns away, continuing toward the taxi stand. "See you around, Jill."

"See ya, Eddy."

"You look worried, Yuk Chu. But I have it all figured out." Ba edges closer to me by using his feet to move the wheelchair forward.

"What, Ba?" I put down my chopsticks, no appetite anyway.

"Don't worry about the business. We have enough money!" He extracts from the pocket of his dressing gown an old black notebook, the kind he's used all his life to keep track of numbers, profits, debts. "Don't you see?" The book falls open to a random place, the page yellowed, ink faded. "It's been a good quarter — we've done well."

"*You've* done well, Ba."

"And one day soon, Yuk Chu, you'll take over for me, just like we always talked about … and … after that …"

"*No, Ba.*" My elbow jostles the edge of my plate, my chopsticks clattering to the floor.

"What?"

It's too much — I can't keep up this charade any longer. I need to get away from this man, the crazed hope and expectation illuminating his gaze, as if in looking at me he sees nothing other than his own future. His own immortality.

"Was it worth it, Ba?"

"Was what worth it?"

"What you did. To buy your escape from Guangzhou. You sold your friends out, didn't you?"

The light fades from his eyes. But he doesn't deny it. "You wouldn't even be here if I hadn't done what I did."

I stoop to pick up the chopsticks. Sauce is splattered all over the floor.

"The next time I'm about to die," Ba says, "I don't want you to call an ambulance."

"What are you talking about?"

"Just let me die."

I can't deal with this man's guilt tactics any longer. Anguish swells in my throat. "You have round-the-clock nursing — the best nursing money can buy. If you're going into cardiac arrest, of course the nurse will call an ambulance!"

He shrugs, his shoulders wilting. "Well, maybe I'll die in my sleep, then."

"Yeah, right. That's like winning the lottery."

The cheque to Mr. Ma remains uncashed. At last, I think I understand his point, his perverse symbolism: not everything has a price tag — some mistakes can't be redressed, for any amount. The satisfaction of delivering this message is worth more to him than a cheque of any magnitude.

So he'll spend the rest of his days in that crumbling little house in the old neighbourhood, keeping watch from his shadowy perch. He will bear witness to everything that happened; he will keep company with the ghosts of the past.

"I guess this is it," Terence says.

We're standing in the middle of a dusty construction site, ragged patches of drywall torn off the exposed bricks, one interior wall knocked down completely. But by the end of next month, it'll be a swanky sake bar.

Feeling sheepish, I apologize yet again for not sticking around to see the project through. I search Terence's face for signs of anger and resentment, but all I see is sad acceptance, mixed with an inexorable glimmer of hope, which only makes me feel worse.

"Next time you're in town," he says, "we'll have a drink here."

"That'd be nice."

"When do you think you might be back?"

He's standing very close now, so close that I can feel the warmth of his humid skin, calling out to be touched. Yet I'm leaving, aren't I? Yes, I need to leave. While I want very much to kiss this mouth — to feel the swish of his tongue against mine, one last time — I remain motionless. The space between our bodies stretches open, like an empty, abandoned field.

"Dunno." I laugh lightly.

"Don't go …"

I brush a flurry of white dust from my black shorts. "I'm sorry — I have to …"

"Then when are you coming back?" he repeats.

"Maybe never?"

His eyes flash. Well, perhaps this is what it takes — a streak of meanness — to get my message to stick.

"Oh, you'll be back. When your father kicks the bucket, you'll be back for his money. Don't kid yourself."

So the meanness cuts both ways. I back away from him, winded.

We stare at each other a moment longer. The tension fades from his face.

"Sorry, Jill … I didn't mean to …"

As I turn away, he puts his hand on my shoulder and I feel my body slackening, melting, knowing it would be the most effortless thing in the world to fall into his arms. But I straighten up, holding on to my resolve. And I find myself wondering, yet again, about what he thinks the deal is between us. Does he view me as a challenge, the ultimate tease? A long-term project? Isn't he getting tired of going in circles here? Or does he think that one day I'll be ready for what he has to offer and fall into his arms forever? And who knows? Maybe I will. Stranger things have been known to happen. At least, with Terence, I'd never have to hide my past, because his own past is covered in just as many faded bloodstains. I can be utterly myself with him; I don't have to pretend to be some person of pristine morals and family background. With him, I'd never have to feign being shocked by things that don't shock me at all anymore.

"Looking forward to going home?"

I don't know what to say to this. And yet, it's a simple enough question. "Things are just easier for me back in Toronto."

I want to leave it at that, but then tears sting my eyes and burst, and it all starts pouring out — all my suspicions about Ba's sins. A jumble of accusations and confessions, which I myself can barely comprehend.

Terence massages the crook of his neck, his gaze drifting away. When he looks back, he doesn't try to hide his emotions. "It's not on you — none of it is. Whatever your father did, *that's on him.*"

I rub at my eyes. "You don't have any guilt about your own family's money?"

"Sure, I do."

"So … how do you deal?"

Terence leans back against the wall. "My therapist has this theory," he says at last.

"I didn't know you see a therapist."

"Yup. An old-school Freudian psychoanalyst. I've been seeing her for about six years." He gives a self-deprecating smile. "Don't laugh at me, okay? I wanted somebody who'd stick with me for the long haul. Guess that's why I chose a Freudian."

"And what's your shrink's theory?"

"She thinks that once I've figured out what I want to do with my dead father's money, it'll cease to be a burden. Instead, the money'll become a source of freedom, or creativity."

"Huh. How very Freudian. But …"

"What?"

"Sounds too easy. And I don't see how it gets around the guilt problem."

"Oh, it doesn't. The guilt's always going to be there, one way or another. But at least, if I'm going to be dealing with guilt, I might as well get something in exchange."

"What you're getting, quite frankly, *is* the money."

"Money's just money. It's what you do with it that matters."

I ponder this. My father would most likely disagree. He never did anything with his money except put it to work making more money. For him, money has a kind of intrinsic value; the numbers in his accounts mean everything to him.

"And what are you going to do with it, Terence?"

"I dunno. Who says I have all the answers? Right now, I just want to build a cool bar where my friends can hang out."

I can't help but smile at this. Typical Terence. "Is that all you want to do with your life?"

He shoots me a withering look, as if to say, *Well, at least I'm doing something.*

And perhaps this is another source of my guilt, which Terence senses. I can't help it. On some level, perhaps I do want the money — I want to do something with it. Even if I, too, haven't yet figured out what.

I think about my father sitting alone at dinner, night after night, slowly dying.

During our last meal together, he attempts to act all gruff. As if to say that if he can't convince me to stay, then fine, I can leave him the hell alone. "I'll be perfectly fine. The doctor says I have the liver of a man half my age."

The smallness of his life — his scuffed slippers, his faded pyjamas, his tiny ceramic dish of soy sauce — weighs heavily on me.

As he continues to talk, the space heater blasts its suffocating cloud. Yet I notice my father shivering.

Toward the end of dinner, he lapses into confusion. "I think ... I think ... your sister's coming home tonight."

"She's not coming, I hate to tell you."

"We'll all be here together, with plenty to eat. A big fish. Me and my sisters."

Past and present blur together in his deranged memory, the fragile idyll somehow kept intact: Ba surrounded by the adoring women in his life, the women he saved.

NINETEEN

B ut as it turns out, I don't get on my plane the following morning. I awake before dawn to the night nurse's feral scream.

I rush into Ba's room and lean down at his bedside and shake his shoulders, gently at first, then harder. His eyes remain closed, just as if he were asleep. While I fumble at his neck for a pulse, I can feel only rubbery puckers of cool skin. And then my hands are shaking too much to be of use, anyway — as I try to dial 999, the phone slips from my fingers and clatters to the ground.

A funny thought skitters across my brain. *Ba has won the lottery.*

"It's my father," I hear myself saying into the phone. "He's died, I think. Died in his sleep."

Ten minutes later, the paramedics arrive and try to revive my father by doing CPR and putting electric paddles to his chest. "You're too late," I hear myself say, but a paramedic holds up a hand to indicate I should move back. It appears that, just maybe, Ba still has a flutter of a faint pulse — *can it be?* As his small, unconscious body is lifted onto a stretcher, I'm trying to answer multiple questions. Although adrenalin is keeping me upright and talking, an unsteady feeling keeps grabbing me around the knees.

Two police officers stride through the door and they, too, begin firing questions my way. While one of the cops stays behind to interview Rina and the nurse, the other one follows me into the elevator with the paramedics and my father's supine body. Whenever a 999 call comes in about a death — no matter how unsuspicious — the police tend to pay a visit, I've heard; they do everything very by the book, these days. Still, I can't believe that they're actually here, or that any of this is happening.

In the ambulance, the cop's all business. A tight little muscle pulses in his jaw as he continues to interrogate me about what happened this morning. It occurs to me that maybe this guy really does view me as a suspect. Does he honestly think that I might have poisoned Ba? Absurd as it is, guilt creeps coldly over my chest; perhaps the cop is right, at some level. If I hadn't upset my father by insisting on returning to Toronto, if I hadn't flung so many accusations at him in recent days, maybe he'd still be breathing normally. Am I responsible for Ba's precarious state, no less than if I'd slipped something toxic into his congee?

"My father's ninety-four and he's been in terrible health ever since his bowels burst earlier this summer." My tears smart and overflow — I can't hold it together any longer.

The cop backs off, though he keeps on watching me. Meanwhile, a paramedic injects my father with something through a long needle.

The next thing I know, the ambulance comes to an abrupt stop. We're at the public hospital in Wan Chai. My father is rushed into the ER.

When I'm allowed to see him again, a thick plastic tube has invaded his throat and his eyes have been taped shut. A chuffing noise fills the curtained-off space, the sound of one of the machines keeping him alive, breathing on his behalf. The monitor beside his bed shows a red line above a blue line, both of them moving in small, sporadic waves. As I watch those two lines doing their thing, I hear a doctor shuffling behind me, a voice telling me that although my father's heart is beating, ever so slightly, the situation is pretty much hopeless. He'll never regain consciousness and probably has very little time left.

A short while later, Ba is moved to a ward on one of the upper floors, beside the Palliative Care Centre. The cop, who must have been in the waiting room all this time, approaches with a stiff wave. He tells me that there's no need for any further police involvement and he'll be leaving now.

Nevertheless, the sensation of guilt stays with me, wrapping around my shivering skin, like a cold, wet towel.

When I call my sister, her phone goes to voice mail; it's the middle of the night in Canada. Then I phone my aunts and tell them to come to the hospital, but they don't arrive in time. So it's just me watching over Ba, as those red and blue lines cease undulating at all and flatten into a smooth, stark horizon. The doctors disconnect all the sighing and beeping machines, leaving us in silence.

The weird thing is that I can still hear him. In the following days, lying in bed in the early mornings, I hear Ba coughing and spitting up phlegm. I hear his wheelchair being pushed from room to room, the soft, scraping sound of the wheels against the floor, the plaintive squeak of some metallic part that needs to be oiled. The click of his spoon against the edge of a bowl, the slurp of a mouthful of watery congee.

I force myself to get up and deal with the list of chores. Picking up the death certificate (cause of death: heart attack). Paying bills. Meeting with the funeral agent, a young, chubby woman with theatrical eye makeup and a stack of brightly coloured binders. She tells me that the soonest we can schedule my father's funeral, at any facility in the city, is in eleven days' time. Then she talks about how for a traditional Chinese funeral — which I know my aunts will insist on — it's important for my father to be buried wearing six layers of clothing, with extra clothes from all seasons thrown into the coffin for good measure. Something about how the thickness of clothing corresponds to the fullness of the life led by the deceased. And four Taoist monks must be chanting throughout the service to keep evil spirits at bay. This I agree to, though I nix the use of musical instruments, since I know from my mother's funeral Ba hated the loudness of it all.

When I phone my sister to let her know the date of the event, I sense a certain hesitancy at the back of her throat.

"You *are* planning to come, aren't you?"

Celeste sighs. "I want to. But in the last couple days, I've been having some complications with my pregnancy ..." Anxiety clouds her voice. While she doesn't want to burden me with the details, the gist seems to be she isn't sure it's safe for her to fly. She needs to consult with her doctor.

"Oh, it's fine if you're not at the funeral." I don't exactly mean this, but I manage to say it anyway. "The baby's health is the most important thing, of course."

Slowly, I walk through the rooms of our condo, staring into space. Ba's old things keep me company on the periphery of my vision. His magnifying glass, weighing down a folded newspaper. His owly reading glasses. His grey plastic calculator.

And then, in a burst of impatience or manic energy — a desire to get this thing over with — I yank open my father's closet and begin rifling through his clothes. I throw everything with stains and holes into garbage bags, and toss the rest in a heap on the bed to give to charity. Meanwhile, I'm on the lookout for his best dark suit, vest, shirt, undershirt, and underwear; I can't imagine what other garments are supposed to comprise the requisite six layers. The well-worn fabrics cling to my hands, leaving them covered in a chalky residue that makes me want to sneeze, though the release won't quite come. A strange, sharp smell — laundry powder mixed with a fine dusting of dead skin flakes — tickles the inside of my nose. Then a heavy feeling comes over my head, but it can't be fatigue, because I only just got out of bed, didn't I?

As I release Ba's threadbare cardigans from their hangers, their arms retain the protruding shape of his bony elbows.

I can't sleep, so I get out of bed and pull on jeans and a T-shirt. I wander down Conduit Road, letting the night air envelop me and carry me forward, in no particular direction. There's no one around, the quivering shadows of trees my only company. It's rare for the city to feel so quiet, so vacant.

A little while later, I find myself at the edge of the university campus. Where the road curves downward, a massive construction site stretches out, like a crater on a dusty planet. Skeletons of a couple new buildings have started to take form, but in the moonlight, they look more like ancient ruins.

I think of our class trip to Italy back in architecture school. When we were passing through a town in what had once been a Roman resort area, my boyfriend and I couldn't resist sneaking out of the hotel in the middle of the night to explore all the places that had been marked off bounds, for archaeologists only. Yeah, right. We were archaeologists, of a different sort. As we clambered up and down over crumbling piles of broken wall, our feet touching the uneven stone floors, tufts of grass poking up here and there, neither of us saying much of anything, it was as though we were descending deeper into ourselves, into the recesses of our own solitary consciousnesses. It made me think of Piranesi's etchings at the end of his life, the walls of Hadrian's villa overrun with dead foliage, built form and organic matter virtually indistinguishable.

And then, my boyfriend — Tobias was his name — turned to me abruptly. The moonlight accentuated the sharp planes of his cheekbones. I could see in his eyes that he was going to say something lovely and sappy. Although I don't remember what he whispered in my ear, I do recall the way his body stiffened when I made a light joke of it, brushing his earnestness off.

I didn't want walking through the ruins to be about anything other than the ruins. What I was seeking wasn't a love sonnet, but more like an elegy. That peculiar feeling of mourning and enchantment. Closeness to the dead. Utter solitude. The distinct sensation that if the whole universe were to end tomorrow, that would be all right — it might even be a relief. Each of us holding on to our secrets until the very end.

And all that'd be left would be this, this trace.

It's cold in here, very cold. The walls of this small room are painted pure white, the lighting soft and diffuse, to give an impression of otherworldliness, perhaps. Through the sliding glass door, I can see into another, much larger white room, with an altar at the far end and rows of empty benches in front. As I exhale, my breath comes out in misty plumes.

But my father should be warm enough in all his layers of clothing, ensconced within his upholstered coffin. I gaze down at his face, freshly restored. His cheeks have regained some of the fullness I recall from fifteen years ago, and his skin has been powdered a peculiar, peachy tone that makes him look like he has a bit of a sunburn. At least he's presentable now. An image of his face, in that half-hour after he died, flashes in my mind; I was sitting at his bedside, waiting for my aunts to arrive, watching the sudden changes come over him. How quickly the skin yellows and clings to the skull, reminiscent of a knotted, ancient tree.

Later this evening during the wake, I'll be expected to stand by the side of the altar and acknowledge all the grieving visitors, who will light joss sticks and pay their respects by bowing. And I will bow in return. There will be a lot of bowing and possibly some kneeling, too, amidst the clouds of incense smoke and melancholic chanting. My joints already ache at the thought of it all.

But now is my quiet time with my father. According to the funeral director, this is my opportunity to add a personal article to the coffin; all the usual things — coins, joss paper, small pieces of red paper to ward off malignant spirits — have already been added.

Folded in my damp palm, I have a small square of satin, in a lush magenta shade. I snipped it from a dress that I found at the back of Ba's closet while clearing out his things. What a surprise to discover that this unsentimental man had hung on to one of my mother's old *qipao*s. Based on its tiny size and body-hugging cut, it must have belonged to her when she was still young and slender.

Tucking the scrap of fabric into the coffin, I lean down, one last time, close to my father's ear. Although I'm not at all sure I believe this, I find myself whispering, "You'll see Mom soon."

Then I slide open the door. Celeste is there, waiting for me. She flew in this morning, having received her doctor's approval. Despite the tiring flight, her face looks rounder, brighter, healthier, along with her whole body. We haven't really had a chance to talk much since her arrival, in the rush of last-minute preparations. The awkwardness of so many unspoken things always there between us.

Now, though, when she sees my weepy eyes, we embrace, we fully embrace — clutching on to each other like we haven't done since childhood. I breathe in the scent of my sister's sweat and greasy hair. I feel her tears dampening my blouse and then realize that I, too, am turning her dress into a soggy mess. The little swell of her stomach nuzzles against me. It's true that there's something comforting about touching a pregnant woman's belly.

"Your turn." I hold open the door.

"I think I'll just stand outside and look through the window." Her hand migrates down to her tummy. "I don't think the baby would like the cold."

We stand in silence, gazing in, for a long while.

"Ba told me he was ready to die," I finally say. "He said, 'Let me die — don't call an ambulance.' And I didn't believe him." Tears sting my sinuses.

"You have nothing to feel guilty about."

But Celeste wasn't there in those final days before his death. She doesn't know how forcefully I pressed our father to admit his sins. Did I suck the will to live right out of him? Or did Ba, at some level, feel relieved that I knew what he'd done? Perhaps it brought him some small degree of peace?

Yeah, right. I'm being far too kind to myself.

"It's okay if you're relieved that he's dead," Celeste says.

Is it relief that I'm feeling?

"Ba's in a giant fridge," I say a moment later. "Remember how fond he was of that old, broken refrigerator in his bedroom?"

"Because he used it as a filing cabinet. His ledger books are there. Just what you want to have next to you when you go to bed at night." Celeste lets out a chuckle, which turns into a whimper, a sigh. "I guess all that junk's going to have to be cleaned out."

"Rina and I tossed a lot of the stuff already."

"But not the fridge?"

"Not the fridge."

"That thing should be enshrined in a museum." Celeste clutches her belly, as though the baby's communicating with her through flutter kicks. Distress twists her lips. "By the way, did you tell Ba that I'm expecting?"

"No, of course not. You said not to."

"Yeah, but now I wish that you had." Her shoulders shake, as she starts crying again, sobs shuddering through her rib cage.

"Hey." I put my arms around her. "Ba's getting what he wanted. He's getting the grandkid he always wanted. That's what matters."

I've missed my sister, I'm startled to realize. After the baby's born, maybe I'll throw myself into being an auntie. I'll coo and tickle and make squiggly lovey faces and even change a mountain of shitty diapers. Maybe Celeste and I will laugh about how Ba never changed a diaper for either one of us, but we're doing this thing our way this time around — we're revelling in being elbow deep in shit. And all this muck is kind of beautiful in its own raw, visceral way, isn't it? The by-product of life, the cycle of life continuing.

Our father — unbeknownst to him — is getting what he wanted. In a way.

"Celeste?"

"Yeah?" She's almost stopped crying.

"I've been thinking. I think we should sell Ba's business. His half of the building."

"Oh … okay?" Confusion sweeps her eyes. "But I thought those units were bringing in a nice income?"

"They are." I shrug. "But I'm just too tired to take over Ba's business."

If ever I've had doubts, I don't anymore. Too much has happened, the blinders stripped from my eyes. I'm no longer the little girl who wanted nothing more than to impress her father by riding so fast around the perimeter of the light-filled kindergarten that his eyes would be forever dazzled.

"Okay, I'm fine with whatever you want." Celeste looks at me strangely for a second, like she can tell there's a lot more behind my decision. But she doesn't want to ask, she doesn't want to know.

"Eddy Chan will buy us out." I have no doubt he'll be interested, particularly if I make him an offer too good to resist. For some reason, I'd rather sell to him than to a stranger. Best to deal with someone I know I can trust, someone whose own interests are equally vested in keeping certain things secret.

And I'm willing to suffer a loss. Maybe I even want to take a loss. As a form of penance. Or a peculiar form of laundering blood money, depending on how you look at it.

"I assume that Eddy's coming to the funeral?" Celeste says.

"Along with his new wife."

"And what about Terence?"

When I remain silent, Celeste keeps looking at me, like she's trying not to smile and risk spooking me.

"Yeah, I invited him," I say finally.

After a few days of cutting myself off from the world after Ba died, I called Terence. Over the past week, he's been there for me, as he's always been, in his steady, calming way.

"How long are you going to stick around, after everything's settled?" Celeste asks.

"Dunno. It's going to take a while to get everything settled."

"Plenty of time for you and Terence to hang out, right?"

I roll my eyes. "Actually, I'm thinking of renovating the condo. Even if we decide to sell, it'll fetch a better price if the place is in a more livable condition. And it has a lot of potential with that view of the mountain."

"Go for it. Give it a facelift. Maybe it'll be so nice you won't want to leave."

"But my whole life's in Canada."

"Is it, though? I don't know about that, Jill."

Her teasing expression reflects a question, a challenge. For an odd moment, she looks a bit like Ba, a gentler, humbler version of him. And maybe she's right. Although I never took his advice when he was alive, now that he's dead, something in the air feels different. The buoyancy in my chest puzzles and frightens me, this upward tug of emotions. Just when I thought I'd been freed, I feel myself being pulled by strange currents back to the very house where I grew up — as if Ba's outwitting me yet again, even from beyond the grave.

I picture myself trying to live within those decaying walls, all the old, dark memories still there. I'll lay my head down on the floor, bewildered, like a child lost in the ruins.

Or perhaps Celeste is right: perhaps some flickering dream can rouse me to rebuild the place and make it my own. I picture Terence and me having dinner on the terrace together, the mountain somehow softer and more undulating with him there beside me.

ACKNOWLEDGEMENTS

Warm thanks to Sam Hiyate and Diane Terrana for their insightful, detailed comments on multiple drafts of this novel, and to Mona Tam for advising me on certain key aspects of Chinese language and culture. Many thanks to Kirk Howard and Kathryn Lane and the fabulous team at Dundurn — including Jenny McWha, Laura Boyle, Elham Ali, Tabassum Siddiqui, and Heather McLeod, as well as freelance editor Jess Shulman — for your dedicated, skillful work in bringing my novel to fruition. Immense gratitude and affection to my partner, Chris Wong, for introducing me to life in Hong Kong, and for encouraging me to write this book. Getting to know your eccentric, formidable father over the course of several visits to Hong Kong and having the opportunity to live with him during the final months of his life provided the kernel of inspiration for this novel, which blends certain facts and recounted tales about his youth with my own purely fictitious, imaginative elements.

I also wish to thank the Canada Council for the Arts, the Ontario Arts Council and the Toronto Arts Council for the generous grant support I received while researching and writing *Red Oblivion*.

Many books and internet resources offered invaluable research materials and sources of inspiration — too many to recount. Book titles that stand out in my mind include: *Wild Swans: Three Daughters of China* by Jung Chang, *Soul Mountain* by Gao Xingjian, *Hong Kong: Culture and the Politics of Disappearance* by Ackbar Abbas, *Collective Killings in Rural China During the Cultural Revolution* by Yang Su, *Canton Under Communism: Programs and Politics in a Provincial Capital, 1949–1968* by Ezra Vogel, and *The Chinese Cultural Revolution as History* edited by Joseph W. Esherick, Paul G. Pickowicz and Andrew G. Walder, in which several essays were useful. My reference in chapter eight to Aldo Rossi derives from his book *The Architecture of the City*, in which Rossi writes, "And always we could see the house of our childhood, strangely aged, present in the flux of the city." My understanding of Hong Kong's rich culture and history benefited from a visit to the Hong Kong Museum of History. That said, *Red Oblivion* is a work of fiction, and its storyline and fictional framework depend, to some extent, upon my imaginative liberties.